A PERFECT ALIBI

By
R.J.Turner

Begins as a mystery, ends as a thriller

Published by Leaf by Leaf Press 2017

Leaf by Leaf Press Ltd, Sycamore Cottage, School Lane,
Gobowen Shropshire SY11 3LD
www.leafbyleafpress.com

Copyright © R.J.Turner 2017

R.J.Turner has asserted his right to be identified as the author of
this Work in accordance with the Copyright, Design an Patents
Act 1988

ISBN 978-0-9957154-0-0

All rights reserved. No part off this publication may be reproduced,
stored in or introduced into a retrieval system, or transmitted in any form
by any means without the prior written permission of the publisher. Any
person who does an unauthorised act in relation to this publication may
be liable to criminal prosecution and civil claim for damages.

Printed and bound in Great Britain by Clays Ltd, St Ives plc

'Life can only be understood backward;
but it must be lived forward'

Soren Kierkegaard

Acknowledgements

I would like to thank members of the Oswestry Writing Group for their interest and support during the writing of this novel and to members of Leaf by Leaf Press for their help and advice with the manuscript. I would also like to thank Nicola Simcock for using her copy editing and proof reading skills in preparing the manuscript for publication. Any remaining errors are entirely my responsibility.

My thanks also go to John Heap for his help with the cover design and to Kirstie Edwards for helping with the general layout of the book. Finally I would like to thank Madeline for her patience while I hide away to write each day.

A PERFECT ALIBI

**By
R.J.Turner**

PART ONE

A GRAVE DISCOVERY

ONE

When the service ended, Jane followed her father's coffin as the bearers carried it across the churchyard toward the place where his wife lay in her grave. Why her father had requested in his will to be buried next to his wife was a mystery, as they had lived separate lives for so many years: separate beds, separate interests, separate holidays and separate friends, though Jane was not sure her father had any friends. Perhaps his wife's death, from colon cancer, three years ago had caused him to remember earlier, better days, so another grave had been dug in this neglected corner of the graveyard.

Out in the cold, drizzly late October air rooks squabbled among the sycamores, still partly in leaf, which surrounded the graveyard and hid the busy road passing nearby. Low clouds loomed overhead, threatening heavier rain. The sandy ground was lumpy where moles and rabbits had burrowed and it would be easy to trip up in one of their holes hidden by soggy turf and damp layers of fallen leaves. The bearers had to tread carefully to keep their balance with the load on their shoulders, even though the corpse was not heavy. Richard, her father, had been a slight man.

In addition to Jane only half a dozen or so of the meagre congregation had braved the untended graveyard and the rain, which had eased off slightly, for the final ceremony at the graveside. The others had walked to the local hostelry where the funeral feast was waiting. Jane knew from experience that funerals always made you feel hungry and thirsty. Even today, when she was the chief mourner, her mouth felt parched and her stomach rumbled; it was nearly lunchtime. She smiled at the thought that her father would have been one of the first to the bar. He would have taken his drink to a quiet corner and observed the proceedings with a caustic eye.

A Perfect Alibi

She had never been particularly close to her father, in fact, she had not seen that much of him in recent years. But she was an only child and even after she moved in with Patrick she had kept in touch with her father by letters – her father despised the internet – which were rarely answered, and by even rarer telephone calls.

Jane had come back to the nearby town of Bridgeport when she was told that her father had had a stroke, and she had stayed in a hotel close to the hospital where he lay in a coma for more than a week. She was the one who was with him when he died and it was she who, with the help of the undertakers and the friendly vicar, had planned the funeral. Patrick was no longer on the scene.

The bearers struggled down the slope to the corner where the grave lay under a row of tall Scots pines. The small group of mourners followed, the older ones supporting each other, desperately trying to keep their shoes from sinking into the soggy earth.

The bearers placed the coffin on the ropes that would guide it into the grave. The undertakers had removed the tarpaulin, which had been placed over there because heavy rain had been forecast overnight. But it came now, instead, as a torrential downpour. The vicar, a mannish woman with a Black Country accent tried to ignore the rain, moved closer to the edge of the grave and spoke the familiar words.

'Man that is born of woman hath but a short time to live and is full of ...'

She glanced down into the grave, dropped her prayer book and screamed. A thin covering of soil had been washed away by the heavy shower, revealing the body of a woman, apparently naked, and indubitably dead.

TWO

The Scene of Crime Team was already hard at work, moving slowly among the gravestones in their white protective suits like ghosts in the thickening mist, when Detective Inspector Dundee and Detective Sergeant Eccles, affectionately dubbed 'the fruitcakes' by their colleagues, reached the graveyard. They had been investigating a case of sheep rustling over Ludlow way when the call came through.

Sergeant Harris had been first on the scene. As soon as the body was discovered someone phoned 999. Of course, when that someone said that a body had been found in the churchyard, there was a snigger at the other end, but eventually they got a serious response and Harris had arrived with PC Grabowski, an attractive young woman, new to the force. Harris was a career copper in his late twenties with plenty of experience. He immediately set up the crime scene and sent everyone who had been at the graveside back up to the church, where Grabowski was collecting their details prior to them being interviewed as witnesses. Harris had phoned CID and SOCO, and had remained at the graveside until they appeared, soon followed by Eccles and Dundee.

Harris quickly brought the detectives up to speed, then went to support Grabowski in the church. The detectives donned their coveralls and overshoes and approached the grave. They were warned to keep clear of the crumbling edges.

The body had not been moved. A photographer lay prone with his camera held awkwardly over the hole, taking a last few photographs of the corpse in situ before a small ladder was positioned so that the police surgeon could lower himself carefully down beside it. The body was small and lying in a foetal position at one end of the grave. Not all the soil had been washed away, but enough to allow the surgeon to make a preliminary examination of the corpse.

Dundee and Eccles tried to be patient while the police surgeon, Gerald Clarke, an irascible man a couple of years off retirement, made his initial observations. They knew that if they spoke too soon, old Clarke would withdraw into his shell, like a hermit crab. At last he looked up and saw the detectives.

'Oh, it's you two, is it?'

There was no way of telling whether he was pleased or not.

'I suppose you want to know how she died, when she died, and what the name of her grandmother's cat was? Well, to be honest I don't have any answers yet. It's a bit of a bloody puzzle this one. That new young pathologist might have more idea when she gets her on the slab.'

With considerable effort Clarke climbed back out of the grave. He was overweight and red in the face. After taking a few deep breaths, he removed his gloves and unzipped the top of his protective suit. A powerful whiff of body odour emerged.

DI Dundee tried to be patient. DS Eccles was fidgeting impatiently beside him.

'Anything at all you can tell us Doc?'

'Well,' said Clarke with a smile, 'She's female.'

Eccles sighed.

'She's young, mid to late teens I would guess. Long blonde hair. Body of one of those models in the magazines.'

Dundee wondered what sort of magazines Clarke might mean.

'There are slight indications of bruising around the neck, but not really strong enough to suggest suffocation. No other apparent injuries. No obvious signs of forced sexual activity.'

'Do you think she suffered?' asked Eccles.

'Of course she did. She's bloody dead!' exploded Clarke, before continuing more calmly. 'Your biggest problem will be identification. Not a stitch of clothing as you can see. No adornments or tattoos. Absolutely sod all for you to go on.'

'Perhaps MISPERS might help,' said Dundee, thinking aloud.

'Hmm, I suppose Missing Persons might have something on file,' said Clarke. 'There's nothing else. Reckon you've got your job cut out with this one. Have fun.'

He said no more and began returning instruments to his bag as he prepared to leave.

Eccles could resist no longer. 'Any idea at all about the time of death?'

'All I'll say at the moment, DS Eccles,' giving her a withering look, 'is that it's not straightforward. Only one thing I'll commit myself to at present, is that she was already dead when she was tipped into the grave.'

'Tipped?' asked Dundee.

'Yes. The way she is lying shows that she more or less fell into the grave and that rigor mortis had not set in at the time. Yet there are other signs – lividity for example – that suggest she had been dead for some considerable time.'

Dundee knew that he was talking about the way the blood of a corpse settles at the body's lowest point.

Clarke closed his bag and began to walk away. He threw one more remark behind him as he went.

'If it's murder, as I suspect, then there's one person with a perfect alibi.'

He nodded towards the coffin which still lay unburied beside the grave.

Dundee was about to speak to the Crime Scene Manager when Jane, who had been given permission by Sergeant Harris to approach the detective, stepped forward.

'Can you tell me when we can bury him? It was his funeral until...'

'You are?'

'Jane Downes. That's my father ... in his coffin.'

A Perfect Alibi

Eccles broke in, 'We're so sorry, Miss Downes, but we had to establish a crime scene. Unfortunately, your father's coffin was within it.'

'Sergeant Harris said I should come and talk to you.'

'I see no reason why the coffin can't be moved once I've had a word with the Crime Scene Manager,' said Dundee.

There were tears in Jane's eyes as she spoke again, looking at DS Eccles.

'I don't know what to do. Everything was going as planned.'

Now, the tears really flowed. Just at that moment the Vicar appeared and put her arms around Jane. She had recovered from her shock at seeing the body and was now more concerned about supporting the bereaved.

'I'm afraid it may be some time, Miss ...?'

'Downes. Jane Downes.'

'Miss Downes, before we can let you use the grave. First we'll have to take the body to the mortuary. And there may be some clues underneath it.'

Jane shuddered. 'I don't want my father to be buried here now. Not after that ...'

'Yes, I quite see ...' said DS Eccles.

'Tell you what,' said the Vicar. 'Let's get your Dad's coffin back in the church while we sort things out.'

She looked imploringly at Dundee, and indicating the Scene of Crime team, said. 'P'raps some of these chaps could 'elp?'

At that moment, they heard the sound of a vehicle arriving at the top of the bank.

'I think that would be a good idea, Vicar.' said Dundee. 'Now the ambulance has arrived we can take the vic ... the victim away.'

'That poor young woman,' said Jane, bursting into tears again.

'You didn't recognise her, by the way?' asked Eccles.

'No idea,' replied Jane, wiping her eyes with her sleeve. 'Mind you, I only glanced down at her for a second. I haven't lived in this area for many years.'

'You Vicar?'

'Well, she's certainly not one of my parishioners. Not one who's ever been to church anyway, but that leaves plenty these days.'

By now the driver of the ambulance, a tiny woman, and two burly paramedics carrying a stretcher, had reached the grave, ready to take the victim away.

'Look, I think it would be best if Miss Downes ...' began Eccles.

'Yes, indeed,' said the Vicar, understanding at once. 'Come with me, love.'

'And soon as we're done with that,' called out Dundee, some of these chaps can bring the coffin up to the church. I shall want to speak to all those who were at the graveside. Oh, and to the gravedigger when he arrives.'

'Of course,' said the Vicar as she helped Jane up the steep bank towards the church. 'Mr Lewis is on the way.'

Dundee turned to his colleague, 'Right Dawn, you go up and start interviewing the witnesses and I'll have a word with Tom.'

Eccles started up the hill while Dundee moved back towards the grave where Tom Phillips, the Crime Scene Manager was waiting.

'Hello, Jack,' he said to Dundee, 'How's things? Those twins of yours at school yet?'

'Just finished their first half term.'

'Wow! Time doth fly, as the poet said. And the lovely Leanne?'

'Fine. She's going back to work soon. Looking forward to it. And it'll certainly help with the bills.'

They went on chatting for a while, catching up on family news. They'd joined the police about the same time. At last they got around to the matter in hand.

The body of the victim had been lifted out of the grave, carefully bagged up and placed on a stretcher. The bottom of the grave, where the body had lain, had been examined minutely.

'Anything at all?' asked Dundee.

Tom showed him a plastic bag, containing two cigarette ends.

'That's it, I'm afraid. And footprints everywhere of course. Most of them from the gravedigger, I should imagine, and some from the mourners who got close to the graveside. Naturally, most of the prints have been photographed and we've made some casts, but I don't think they'll be much help. Reckon she was rolled in from some distance away, like the Doc said. I suppose they might find a few prints on her body, when they get her to the morgue, but I doubt it.'

'Do you think, like the Doc, that she was already dead?'

'Yes, but there's something odd about that. Doc said that rigor mortis had only just begun to set in, probably after she was put in the grave.'

'Peculiar that,' mused Dundee, making a note in his book. 'Well, I'd better get up to the church and help with interviewing the witnesses. Must be a fair few, but I don't think they'll be much help. And somehow I don't think there'll be any other witnesses who were around here last night.'

They heard the ambulance start up.

'See you back at the ranch,' said Dundee as he began to climb the bank, then he remembered, 'Oh, Tom. Could some of your guys bring that coffin up to the church when you've finished here?'

'Of course. That's one witness who won't be saying much. See you, Jack.'

Just as DI Dundee set off for the church he saw a man sneaking up the back way to the graveyard. Dundee hurried over to him.

'That's as far as you go, Matthews.'

Dundee had known this man since he first moved to the valley. He was a reporter from the Star. He had disliked the man since the first time they'd met. Now, he despised him and Matthews knew it.

'OK. OK. I won't enter the crime scene, but I want to know what's going on. I've every right.'

'Wait for the press conference.'

'Is it a murder?'

'No idea yet.'

'Who is she?'

'A young woman. OK, that's enough. Just piss off now and let us get on with our job.'

'No need to be offensive. All I'm doing is *my* job.'

'Yeah, well, I've seen the way you write about us. In fact, about me in particular.'

'Bound to. You always seem to be involved.'

'I suppose so. Anyway, that's all I'm giving you at the moment. So, on your way, Matthews.'

Dundee knew he shouldn't be speaking like this. He usually made sure it was DS Eccles who spoke to the guy. Something about Matthews always riled him.

'Is DS Eccles about?'

'Yes, in the church. But she'll be far too busy to speak to you.'

'Maybe. I'll wait and see.'

As Dundee moved back to the grave he spoke to one of the SOCOs and asked him to make sure that Matthews didn't come any closer, but when he looked back to where Matthews had been standing the guy had disappeared and there was no sign of him as Dundee entered the church.

A Perfect Alibi

'Good riddance,' muttered Dundee.

He could see that the interviews were well in hand. The Vicar had made tea and the witnesses sat spaced out in the rear pews to avoid any collusion.

A young PC was helping the last witness, the kind of frail old lady who probably managed to attend every funeral, back to her pew. Then she checked her list and asked the next witness to accompany her into the vestry. Efficient as well as attractive, observed Dundee.

Sergeant Harris came over.

'The undertaker's men had to leave. Another funeral. But they were happy for you to come and speak to them at the office when that one's finished. Jones & Parry it is. Bridge Street.'

He handed a business card to Dundee with the men's names written on the back. The DI put the card in his pocket and as he glanced up he saw another man enter the church. This one, probably in his late sixties, was a large man, in what looked like a velvet jacket stretched across his considerable girth and with purple cord trousers and yellow boots beneath. Upon entering the church the man removed a large black hat which allowed a mop of silvery curls to flop down to his shoulders.

Sergeant Harris accosted the man, and when he explained that he was the gravedigger, Harris took him over to the DI, who in turn led him to a quiet corner of the church. Dundee introduced himself and showed the man his identity card. The man looked absolutely nothing like a gravedigger and when he spoke it was in a loud voice with a slight Welsh lilt.

'Ah yes, Detective Inspector. My name's Lewis, Angus Lewis. Bit of a mash-up that, the moniker I mean, Scottish and Welsh. But that's what my parents called me and I'm stuck with it. The Reverend Edwards telephoned to say you wanted to see me. Ghastly business, this body in the grave. Alas poor Yorick and all that.'

'How long have you been digging graves, Mr Lewis?'

The man looked puzzled for a moment.

'Oh, I see. Not what you expected. Should be a burly yokel, eh? Or a village ancient? You may well have seen me on the stage, mainstay of the dramatic society in Bridgeport. Strangely enough my last part was in The Scottish Play. Lots of horrid murders in that.'

Dundee had never been to see any of the dramatic society's productions but he could well imagine this guy treading the boards.

'So, how come you're digging graves?'

'Matter of making ends meet, Detective Inspector. The pension barely covers the alcohol intake, let alone the rent. And I used to quite enjoy the task. Time to philosophise as I dipped my spade into the earth, or to learn my lines among the quietest of company. But not for much longer I'm afraid. I'm beginning to suffer the slings and arrows of old age.'

'When did you dig this grave?'

'Last evening. With the help of young Peter Staines. A lovely lad. What he lacks in the brain department he makes up for in looks and muscles. And he's quite content with a couple of pints for his assistance. Poor lad's on the dole as they call it.'

'I shall want his address.'

'And you shall have it.' He took a notebook from his pocket, wrote the address and with a flourish, ripped out the page and handed it to Dundee.

'Do you smoke, Mr Lewis?'

'Never! Would ruin the breathing. So important for an actor. I was almost a professional, you know, many years ago.'

'What about young Staines? Does he smoke?'

'Yes, unfortunately, like a reeky chimney. Why do you ask?'

'We found a couple of cigarette ends in the grave.'

'That wouldn't be Peter. I would never allow it. Too disrespectful.'

'Did you see anyone when you were digging the grave?'

'No. Mind you, the dark night had fallen. We had to use the lamp with a little generator to power it.'

Dundee thanked Lewis and informed him that the Reverend Edwards would like to speak to him.

'Ah, dear sweet Angela. A saint. A veritable saint.'

Later DI Dundee and DS Eccles went to interview the two men from the firm of undertakers who had arranged the funeral of Richard Downes, but they were unable to tell them anything they hadn't learned from the other witnesses.

Afterwards, they went to talk to Peter Staines, who lived on a small council estate at the edge of the village, but here they were in for a surprise. They were met at the door by a scrawny woman in her late forties, guessed Dundee, with screwed up eyes and a cigarette between her lips.

When the detectives showed their ID cards and explained why they were there, the woman threw her fag down on the step, squashed it with her slipper and invited them in.

'Funny thing is ...' she began, then paused to cough till she was red in the face, 'I were about to contact *you* lot. See, Pete ain't bin 'ome. I mean, he often stays out most of the night, some girl or other I suspect, but he's always back for breakfast. Not today though. And that's really unusual. He's a good lad is Pete. Best of my kids by far. Always lets me know where he is, 'cause he knows his Mum'll have nice meal ready for him. But I've been phoning his mobile all day and there ain't been no reply.'

THREE

Jane had collected the key from the solicitor a few days before. He had explained that her father had left her the house in his will. This could only be made official following the probate process, but the solicitor was sure there would be no objection to Jane staying there overnight. She pushed open the heavy front door, which was obstructed by the usual pile of junk mail scattered across the Minton tiles. The large Victorian house was dark and cold. She located the light switch, and when a weak bulb was illuminated – thank goodness the power had been left on – she piled the mail on to the hall table. The house was cold, she assumed, because the heating system had not been set, so she must find the boiler and start it up.

She wished, momentarily, that Patrick was with her. He was so good with anything mechanical. Then she decided that she must learn to cope by herself. She never wanted to see Patrick again.

The kitchen had been modernised quite recently, despite her father having told his wife, when she was alive, that it was not necessary. She remembered that the boiler was in the utility room at the side and that it was very up-to-date and easy to operate. Her father would have made sure of that. He hated anything technological, still used a typewriter for his writing and could barely use a mobile phone. Soon she felt the warmth spreading through the radiators, but she would keep her coat on until the house had thoroughly warmed up.

She took the kettle from the work surface and swilled some fresh water around inside before half filling and switching it on. There was a jar of instant coffee in the cupboard. She saw that her father's cleaning lady, a Mrs Bennett if it was the same one, had sensibly emptied the fridge and switched it off, so she would have to drink the coffee black. The house was warming up nicely

A Perfect Alibi

now, so she sat at the kitchen table, sipped her coffee and thought about everything.

What a dreadful day it had turned out to be. The funeral had gone quite smoothly until that poor girl's corpse had been found in her father's grave. She got the impression from something she had overheard that the girl may have been murdered. But who would have killed her and why had they put the corpse where they had? Perhaps a ready-made grave was an obvious place to dispose of a body. Apparently, they had intended to cover the body with soil from the heap at the side, but the sudden shower had washed most of it away.

Well, her father would be buried tomorrow. The gravedigger had told the vicar that he would prepare another grave in the newest part of the graveyard and the wonderful Reverend Edwards, who had been so kind and helpful, would hold a little private ceremony at noon. There would be no other mourners.

Jane's stomach rumbled and the sound echoed around the empty house. She remembered that she had not eaten properly since breakfast, when she had not been in the mood for much, so she'd only had a cup of tea and a couple of biscuits all day.

There was nothing to eat in the fridge, but she remembered that her father more or less lived on prepared meals from the large chest freezer in the cellar, which had been damp-proofed, painted out and fitted with racks for his plentiful supply of wine. She smiled as she remembered that he kept the key in his desk. Perhaps he thought Mrs Bennett might steal some of his best wines. It had nearly caused the poor woman to give in her notice, but Dad paid well and he used so little of the house that her work was soon done.

Jane was surprised to find that the cellar door was unlocked but was disappointed to discover that the freezer was completely empty, though still switched on. She chose a bottle of claret and went back to the kitchen. She would open the wine, leave it to reach room temperature and order a pizza. When it arrived, she would eat the lot and get merry on the wine.

The landline was still working and there was a local free paper among the junk mail, with a whole page of take-away food outlets in Bridgeport. She chose a pizza place and ordered her meal, which she was told would be with her in less than half an hour.

Before returning to the kitchen she sorted through the mail, making one pile of the few real letters to her father and another ready for the bin. She couldn't face opening her father's mail, so she just left it on the table and looked for a wine glass and corkscrew. She knew that she ought to wait for the food to arrive. Drinking on an empty stomach was never a good idea but the food would be here soon and it had been such a dreadful day.

She poured herself half a glass, drank it down and felt it flushing through her bloodstream. Suddenly, she felt full of self-pity and burst into tears. Here she was at 38 years old, an abandoned woman and an orphan. It was the usual story. After ten years of living together Patrick had gone off with a younger woman, in fact you could hardly call her a woman, just a girl, with long hair and short skirts, who had just been given a temping job at his office.

Her dad had been right all along. He had hated Patrick from the start. Would not allow her to bring him home and would not visit her in London while she lived with him. Mum on the other hand really liked Patrick and the three of them met quite often. Even when Mum showed the first signs of her illness she would make the effort to visit and Patrick's charm would bring back the sparkle into her mother's eyes. But Dad had insisted that Patrick was a fraud and that it would end in tears. Now, of course, it had.

The doorbell rang. When Jane stood up to answer it she found that she was already a little dizzy. She turned the hall light on and put the door on the chain before opening it. After all, this house was rather cut off from the rest of the village and its isolation was increased by the surrounding trees.

'Your pizza, Miss.'

She liked being called Miss. Through the gap in the door she could see the little delivery van with the company name painted on the side.

'Just a moment ...'

She fetched her purse from the kitchen, removed the chain and opened the door. When she saw that her pizza had been delivered by a tall, dark and quite handsome young man, she almost asked him in. My God that would be one in the eye for Patrick she thought, but no, there was her father lying in his coffin, still waiting to be buried. It just wouldn't do. And anyway, what on earth would this young guy with his sexy smile see in a woman of her age?

She paid for her dinner and sighed as the young man drove away.

When she had eaten most of the pizza, helped down with large gulps of wine, she began to sort through her father's mail. There were two utility bills, a cheque from the public lending rights office, a letter from his publisher reminding him that the expected manuscript was well overdue and a letter from a reader pointing out some petty inaccuracy in one of his novels. Dad used a nom de plume and all correspondence had to go through his publisher. He sneered at the idea of social media and author's blogs and all that dumbing down as he called it. Perhaps that was why his novels hadn't sold so well in recent years.

There was just one letter left. In a small, scented envelope, not stamped and with her father's real name and this address. Inside was a single sheet of lined notepaper with a message written in a neat hand.

You bastard! I know what you have been doing. You won't get away with it.

Jane felt disturbed. Surely it could have no connection with that body in the grave? So, what on earth was it about? There was no way her father would have anything to do with murder, except in his novels. And anyway, he had a perfect alibi. He had been in hospital for almost a fortnight and then lay at the undertakers for another week while the funeral was arranged. No, it must be something to do with his life in the village. He had never been particularly popular, even less since his wife had died, because everyone liked her and he made no attempt to be liked by anyone. Yes, thought Jane, it must be something like that. She crumpled up the letter and threw it in the bin.

She found that she was now quite sober so she picked up the other letters and took them to her father's study, a pleasant room at the top of the stairs, which in daylight had a fine view over the garden. The study was lined with bookshelves, one of which was reserved for her father's own books, several copies of each, with their gaudy covers, racy titles and his nom de plume, Dirk Barker, in eye-catching print.

As she placed the letters on her father's old oak desk, Jane was surprised to see that the typewriter had gone. Instead a slim, shiny laptop stood in its place. Perhaps her father had gone online after all. She was tempted to open the laptop and see what he had been working on, but this seemed too much of an intrusion while he still lay unburied in the church.

There was a neat pile of papers beside the laptop, which appeared to be the manuscript of a novel called *The Girl With Long Fair Hair*.

Jane sat down at the desk and began to flick through the pages. It was very similar to his other novels, except that there was no murder yet and the hero seemed to have many of her father's characteristics, though in a younger man. She had never really liked his novels, finding them formulaic and rather nasty. This one seemed more true to life. She flipped through a few pages, searching for the murder, but could not find it. That was strange. How could you have a whodunit when nothing had been done? She skimmed on to the last page. The novel was unfinished. It stopped abruptly mid-sentence. And her father had scribbled something in pencil across the page.

I just can't do it anymore!

Jane frowned, as she went back downstairs, wondering what 'it' was. She took another gulp of wine. But surely it was obvious. Her father had been suffering from writer's block.

Suddenly, a wave of weariness overcame her. It had been a long difficult day and she couldn't face any more puzzles. It was time to find somewhere to sleep. She couldn't possibly sleep in her father's bedroom, where the cleaning lady had found him lying on the floor after his stroke, but the other bedrooms were unused, and none of the beds were made up. Jane went back downstairs, cursorily checked that the doors were locked, filled another glass of wine and swallowed it before going into the sitting room and almost falling on to the large settee. She was too tired to undress, except for kicking off her shoes. The heating was still on so she didn't need any blankets. Soon, she was fast asleep.

Sometime in the night she was woken by a sound; the creaking of a floorboard or the soft squeal of a door hinge. A short while later she thought she heard a car drive away. But she heard nothing else and soon her heavy eyelids closed again. Next time they opened she heard birdsong and saw light flooding in through the windows, where she hadn't bothered to close the curtains.

For a moment she wasn't sure where she was. Why was she lying on a settee in her clothes? Where was Patrick? Why was it so quiet? There was always noise in the morning from the busy road outside their flat. Should she be on her way to work?

Gradually it came back to her. This was her father's house, well, hers soon. Patrick was somewhere else, probably having sex with that girl. Jane's body felt stiff from sleeping on the settee and when she turned slightly, pain shot through her head and she saw a stained wine glass and an empty bottle beside her on the carpet.

'Christ, Oh Christ,' she said aloud. 'I have to be at the church. Dad's funeral!'

Then she glanced at her watch and saw that it was only 8.30am.

'Thank God for that!'

Under normal circumstances she would have been late for work, but she had given in her notice when her dad became ill. She had become bored with the job anyway and had enough savings to last for a while.

Gradually, she became fully awake. She made another black coffee and sat at the kitchen table thinking about that strange note and the words scribbled on her father's manuscript. She wondered again if it could possibly have any connection with that young woman's body in her father's grave. She began to feel that she needed to talk to someone, but who? Then she remembered that woman detective, with the name of a cake – Eccles, was it? – who had been so helpful and supportive yesterday. She had the detective's card in a pocket somewhere, but why should she tell anyone? What did her father's business have to do with anyone else? Anyway, the most important thing today was to complete his internment.

She swilled out the coffee cup, fetched her case from the car, showered and changed into casual clothes. There was no need to wear anything more formal today. There would only be herself, the vicar, the gravedigger and a couple from the undertakers to push the coffin on the bier along the gravel path to the new grave.

She felt much better now. The shower and another coffee had almost cured her hangover. Suddenly, she remembered waking briefly in the night. There had definitely been the sound of a floorboard creaking or a door opening. Perhaps she ought to check. She started on the ground floor. There was the front door, still locked, and the back door, also locked. There was a corridor, leading off the hallway to the sitting room, a formal dining room and another reception room that her father hadn't used. At the end of the corridor there was a heavy curtain concealing an internal door to the garage. She pulled the curtain aside and discovered that the door was unlocked.

'Damn! I should have checked.'

She opened the door and saw that the car was not there and she wondered where it might be. He was very fond of his rather outdated and uneconomical car which was one of the last, mainly, British cars to be made. Anyway, for whatever reason, it had gone. When she checked the garage doors she found that they were unlocked as well.

Now, she really began to worry. There wasn't much of value in the house because her father was not into antiques or expensive watches or anything like that, but she didn't like the thought that someone had been in the house while she was sleeping. She was slightly reassured when she checked the downstairs rooms and found that nothing seemed to have been disturbed. Upstairs, she went straight into her father's study and saw at once what was missing. There was a space on her father's desk where the laptop should have been.

The doorbell rang. When she looked out of the landing window Jane saw a battered delivery van parked on the drive. She hurried downstairs and unlocked the door. The driver, almost as scruffy as his van, handed her a bulky parcel without bothering to check whether she was the proper recipient, then turned without a word and drove away.

Jane took the parcel into the kitchen and found a pair of scissors in the table drawer. She carefully slit open the brown paper and pulled it apart. When she saw the contents she sat down heavily on one of the chairs and her head span. The parcel contained a woman's clothing, washed and ironed, with a pair of knickers and a bra on top.

FOUR

That evening's Press Conference was an embarrassment for Detective Chief Inspector Wentworth. He tried to hold back as much information as possible, but what information did they have? A young woman's body had been found in the graveyard of St Michael's Church. Her identity had not been established. The post-mortem was taking place at that moment but the results would not be known until the morning. Coincidentally, a young man called Peter Staines had gone missing but there could be many reasons for that.

When questions were allowed, Matthews, the reporter from the Star, asked who was heading the investigation, and when told that it was Detective Inspector Dundee he said sarcastically,

'Oh well, that's all right then.'

But his jibe did not raise as much laughter as he'd hoped, because most of the press were from further afield and had never heard of Dundee.

In fact, DI Dundee had just donned the correct gear of overall, gloves, mask and rubber boots for the mortuary. He had watched enough post-mortems not to be phased as the pathologist went about her work. It still embarrassed him to think how sick he'd been the first time he had attended one. Avril Denton, the new pathologist was relatively young, recently appointed, and from their dealings on a couple of cases, Dundee already had a high opinion of her. Together they looked at the young woman's corpse.

'This is a very strange business, Detective Inspector. As you can see there is very little sign of decomposition, yet there are other indications that the woman has been dead for some time. My esteemed colleague, Dr Clarke – Dundee wondered what she called him in private – told me that rigor mortis had only just set in when he first examined the corpse.'

'Hmm,' muttered Dundee.

'There is nothing on the corpse to identify her, but that's your job anyway.'

'Cause of death?'

'Another puzzle. You can see slight bruising on her neck but nothing to suggest that she was strangled. And if you look at her thighs and buttocks you can see several puncture marks that may suggest drug use, but it will require blood tests and an examination of her stomach contents to discover whether there is any evidence of narcotics or poison.'

The Pathologist examined the corpse's vaginal area, then stated, 'There's no obvious evidence of forced sexual activity, but I'll take a swab and see what we can find.

'So, to sum up,' said Dundee, 'we don't know who she is, how she died, or how long she's been dead.'

'That's about it.'

The post-mortem continued with the usual cuts to the corpse and the removal and examination of the organs, but the tests on blood, stomach contents and vaginal swab would take a while longer.

Dundee thanked the young pathologist and went next door to the office to check his notes. He took off the special gear, threw it in the bin and washed his hands thoroughly before completing his report, leaving it on Wentworth's desk and going home.

Dundee arrived at the station early next morning. There was a lot to do. The young woman whose body had been discovered in the grave had to be identified. And the lad who had helped Angus Lewis, the gravedigger, had to be found. Of course, his disappearance made him the chief suspect.

In some ways Dundee was glad to be at work. Good to have something else to occupy his mind. He and Leanne had been bickering again. It was happening too often recently. And the kids would notice eventually. They seemed to be pleased to be going to school. That wasn't right.

Dundee wasn't sure what the problem was. Just the seven year itch perhaps? That was how long they'd been married. But he hadn't started looking at other women, had he? OK, so she wasn't quite the lovely Leanne anymore, as Tom had called her yesterday. She'd put on weight with the twins and couldn't seem to lose it again. And a permanent scowl spoiled her pretty face these days. Perhaps he should give her more of his time, take her out somewhere special or get to bed earlier and share some sex. It had been a while. But it was difficult when he was always on call. And now especially, with this unexplained death.

He parked in his spot at the station and walked over to the doors at the rear of the building. A young woman was walking just ahead of him. Nice figure, he thought. She turned as he caught up with her. Had she been waiting for him?

'Good Morning, Sir.'

It was that young PC he'd seen at the church yesterday. Slim and shapely, with a rather pale face framed with soft brown hair, large blue eyes and generous lips curled in a welcoming smile. Eccles had told him her name on the way back from the church yesterday, and said how helpful she'd been. She was, apparently, of Polish descent.

'Morning. PC ... er ... Grabowski isn't it?'

'Yes, Sir. Bit of a mouthful. You've got a good memory.'

'Not really. You're new. That's unusual when they always seem to be cutting staff. And you are ...'

He was going to say 'very pretty' but knew that wasn't the right sort of thing to say these days.

He thought the young woman blushed slightly.

'And you're connected in my mind with that nasty business at the church yesterday.'

'Oh, I see.' She seemed rather disappointed.

'Well, I must get on. See you around.'

He hurried past her to avoid further embarrassment.

When he entered the CID room, slightly later than usual, DCI Wentworth had gathered the team together in front of the whiteboard. They were all in early today. Amazing what the death of a young woman could do to break the boring routine.

'Ah, Dundee, glad you could join us.' Dundee looked guiltily at his watch in case it was later than he thought. No, it was just Wentworth being sarcastic. Dundee found an empty seat next to Eccles as Wentworth continued.

'DI Dundee attended the post-mortem last evening and I have his report here.'

He began to read the report.

'The pathologist tells us that the victim was between 18 and 22 years of age and ...' he paused dramatically, 'she had probably been dead for at least a week.'

Dundee interrupted, 'Yet the body looked so fresh.'

'Trust you to notice that she was a looker, Dundee.'

Dundee was really beginning to dislike Wentworth. He had been foisted on them when their usual DCI, Diana Pearce, had taken maternity leave. But he decided it wasn't worth letting his dislike show.

Wentworth muttered something under his breath, then continued.

'There were no signs of any fatal injuries, and only some slight bruising around the neck, but not enough to suggest she had been strangled. Oh, and a lot of puncture marks, especially on the thighs and buttocks, but none of these looked particularly fresh. She was probably a user, but it's not clear yet whether drugs caused her death. The body snatchers may have a better idea when they've tested her blood and analysed the stomach contents.'

Wentworth paused for a moment, as if enjoying his performance in front of a captive audience.

'Miss Denton sent some extra information by email this morning. There was some evidence of sexual activity, but no suggestion of sexual violence and no sperm, which probably suggests that precautions were taken.'

'So, it was consensual, you mean?' Eccles asked.

'Apparently.'

Eccles looked puzzled.

'Are we getting anywhere with identification, Cheesy?' asked Wentworth.

You wouldn't have immediately placed Simon Cheshire as a computer nerd. In his fifties, with thinning grey hair and always smartly dressed, but he was the expert with such enquiries.

'Zilch so far,' said DC Cheshire. 'Certainly nothing local, so I'm widening the search.'

At that moment DS Eccles's phone rang. She apologised to Wentworth, then got up and walked away to take the call.

'So,' Wentworth continued, sticking a photo of the victim on the whiteboard, 'We're going to have to start taking her picture around the pubs and clubs. Surely someone would have noticed a good looking girl like that, wouldn't they Jack?'

Dundee was about to respond angrily to Wentworth's insinuation, but Eccles returned.

'That was Jane Downes.'

'Who?' asked Wentworth.

'The daughter of the man who was supposed to have been buried yesterday,' explained Dundee.

'She sounded very upset.' said Eccles.

'OK, Dawn, you and Jack had better follow that up. Probably just wants to chat about the funeral that didn't happen. Cheesy, you get on with your enquiries.'

DC Cheshire nodded. Now, Wentworth turned to DC Murphy.

'What about this lad ...' he consulted his notes, 'Staines. Any luck there?'

A Perfect Alibi

'Not so far, Sir. Except that the regulars at his local were very surprised when he didn't turn up night before last for the darts match. Seems like he's their best player. But they did say that he's a great hit with the ladies, so we should *cherchez la femme* as one of the more educated drinkers put it.'

'Well, you and Jones go on with that. We need this lad and we need him fast. The rest of you pick up a photo and get out on the road.'

FIVE

Dundee sat comfortably beside Eccles as she drove the squad car out of town, over the bridge across the river, where the water level was high after all the recent rain, and turned north, following the river upstream into wooded hills. He could relax again now he was away from Wentworth. Suddenly, DS Eccles asked.

'You're not keen on the DCI?'

'I hate his guts.'

'Well, there're plenty of those, hanging right over his belt.'

Dundee smiled. Eccles continued, 'You know he's just jealous don't you? 'Cause you're younger, better looking and you're happily married, not twice divorced.'

Dundee wasn't so sure about the happy marriage, but he smiled again.

'How d'you know all this?'

'I keep myself informed. Good for my career.'

They drove on in silence for a while, interrupted occasionally by the police radio, but none of the messages were relevant to them. They'd given up trying to share music. Their tastes were just too different. Dundee was into country and western. Eccles liked hip-hop and rap. Anything edgy and fast.

'So, what did Miss Downes say in her call?'

'Said she'd got something to show us. And she'd had a burglary. Oh, and her father's car may have been stolen.'

'Christ! That poor woman! An aborted funeral and now a burglary.'

'I've been doing some research. The guy who was going to be buried. Do you know who he is or was?'

'Of course. Richard Downes.'

'Well, yes. But he was also Dirk Barker.'

'Who?'

'The crime novelist. That's his nom de plume.'

'Crime novels! I never read them. Load of rubbish!'

'What about Sherlock Holmes?'

'Ah, that's different. That's a classic. Are you telling me you read that stuff?'

'Sometimes. There're some recent writers I really like. Their stories are always set in a specific part of England. One always writes about Yorkshire and another sets his stories in the Peak District. Then of course there's Rebus in Edinburgh. Oh, yes and we've got our own author who lives across the other side of the county and uses that area for his novels.'

'Near the Welsh border you mean?'

'Yes, and sometimes over it.'

'All those places beginning with two Ls. I took Leanne and the twins over there last summer. There's this fantastic waterfall. Another place beginning with double L. Do you know it?'

'Llanrhaeadr,' Eccles said. 'Yes, I walked over the Berwyns from there. With Trish, before she moved on.'

There was a note of sadness in her last remark. Dundee knew that DS Eccles and her partner Trish had fallen out, so he quickly changed the subject.

'D'you reckon you can learn anything from this crime fiction stuff?'

'Not really. It's just a game. Relaxation.'

'And what about this ... er ... Barker? Is he any good?'

'I've only read one of his. I didn't like it. There was a sadistic feel about it.'

'Hmm ...' murmured Dundee.

They were approaching the village now and Eccles slowed to 40 as they passed the 30mph sign.

'What about this Pete Staines?' she asked.

'Well, he's got to be top of the list. I mean, he knew there was an empty grave, 'cause he'd helped to dig it. Now, he's vanished.'

'Ah, here we are. The Old Vicarage.' said Eccles as she drove through the gates and braked sharply on the gravel driveway.

It was obvious to the detectives as they entered the house that Jane had been crying. Her eyes were red-rimmed and she kept dabbing at her cheeks with a soaked handkerchief. Eccles immediately went to comfort her.

'It's always disturbing when you discover someone else has been in your house. You can feel violated. Has much been taken?'

'Only one thing as far as I can tell. I'm just being silly really.'

Jane led them upstairs and showed them the empty space where the laptop had been. The thief had not taken the mains lead or the mouse, which remained redundant on the desk.

'Don't touch anything in here,' said Dundee. There may be fingerprints. I'll call SOCO.'

He moved away a little and made his call.

'What's that pile of papers?' asked Eccles.

'Dad's latest novel. I don't know whether you know, but he wrote crime novels under another name. It's not finished. I glanced through it last night.'

She didn't mention the note her father had scribbled on the last page. Or that strange letter among the post.

'Do you think, when SOCO has finished, I might take a look?'

'That's fine by me,' said Jane.

Dundee heard Eccles's request and thought that reading the unfinished manuscript of this bloke's novel sounded like a complete waste of time, but her methods often surprised him and sometimes bore results. She had just revealed her interest in crime novels, so it made sense she would want to have a look at it.

'Did you see what was on the laptop?' he asked Jane.

'No, I was too tired.'

'Well,' said Eccles, 'There was obviously something on it that someone didn't want us to see.'

'Is anything else missing?' Dundee asked. 'I mean in the rest of the house?'

'Nothing at all. So far as I can tell.'

'Any sign of a forced entry?'

'No. That's why I feel so foolish. You see I checked the front and back door, but I forgot that there is a door from the garage. It's hidden by a curtain.'

'And that door was unlocked?'

'Yes.'

'Was there a car in the garage?'

'Well, my father's car should have been there. But it isn't. I wondered if he'd sold it. It's quite old. Or perhaps it's in a garage being repaired. They'd be waiting for him to collect it. Unless they've heard about his death.'

'What sort of car was it?'

'One of the last cars made by Rover. Quite a big car. A 75 I think it was called. Mind you, he might have changed it without my knowing. It's a while since I was here. He usually insisted on a British car but that would be difficult now, wouldn't it? There's probably some paperwork somewhere.'

'Was the garage door locked?'

Jane shook her head.

'It sounds very much as if this had been planned.'

'Did you hear anything last night?'

'I think so, but ... well, you see, I'd had a few glasses of wine. I was upset.'

'What do you think you heard?'

'Possibly a door opening or a footstep on the stairs. And there might have been the sound of a car driving off. But I thought I was imagining things and I went back to sleep.'

'Well, thank goodness only the laptop was taken. I mean, it's not as if your father needs his laptop any more. And I'm sure you have your own computer.'

'Yes, I have a tablet, but it's not really that. It's what was delivered this morning.'

Jane began to sob again.

'It's horrible! Horrible!'

'You'd better show us.'

'Yes. It's in the kitchen.'

Jane led them downstairs and pointed out the package on the table. Eccles bent over to study its contents.

'Oh my God!' she exclaimed. 'I see what you mean.'

Dundee had a look as well, taking care not to actually touch the clothes. He sensed from even the slightest glance that these were the sort of clothes that a very young woman, like the body in the grave, might well choose to wear, especially the flimsy underwear. He knew that Leanne would not wear such stuff and she was only in her mid-thirties.

'Who was the parcel addressed to?' asked Eccles. She didn't even want to disturb the wrapping to find out.

'My Dad. His real name.'

'Who delivered it?'

'A man in a scruffy white van. I assumed it was from a laundry. But there was no name on the side. I only thought about that later.'

'Did your father use a laundry?'

'I don't know. But I'm sure Mrs Bennett will.'

'Mrs Bennett?'

'His cleaning lady.'

'Well, we'll obviously need to speak to her.'

'She lives in the village.' Jane unpinned a card from a notice board on the kitchen wall. 'Here we are. 45, Wainwright Close. On the council estate. Do you know it?'

A Perfect Alibi

Both detectives nodded. That estate was their next destination, to continue the search for Peter Staines. They heard a vehicle arrive outside.

'That'll be SOCO,' said Dundee.

'What's happening about your father's funeral?' asked Eccles.

'I'm meeting the vicar at the church at half past eleven.' She glanced at her watch. 'Damn! It's already five past.'

'You get on your way,' said Dundee. 'I'll speak to SOCO. They'll look for prints upstairs and' – Dundee indicated the parcel – 'they'll bag these up and take them to the lab.'

The doorbell rang. Eccles noticed that Jane Downes jumped slightly. She was not surprised. The woman must be under considerable stress. Dundee went to let the SOCOs in.

'Look,' said Eccles, 'this must all be very unpleasant for you, Miss Downes. I suggest that after the funeral you book into a hotel for the night. We'll make sure that everything is secure here. And we'll probably leave someone to watch the property. Just in case the burglar returns. But please let us know where you're staying. I'm afraid we may need to speak to you again.'

Jane smiled for the first time that morning and went to pack her bag. Something told DS Eccles that this would not be the last time she and Dundee visited the Old Vicarage.

As Eccles drove, Dundee contacted the station telling them to ask around the garages and look out for an abandoned Rover 75. These days a car like that would stick out like a sore thumb.

When they reached the small council estate they called first on Mrs Staines. She came to the door wreathed in smoke as usual.

'Have you found him? I've been worried sick.'

'I'm afraid not. You haven't heard from your son?'

'Not a dicky bird. I've phoned and phoned.'

'Could your son drive?' asked DI Dundee.

'Don't be daft. How's he gonna afford fucking driving lessons or buy a car on jobseeker's?'

'I thought perhaps with odd jobs. I know he helps the gravedigger.'

'What? Old Angus? He don't get more than a pittance from the church. Got his pension ain't he? Buys Pete a pint or two for his help, that's all.'

'Does he have any other part-time jobs?'

'Well, he was helping that writer chap over the other side of the village. Spent quite a lot of time up there recently. Don't know what he did, mind you. Of course, the old bloke's dead now, ain't he. But I don't suppose he paid well. You know what they're like, these arty types.'

'Well, thank you, Mrs Staines. We'll let you know of any developments. And you'll contact us if your son gets in touch?'

There didn't seem much point in continuing this conversation so the detectives moved on to Wainwright Close.

They reached number 45 with its neat front garden leading to a newly painted front door. There was an aggressive yapping from inside when they rang the bell. Then a ladylike voice told the dog to be quiet and asked them who they were. The yapping turned to a low growl.

'Is that Mrs Bennett?' asked Eccles in her gentlest voice. 'This is Detective Inspector Dundee and Detective Sergeant Eccles. If you open the door we can show you our ID cards.'

'Very well. I'll just put Sophie in the other room then you can come in.'

A door inside the house was opened and closed and the growling dimmed, then turned to yapping again as Mrs Bennett opened the front door.

She checked their cards, ushered them in and took them through to a conservatory built on to the back of the house. It was small, very warm and crammed with wickerwork furniture.

A Perfect Alibi

'I'm sorry about Sophie. But she's such a good little guard dog. And since my husband died ... Would you like some tea?'

Dundee was about to refuse, but Eccles jumped in,

'That would be lovely Mrs Bennett. Only milk for me, but my colleague takes sugar ... two spoons full.'

Mrs Bennett went into the kitchen. Dundee was about to protest but Eccles whispered, 'best way' and he realised she was probably right. Soon Mrs Bennett returned with three cups on a tray and a plate of biscuits.

Dundee was about to dunk one of the biscuits in his tea when Eccles shook her head. She opened a notebook and asked,

'Mrs Bennett, I believe you used to work for Mr Downes at the Old Vicarage.'

'That's right. I'm Mavis by the way. Yes, I used to go in three mornings a week to sort him out. It was me who found him, poor man, lying on his bedroom floor, totally incapacitated as they say. I called the ambulance and telephoned his daughter straight away.'

'It must have been a terrible shock for you, Mavis.'

'It certainly was. He'd become a bit of a recluse lately, you know, never went out anywhere, but he hadn't shown any signs of being poorly. Then bang, he has a stroke. And I'd not long lost my hubby.'

'Did you lock up after the ambulance had gone?'

'Oh yes. I checked around, emptied the fridge, washed up a few things, you know.'

'What did you do with the stuff from the fridge?'

'Well, there was only half a pint of milk left, some cheese, a few tomatoes in the bottom part and a tub of margarine. I poured away the milk and brought the rest home. I'm sure he wouldn't have minded and I do hate waste.'

'Of course. You did the right thing,' said Eccles in that same soft voice.

Dundee was feeling uncomfortable in the heat. He loosened his collar and spoke for the first time.

'When you'd locked up, what did you do with the key?'

'I put it in that special hiding place in the garage. Really clever place it is. See, Mr Downes showed me how to wrap the key in foil and put it on top of one of the low beams in the garage. You couldn't see it at all from below. I had to climb on a little stepladder, put the keys up there, then move the ladder away. He told me that I was the only other person who knew where it was. I was going to tell Jane, his daughter, at the funeral, but after what happened, I completely forgot.'

'Never mind,' said Eccles. 'We'll let her know.'

'Did Mr Downes use a laundry, Mrs Bennett?' asked Dundee.

Mrs Bennett paused for a moment, then answered, 'Oh yes, That place called Best Wash in town. They used to pick up on a Monday and bring the clean stuff back on Thursdays. But I wasn't there last Monday so there won't have been anything to bring back. Oh dear, that stuff will still be in the laundry basket.'

The detectives shared a glance, thinking that was another job for SOCO, then Eccles said, 'Don't worry, Mavis. We'll see that it's dealt with.'

As the detectives left, there was a paroxysm of yapping from the other room as Sophie's guard-dogging skills went into overdrive.

SIX

When the detectives got back to the station, uniform branch were changing shifts. Out of the door came PC Grabowski giving them both another of those enchanting smiles. Dundee glanced at Eccles and saw a slight blush colour her cheeks. He knew that his colleague's interest was in her own sex rather than his, but he was not sure about Grabowski. The fact that the fruitcakes had been partners for a good while had been reassuring to Leanne. She had seen so many working relationships become something more. At least that wouldn't happen with her husband and Eccles.

They had gone past the young woman when Dundee glanced back and saw Grabowski watching him.

As they climbed the stairs to the CID room Eccles suddenly asked, 'How's your wife, Jack?'

'Fine. Leanne's getting used to the kids being at school. She's going back to work soon.'

'Well, you need to be careful. That girl's got the hots for you.'

'Which girl?'

'Oh come off it Jack. The one we just passed.'

Now, it was Dundee's turn to blush.

'What on earth would she see in an old bloke like me?'

'Oh, you're not so bad for a man approaching middle age. Tall and slim and not much grey hair as yet. I've heard a few bits of gossip in the common room. I'm not interested for obvious reasons but ...'

'You're talking rubbish, Dawn.'

'Some girls go for older men. Agnieska certainly does. That's her first name by the way. Pretty isn't it? Mind you, she gets called Agnes most of the time. She's not interested in me, unfortunately, but I've seen the way she looks at you.'

'Well, d'you think you could have word, Dawn. I mean, warn her off.'

'No way, Jack. You do your own dirty work.'

Jack thought about Dawn's words as he entered the CID room. He decided he'd get home early for a change, buy a bottle of wine, have some quality time with Leanne and perhaps, if he was really early, he could put the twins to bed.

It was very quiet in the incident room and the few officers there were peering at screens or writing notes.

'Where's the DCI?' he asked generally.

'Already gone,' replied Cheshire. 'Some function at the Town Hall. All dressed up he was.'

'Thank God for that,' muttered Dundee. He called those present over for a quick conference. He told them what he and Eccles had discovered, which wasn't a lot and didn't take much telling.

'Any luck with MISPERS, Cheesy?'

'A couple of possibles down London way. They're sending descriptions, but no photographs unfortunately.'

'Any luck with the pubs and clubs?'

A couple of the footsloggers shook their heads.

'What about Staines? Anything to report, Dave?'

'Not a sausage,' said Murphy. 'But if that car turns up ...'

At that moment, the desk sergeant entered with a parcel addressed to Eccles.

'From SOCO Miss,' he informed her. 'Only two sets of prints. That writer chap for one and the other ...'

'His daughter, I expect,' said Eccles.

'If you say so ... Anyway, SOCO said you could have it now.'

'Thanks Bill.' He left. Eccles took the parcel to her desk and undid the wrapping.

'Right then,' said Dundee, 'I reckon we can all have an early night.'

There were joyful mutterings all round and the CID room began to empty quickly.

'What about you Dawn?'

'I'll stay a while. Give this manuscript a whirl.'

'Now, that's devotion to duty I must say.'

'You get home and be nice to that sweet wife of yours.'

By the time Dundee had made a few notes for DCI Wentworth and was ready to leave DS Eccles was deep into the manuscript.

Dundee drove one of the pool cars towards the edge of town. Leanne needed their own car with the twins to transport everywhere and it was beginning to show its age. They had bought the house from new when this road had been built just above the water meadows. It was really more than they could afford but with that view across the river and the wooded hills beyond they just fell for it.

Dundee had moved here from the Black Country but he knew the valley well. His father had often brought him here at the weekends to fish in the river. Dad was glad to get away from the drab streets of the Willenhall estate where they lived and the foundry where he had worked for most of his life. They would sit on the riverbank, whatever the weather, and feel the peace of the place and the clean air raising their spirits. He also knew that his father was relieved to get away from his mother, who preferred bingo and a night down the pub to the attractions of the countryside. Dundee lost interest in fishing when he reached his teens, but he never lost his love of this valley.

He was 17 when his dad died of fags and disappointment. When Mum brought a new man home Jack moved out, and applied to join the police. He started his training in Darlaston but when he saw this post advertised in the valley he jumped at it. Of course, he was ribbed by his colleagues who thought he must be mad to move to 'Dullshire' as they called it and his superiors saw it as a bad move for someone with a promising career.

A year or so later he met Leanne at a dance. They clicked straight off and six months later they moved in together. At first they lived in a flat near the town centre and saved as much as possible from their combined wages. His dad had left nothing and his mother had moved to Birmingham with her new man. Leanne's parents were just stingy. Leanne was a hairdresser so she earned very little and even with Jack's move to CID and then promotion to Sergeant it was ages before they could afford to get married and put down a deposit on a house. Almost as soon as they moved in Leanne got pregnant and when the twins were born she left the hairdressing salon to look after them and they continued to struggle financially. Things improved slightly when Jack was promoted again to Detective Inspector. Now, just as Leanne was going back to work and things might become a little easier all round she seemed to have become discontented.

Dundee stopped at Sainsbury's and bought a bottle of wine. He was about to buy chocolates as well but then remembered Leanne's expanding waistline and bought flowers instead. When he got home she was sitting in the kitchen, flicking through one of those celebrity magazines and the kids were in the next room watching TV. She gave her husband a quick smile to show that she was pleased to see him home early for a change, then that smile widened as he placed the bottle of Rose – Leanne's favourite – on the table and handed her the flowers. She got up and they hugged as they had not hugged for ages. Suddenly, Leanne's smile disappeared.

'I didn't know you'd be coming home early. I haven't prepared a meal.'

'Have the kid's eaten?'

'A while ago.'

'Well, why don't we have a take-away? You order and I'll say hello to the twins.'

'Indian or Chinese?'

'Whatever. You choose.'

She made her way to the phone in the hall while he went into the lounge. At first the twins grumbled as he forced his way between them on the sofa, but soon they snuggled up against him, Sean placing his favourite toy car in his dad's lap and Karen placing her tiny hand on his. He tried to talk to them, but he could not make them take their eyes off the screen, so he decided to watch the programme with them. It was an action packed American cartoon full of weird characters. He couldn't follow it at all. At last, the cartoon ended. Jack grabbed the remote and switched off the TV. At first, they both protested then they both tried to give him their important news simultaneously.

'Mrs Reynolds gave me a gold star today,' said Karen, while Sean said, 'Wayne's my best friend. He's ace!'

The doorbell rang and he heard Leanne paying for the takeaway. Then she called, 'Bedtime, you two.'

Dundee expected another protest, but the twins took him by the hand and led him upstairs. They were already dressed for bed. They still shared the same room. Jack was supposed to be turning the office into a separate bedroom for Karen when he had the time.

'Huh! When he had the time!'

When the twins got into bed he'd expected them to demand a bedtime story, but it appeared that going to school had worn them out. Sean had taken back that special car and brought it upstairs. Now, he lay down in his bed and ran the little model across the pillow, while he made an engine noise. Karen tucked her favourite doll in beside her. Almost before he leaned to kiss her cheek his daughter's eyes had closed and when he went to kiss his son Sean turned away muttering, 'Night Dad.' Perhaps he thought he was already too old for goodnight kisses.

Jack turned out the light and moved back on to the landing. Whatever was happening between their parents did not seem to have been noticed by them. They seemed as happy as ever.

As he came back downstairs he saw Leanne waiting at the bottom, with a finger to her lips. A wonderful smell was wafting up from the kitchen. When she smiled, Leanne looked more like the girl he had fallen for all those years ago. She directed him into the little dining room. He had always meant to knock down the wall and turn the area into a kitchen-diner, but he had never had the time. Now, they rarely bothered to use the dining room unless they had visitors. But tonight, Leanne had put the flowers in a vase, set them on the table and lit a candle next to them. Leanne served the meal on warm plates and Jack poured the wine. They ate in silence for a while, then Jack noticed that Leanne's glass was already empty and leaned over to refill it. Her face was quite flushed and she was smiling. She had undone the top two buttons of her blouse, probably to cool herself down, and he found himself looking at her breasts, fuller now, but still firm and shapely. He felt himself becoming aroused and went around to her side of the table. He lifted her gently from her seat and sat her back down on his knee.

'Shouldn't we clear the ...'she began, but now, he had undone the other buttons of her blouse and put his hand inside to feel her breasts. Leanne moaned and pressed her lips to his. He unclipped her bra and soon his hand was stroking her unfettered breasts and feeling her nipples harden.

Suddenly, his phone rang. He tried to ignore it but it rang on and on. The moment had been spoiled.

'Shit! Shit! Shit!' he exclaimed as he went into the kitchen and reached into the pocket of his jacket which he had hung on the back of a chair. He saw that the call was from Eccles.

A Perfect Alibi

'Jack, I'm sorry to spoil your evening but I have to see you. Meet me at the Old Vicarage as soon as possible.'

When he went back into the dining room Leanne had slumped back on her chair, her smile had gone and the scowl had returned.

SEVEN

It was raining again as Dundee drove out of town. Much more of this, he thought, and the river will flood its banks. This had been a regular occurrence during the last few years. He had never regretted moving to the valley, but he knew that its beautiful river had a downside too.

His evening at home had ended in disaster. Leanne had not spoken to him as he'd got ready to leave; she had merely stomped off to bed. He had cursed Eccles and hoped that what she had discovered was really useful. She was just too bloody zealous at times.

There was very little traffic on the road and when he reached the village it seemed to be totally deserted. At first he missed the turning to the Old Vicarage because of all the trees, but at last he recognised the white gate, drove up the drive and parked next to DS Eccles's little sports car. She loved that car and it seemed to match her personality; fast and smart.

Eccles had heard Jack's car arrive and came to open the door. She was dressed in jeans and sweater, which emphasised her stately figure and her black hair was pulled back in a severe pony tail. Her face had a well-scrubbed look without any makeup. He was reminded briefly of Xena the Warrior he had once seen on TV.

'OK, what was so bloody urgent you had to spoil my evening?'

'I'm sorry Jack, but really it couldn't wait. Come and sit in the kitchen. I brought a flask of coffee.'

They sat at the kitchen table, sipping their coffees, while Eccles began to explain.

'First of all I read through that manuscript. There were only 50 or so pages.'

'And?'

'It's very peculiar. I don't think the daughter read it properly or she was not prepared to accept the implications.'

'What the hell is it about?'

'Well, of course it's fiction but, for a start, the story is set in a village, mainly in a house like this one. The story is told in the first person. He and his wife lived separate lives. He hated her for some sort of humiliation she'd put him through years ago. He is delighted when she gets ill and dies. Now, he wants a woman just for sex, with no strings, and the younger the better.'

'Do you think Downes was like that?'

'I don't know. But we're going to have to talk to his daughter as soon as possible.'

'So, what happens?'

'Ah, this is where it gets really interesting. The guy searches the internet and makes contact with a gang that is trafficking girls into the country for strip clubs, and worse. He hands over a fair amount of money and this gang delivers a girl to his house, where she is locked up, drugged and forced to have sex with him. Most of the time she is too out-of-it to resist. That's where the story breaks off. Oh, and there's this strange note in handwriting on the last page. I copied it out for you.'

He read the strange comment that the author had written.

'I just can't do it anymore.'

'Sounds like he's run out of ideas. Or perhaps he can't be bothered to write anymore.'

'Perhaps?'

'Is this Richard Downes's handwriting?'

'Well, forensics told me that there are only two sets of prints on the manuscript, and one's his. They compared it with the hundreds of other prints around the house. The other set will be Jane's I expect. She said she'd skimmed through it.'

Dundee became thoughtful but finally said, 'Look. This is fiction. It's just a story. The guy was a bloody writer. A crime writer! Don't you think you're jumping to some incredible conclusions?'

'Maybe, but then I found this.' She placed the note that Jane had tossed into the bin on the table and flattened it out.

Dundee read it out loud, *'You bastard. You won't get away with it'* and nodded briefly.

'I'm beginning to think our Miss Downes isn't telling us everything.'

Eccles continued, 'Then I thought about those clothes that the laundry – well somebody – delivered. They were the kind of clothes a very young woman would wear.'

'The lab should have something on them pretty soon. You know, I'm beginning to see what you mean.'

'There's more. I want to show you something. This way.'

She opened the cellar door and turned on the light. He followed her down the steps.

'Well?'

'What do you see?'

'A damned good supply of wine.'

He took a bottle from the rack.

'Pretty expensive stuff.'

'And?'

'A large freezer.'

'A large, empty freezer, but still switched on.'

'Ah! Right. We need SOCO here first thing tomorrow.' He glanced at his watch. 'Actually today!'

'And we have to call at The Crown. I had a text from Jane Downes. That's where she's staying.'

It was after 2am when Dundee got home, so he didn't disturb Leanne and lay on the sofa instead. It was too short for him to stretch out properly and he couldn't get to sleep for ages. Partly, it was this case. It was very strange. Generally, the few murders he dealt with were the result of anger or jealousy and often fuelled by drink. You know, a guy comes home early and finds his wife having it off with one of his friends, so he bashes the guy or his wife or both with something handy as a murder weapon. Or an argument in the pub gets out of hand and someone just happens to have a knife. But this was something else. A beautiful young girl, died in an unexplained way, and dumped in an empty grave. A note and some woman's clothing sent to a local writer who was now dead himself.

When he finally dozed off he saw the dead girl again lying slumped in the grave but her face became that of PC Grabowski. He woke with a start. When he woke up properly he couldn't face Leanne or the kids. Luckily, it was Saturday so they would be lying in. He crept up to the bathroom, shaved and showered, put the same clothes back on, to avoid going into the bedroom, and left the house. He drove to Eccles's flat and they went straight to The Crown to talk to Jane Downes.

EIGHT

Jane had slept surprisingly well. Her father had been buried at last, with the minimum of fuss. The press had not been too intrusive. Some guy called Matthews had phoned, asking her how she had felt when the body had been discovered in her father's grave. She had told him that naturally she had been upset, but her father had now been buried properly and she simply needed to be left to grieve. He asked about her father's writing and whether there was another of his novels on the way. She told him that he would have to contact the publishers about that. The reporter did not seem to have connected the dead girl with her father, except in the use of his grave, thank goodness.

She got up early and looked out of the window on to Bridgeport High Street, sparkling in morning sunshine after another night of rain. The wide street was still fairly quiet at this early hour but the stallholders were beginning to set up for the Saturday market. Scaffolding structures were being bolted together and brightly coloured awnings were stretched across the top and sides. In the middle of the street stood the old Town Hall, raised on stone arches so that traffic could pass underneath, but on market days no traffic was allowed through because the space was filled with stalls.

There were not too many empty shops in the High Street as the town attracted many tourists, especially with its restored railway line offering trips down the valley on trains pulled by one of an impressive collection of steam locomotives.

The old town held many memories for Jane. She had attended the Girls High School and made good friends. She had done well in her exams, enabling her to go on to university.

She remembered the many Saturdays when, as a little girl, she would come into town with Mum to help with the shopping and then go for coffee and cakes in the town's poshest restaurant.

A Perfect Alibi

When she reached her teens she would come in on the bus alone and meet her friends. They would window shop, have coffee in one of the more up-to-date cafés, then stroll around Woolworths, long closed now, and spend their pocket money, but as they grew older their attention was directed more at boys. It was at the local cinema that she had her first kiss and in some bushes down by the river she had had her first very clumsy experience of sex.

She blushed as she remembered a very embarrassing incident in Woolworths. She had become mixed up with a rather unsavoury group of girls, as a rebellion against what she considered to be her very middle class upbringing. These girls had dared her to steal some make-up – they were regular shoplifters – and foolishly she had agreed. Of course, because she was inexperienced she been caught and taken to the manager's office. Doreen and Trixie had disappeared.

Her father was called and he arrived, seething. He was terribly angry because she had embarrassed him, but with his cultivated accent and patronising attitude to the store detective he got her off with a warning, but he didn't speak to her as she cried her way home, and he would not speak to her for weeks afterwards. She was not allowed to go to town on her own for six months, but Mum took her in the car with strict instructions not to get mixed up with those girls. When she saw them they ignored her and went sniggering away.

And there were other more distressing memories. A school friend who drowned when the river was in flood and a favourite Aunt, one of very few relatives living in the area, who had been killed in a car accident.

She had stayed at The Crown when her mother died, rather than be a burden for her father. Actually, her father had made it clear that he would not welcome a visit anyway.

She had brought Patrick to Bridgeport once, and they had stayed at The Crown. She had taken him around to see the sights; the old castle, the Cliff Railway, the park on the hill overlooking the lower town, and the restored railway, which he loved.

Jane had decided to sell the Old Vicarage as soon as it became legally hers and use the money to begin a completely new life, as far away from Patrick as possible. As soon as she had breakfasted she would go to one of the estate agents and ask them to value the house, even though she would not be able to put it on the market until probate was completed. Then perhaps she would look for a flat or a much smaller house to rent while she considered her future.

It was while she was enjoying a light breakfast that she received the message from Reception that DI Dundee and DS Eccles would like to speak to her.

It was quite cramped in Jane's room. Dundee sat on the tiny stool in front of the dressing table, his long legs stretched out. Jane sat on the one easy chair underneath the window and Eccles sat on the bed, still unmade. The atmosphere was fairly informal.

'So, you finally got your father buried?' asked Eccles.

'Yes. It was simple and quick. Luckily the rain held off.'

'Miss Downes,' began Dundee in a more formal tone, 'We'd like to ask you a few questions. Firstly, why didn't you tell us about the note to your father? The one you threw away.'

'Note? Oh that. Well, there was so much going on. I completely forgot.' She paused, 'You've been back to the house? Why?'

Eccles said, 'We were puzzled by a few things.'

There was a growing tension in the room. Jane began to feel uncomfortable.

'What things?'

'Well, for a start I read that manuscript. I found it disturbing. Then there was the handwritten comment at the end.'

'Well, I must admit I didn't give the story much attention. I was tired and ... to be honest I never really liked his novels.'

Dundee said, 'Tell us about your father.'

'What about him?'

'Well, to begin with, how did you get on with him?'

'Why? What has this got to with anything?'

'Probably nothing. But just humour us for the moment.'

'Very well. If I must.'

Eccles noticed that Downes had gone rather pale and that there seemed to be tears brimming in her eyes.

'My Dad and I never really got on. I mean, as a baby he just found me a nuisance. You know, sleepless nights, smelly nappies. Our house was quite small in those days. Mum told me that he would always leave the room when she had to change me and he hated having to babysit for more than a few minutes. The trouble was that he was teaching then, at the boys' school and trying to write as well. It must have been hard. Mum did everything for me.'

'So, he hadn't had a book published then?'

'Oh no. I was about five or six when that happened. I remember it well. For a while the house was a happy one. Dad had some money, and I had started school so Mum was able to work again.'

'I bet that was a relief,' said Dundee thinking of himself.

'What did she do?' asked Eccles.

'She was a legal secretary. Bradley and Dibbs in town. Are they still there?'

'Yes. Mind you it's Bradley, Dibbs and Parker now.'

'Dad was given a good advance for his next novel and we moved to a slightly larger house in Back Lane, near the church. For a while we were quite a happy family. Mum became involved in village activities. The WI, the church choir and so on. Dad even went to the pub from time to time.'

'But the good times didn't last?'

'No. I was about 13 or 14. I'd been at the High School for a couple of years. A school friend had been to stay for the weekend. Moira Evans. She was very pretty, with long fair hair and a lovely figure and she was a bit precocious. Mum had just brought me back from my music lesson. The lesson had been shorter than usual. When I went up to my room to change I heard this terrible row downstairs. I rushed down and saw them standing in the kitchen. Dad's face was scarlet. Mum's deathly pale. They stopped shouting when I entered. Dad stormed off. Mum sat down and burst into tears.'

'So, what was the row about?'

'I don't know. But I was never allowed to have friends to stay after that.'

'Hmm,' said Dundee.

'In my mid-teens I became rebellious. I defied my dad in every way. You know staying out late, drinking, smoking, sometimes dope, several boyfriends; the sort of boys Dad did not approve of. Mostly he turned a blind eye, glad to be rid of me for the evening but one night when I came home really late, my dad hit me, hard, across the face. Called me a slut! Said, I had really disappointed him.'

'Where was your mother?'

'Oh they were living separate lives by then; she must have been out that night.'

'So, what happened when you told her?'

'I didn't and the strange thing was that my father saying I had disappointed him brought me to my senses for a while. I began to study again. Worked hard for my A-levels. Got good results. Then I disappointed him again.'

'How?'

'Because I chose science subjects and applied for a university with a good reputation for science. He hated anything like that, didn't understand it at all. He even threatened to cut off any financial support.'

'Would he have done that?'

'Probably not. But I was just a kid. I wasn't sure.'

'Do you know Jane. I don't think you father sounds like a very nice man.'

Jane noted that this was the first time that Eccles had used her Christian name.

'That's unfair. He was just my dad. He had his faults. I'm sure all fathers do.'

Eccles thought about her own father's homophobia and the disaster her coming out had been.

Dundee hadn't spoken for a while. Now, he asked,

'Did you go to university?'

'Oh yes. Mum made it clear that I was to do what I wanted. He was not to interfere. She seemed to imply that if he did anything to stop me she had ways of making life very difficult for him. So, he backed down and I went off to uni, got a fairly good degree and a job in a research laboratory.'

'What was your research?'

Eccles knew that this was simply curiosity and would not help them with the case.

'Oh this and that. Obscure and unimportant. It was just a job. Meanwhile I became close to Mum again. She visited me often and loved London, where I'd moved to, and really enjoyed being away from Dad.'

She paused.

'Then I met Patrick. He was everything that Dad hated. He'd been to public school. He worked with computers. He had a German car. And worst of all he was quite well off. So, I moved in with him and contact with Dad became minimal. I only visited him a couple of times in ten years. I wrote very occasionally and phoned a few times. Now, Patrick has left me and Dad is dead.'

Eccles saw that tears were brimming again. She wondered which of those events had caused them.

There was an awkward silence in the room, then Eccles nodded at Dundee and said, 'Thank you, Jane. You've been very helpful.'

'I don't see how. I mean you can't possibly think that my father had anything to do with the death of that girl.'

'I shouldn't think so,' said Dundee. 'But I think someone is trying very hard to convince us that he did. There's the stolen laptop and that parcel of clothes. We just have to look at all angles. Will you be staying at The Crown, or moving back to the Old Vicarage?'

'Oh no! I'm putting the house on the market as soon as I can. I'm staying here for a while, but I shall be looking for somewhere smaller to rent until it's sold. I've given in my notice at the lab. And I won't be going back to London.'

NINE

Peggy Dickson called to her dogs and set off on her morning walk up the hill. This was her hill. She had lived here for most of her life. She knew every inch of it. This morning they would follow the path around the plantation of conifers and reach the top from there.

It was a lovely day, cold and clear. She had heard it said that there was nothing higher between here and the Urals and this morning she could believe it. Bridgeport, the nearest town, was hidden in a deep valley gouged out by the river. Beyond that she could just make out a group of tall buildings, probably high rise flats, marking the beginning of the Black Country.

Peggy had suffered a broken night. She was a light sleeper but her cottage was so isolated that she was rarely disturbed. Sometime after midnight she had heard a car go past the cottage in low gear because the lane was steep. The headlights briefly flickered across her ceiling as it went by.

She could not get back to sleep, waiting for the car to come down again. But it didn't return. Then, even more strangely, she heard another vehicle with a larger diesel engine, possibly a van, growling slowly up the slope. Disturbed, she sat up in bed. The luminous hands of her alarm clock showed it was 1.30am. She never used the alarm because she had always been an early riser. About half an hour later she heard the larger vehicle descend, but the car did not return.

She needed this brisk morning walk to clear her head. As she reached the steepest part of the path the two younger dogs ran in front of her, nosing into the bracken, making useless forays after rabbits, while the older dog loped gracefully beside her.

At last, she reached the top of the hill. Here there were obvious signs of the industrial beehive this had once been, with heather covered mounds that disguised the spoil heaps from coal mining days and deep black pools filling the quarries where limestone had once been extracted.

She thought again about that car. There was no sign of it now. Joyriders? She had known about them during her few brief years in Birmingham as a student nurse, with a spell in A&E. But surely they just abandoned their stolen vehicles and fled or torched them. Wasn't that the term used? Then she thought about a courting couple, or perhaps an adulterous relationship. But they must have been damned hardy coming up here for their pleasure on a chilly autumn night. And why hadn't she heard them come back down? There was no other way off the hill for a vehicle and she hadn't gone back to sleep.

The dogs lay on the ground beside her, panting hard, with their tongues lolling from their jaws. She thought about the time her family had gathered here to scatter her mother's ashes. That was 15 years ago. Peggy, as the unmarried daughter, had given up her nursing career, and her little flat in Edgbaston, to come home and look after mother when she first became ill. Her father had been killed a few years earlier in a shooting accident. He was a gamekeeper. His body was not discovered for a few days and the animal world had begun to take its revenge.

Peggy could not return to nursing but she found a job as a receptionist at the surgery in the village at the bottom of the hill. Shewasas past retirement age, but they had persuaded her stay on. She had looked after her mother for 17 years. Now, she knew she would never leave here until her own ashes blew away in the wind.

Standing on the highest point of the hill, where sheep and picnickers had cleared the bracken from a wide circle of turf, she noticed a shadow moving around her and when she looked up into the clear sky she saw a buzzard circling above the largest pool. Suddenly, it dived and lifted some small prey from the grassy edge of the pool. It was then that Peggy noticed the tyre tracks, leading off the lane and running straight down to the water's edge.

The dogs rose eagerly to join her as she stumbled down the steep slope, following the ruts cut deep into the turf. Her heart was beating fast as she approached the pool. The tracks led straight into the water, which was rippling in the breeze. Then the wind dropped, the water became still and Peggy caught a glimpse of something metallic just beneath the surface. She guessed what it was and gasped, filled with horror at the thought that someone or more than one person might be still inside. Moving as fast as her 69 year old body would allow, she made her way back to the cottage to call the police, her dogs hurrying after her, obediently.

Back in the incident room DCI Wentworth asked, 'So, where are we now? Dundee?'

'Eccles and I are beginning to think that someone is trying very hard to frame Richard Downes for the girl's death. His daughter Jane has told us about her father. He was not the nicest of men ...'

'That's putting it mildly,' interjected Eccles.

'He might well have had some dealings with the girl. Have we identified her yet?'

'No.' said Cheesy.

'But,' said Wentworth, 'we've had an interesting report from the lab. Apparently, all those clothes were purchased abroad. Which suggests that the girl was foreign.' He paused, as if thinking. 'Young, pretty, as Jack has observed, and foreign. What does that suggest?'

'Mmm,' muttered Eccles, 'au pair, language student, brides for sale, sex work ...'

'Right then Cheesy, get on to any au pair agencies and language schools, and see if anyone resembling her has gone missing. Oh, and look into brides for sale. We'll contact Vice and see if they know anything about local traffickers for the sex trade.'

'OK Boss.'

Dundee broke in, 'And how about Peter Staines? When a young girl is found dead and a young man is missing, there's a good chance they're connected. We need to find him. Even if he's not directly involved he may know something.'

'Well, let's get the feelers out on all of this, but to be honest, if we don't get some leads soon I'm thinking of passing this one up. We're not really getting anywhere. I felt a right tit when the Chief spoke to me this morning. I had to tell him that our progress was about as significant as a silent fart.'

Wentworth's phone rang.

'Yeah, Wentworth here. Go on ... I see. Thanks.' He closed his phone and smiled around at the assembled group.

'That was uniform. Someone has just reported an abandoned car dumped in a pool.'

'Where?'

'Would you believe. On top of the fucking Brown Hill.'

Not many people visited Brown Hill anymore, except for one day a year when a sponsored walk took place and thousands made the journey from Bridgeport to the top of the hill and back again, 22 miles in all. But the walkers dotted about the bracken and heather today were not enjoying the sort of walk that would give them a sense of achievement and their chosen charity a healthier bank balance. No, these walkers were moving carefully line abreast across the hilltop inspecting every gorse bush, tapping down every clump of bracken or heather and looking into the few ruined stone structures remaining from those long abandoned quarries and mines.

The car had been pulled out of the pool and taken away for careful examination. It was a Rover 75. There was no one inside it. There were figures in wet suits diving into the dark water where the car had sunk. They'd been at it since Peggy's call that morning had brought the police to the scene. The mobile cafeteria would be doing a good trade when the whistle blew for another break.

The weather had turned. The wind was blowing straight from the north-west. Low clouds threatened rain or even sleet. Dundee and Eccles sat in their car, just outside the crime scene tape, with Peggy Dickson on the back seat. She was very agitated, nearly spilling the steaming tea from her plastic cup.

'Oh my God, I hope they don't find him in the pool.' said Peggy. 'The driver I mean. Were you looking for that car? Is the driver in trouble? Perhaps he, or she I suppose, just dumped the car and ran away.'

'That's a possibility,' said Eccles.

'Peggy ... I can call you Peggy?' asked Dundee.

'Of course.'

'You did very well, noticing the car, and reporting it straight away.'

'Is the owner in trouble then?'

'Well, we certainly need to speak to the driver.'

'So, you know who the car belongs to?'

'We're not absolutely sure. But once we check the records ...'

'Someone will be very upset, I reckon. If the car was stolen.'

'I don't really think he'll care. I'm afraid, he's dead.'

Peggy muttered a shocked, 'Oh!'

The window on the leeward side of the car was open. They heard a shout from someone in the pool. Other figures rushed across then shook their heads and walked away again.

'Probably a dead sheep,' said Peggy. 'They're always falling in. There should be a fence.'

Dundee turned around to look directly at Peggy.

'Peggy, I want you to think very carefully. Have you noticed anything unusual up here in the last few days? Any strangers? An unusual vehicle passing your cottage? Anything at all?'

'Oh, yes. Something very odd indeed. Early this morning, very early ...' She stopped to think. 'About half past one. I heard this car going past my cottage. It was in a low gear 'cause the lane's quite steep. It woke me up. Soon after, another vehicle passed by. It was bigger, with a noisier engine. I think it might have been a van. A bit later the van came back down, but not the car. I'm a light sleeper these days, so I'd have heard it if it had. And it couldn't have gone down another way because the lane past my place is the only way you can drive to the top. So, I suppose that car ...'

She indicated the pool from which the car had been recovered.

'That's very interesting,' muttered Eccles, writing in her notebook. 'Thank you, Peggy.'

Dundee got out of the car and spoke to the officer in charge of the search. His hands seemed to describe a bigger vehicle and then he pointed at the ground. The officer called half a dozen men to the spot and they began to examine the turf very carefully.

When Dundee returned to the car he said, 'Now, Peggy, we'll have to get you to make a written statement. We'll drop you at your cottage and do it there. Save taking you to the station. Is that OK?'

While they shared a much nicer cup of tea, Peggy made her statement and signed it.

'Can we give you a lift anywhere, Peggy?' Dundee asked.

'No thanks. My dogs will be going spare. They haven't had their afternoon walk. I'll have to put them on the lead and take them down to the village, I suppose. They'll hate it, but they must have their exercise.'

She saw them to the door and Eccles shook her hand.

'Thanks, Peggy. You've been very helpful.'

A distraught Mrs Staines had seen their car draw up outside. She came to the door with a cigarette held in her shaking hand.

'Have you found him?'

'Not exactly. Can we come in?'

She threw the fag on to the path and ushered them in, looking up and down the street before closing the door.

'Bastard neighbours are watching like hawks. I'm a prisoner in my own home.'

She took them into a sitting room, filled with junk. She moved a complaining cat off the sofa, which strode away with its tail in the air, before settling in a corner, scratching itself. Dundee and Eccles both thought about fleas as they sat down. Mrs Staines lifted some magazines off an easy chair, chucked them on the floor and took their place.

'You said, "not exactly". What the fuck does that mean?'

She took another cigarette from a packet in her apron pocket and tried to light it, but her hands were trembling too much.

'Mrs Staines, are you sure your son couldn't drive?'

'S'far as I know. I mean, you know what lads is like. Why?'

'Well, we've found a car. It belonged to that writer who has just died. The one you said your son had been helping in some way.'

'If you think my Pete would have pinched his car you'm barking up the wrong tree. He would never ... So, where was this car found?'

'In a deep pool. On top of the Brown Hill.'

Mrs Staines's mouth opened and stayed open.

'Top of the Brown Hill! What the fuck's going on?'

'I wish we knew, Mrs Staines. The whole area is being searched at this moment. We wondered if your son knew anybody living in that area.'

'Well, he might of. I mean he's an adult. He don't tell me everything. Might have a girlfriend up that way, I suppose. He's very popular with the girls. But he don't take them seriously, he's never brought one home.'

She got up from her seat, threw the unlit cigarette in the empty grate, picked up a framed photo from the mantelpiece and handed it to Eccles.

'See. That's my Pete.'

The photo showed a good looking lad about 20 years old. Probably worked out regularly. Dressed in expensive casual clothes. His smile said, 'I'm a great guy.' He didn't set Eccles's heart thumping for obvious reasons, but she smiled obligingly and passed the photo to Dundee.

'I see what you mean, Mrs Staines. Have we already got a picture at the station?'

'Yeah, Sergeant Harris and that young woman with the foreign name took one with them.'

Dundee felt warmth spreading to his face.

'Would you mind if we had a look at your son's room?' asked Eccles.

'To be honest, I'm past caring what you do. I mean, my lad's gone missing. I don't know what the fuck's happened to him. I'm at my wits end. You get in there and find anything as might help.'

'Thank you, Mrs Staines. We will do everything we can to find your son.'

'I'll show you his room, but I don't know what you're looking for. He won't let me in it, even to clean around.'

She lit another cigarette, then led them upstairs, the climb causing a bout of coughing, and opened a door off the landing.

'Have a good gander. But don't take nothing without asking. I'll be downstairs. There's a programme I watch about his time.'

The first surprise as they entered the room was that unlike the rest of the house this room was incredibly tidy.

'Do you think his proud Mum has had a tidy up in case there was something she wouldn't want us to see?'

'Drugs you mean?'

'Possibly.'

'No, I think this is young Pete's handiwork. I mean look at these DVD's. They've all got stickers with the date on them. And they're in alphabetical order. This is one very methodical guy.'

Eccles opened the wardrobe.

'Hey Jack, look at this.'

He joined her and ran his hands along the clothes neatly hanging up inside.

'I don't know much about fashion,' he said, 'But going by these labels I'd guess this stuff is pretty expensive.'

'Yes,' said Eccles. 'I know that we all have different priorities, but most of this stuff's way beyond someone on jobseeker's.'

'Nicked?'

'Could be. And look at those trainers. One pair of those would cost a hundred quid at least. And there's a couple of pairs, as well as these fancy shoes.'

'Hey look,' said Dundee. 'What's in that box?'

'Let's have a gander as the lady of the house put it.'

They took out the box, set it on the small table, and flicked through the contents. There was a series of hanging files. Dundee opened one and burst out. 'Bloody hell!'

'What?'

'Guess what his bike cost?'

'No idea. I'm not into bikes. I prefer hiking.'

'Over a thousand quid!'

Eccles whistled, 'Wow, someone's been digging a lot of graves.'

Dundee picked out another file; inside was an envelope. He used his pen to lift the unglued tab and gasped.

'Christ almighty!' he exclaimed. 'Here, have a look, but don't touch.'

Eccles whistled again as she peered into the file. She guessed there must be at least a thousand pounds in crisp twenties.

'Look, I know that doting mum said we shouldn't take anything, but I think forensics should have a look at this.'

He pinched one corner of the envelope between thumb and finger and slipped it into his jacket pocket.

As they went downstairs they could hear a television burbling loudly. Eccles knocked on the sitting room door.

On the screen an obese young woman was haranguing a weedy looking young man.

'He's been knocking off her best friend,' Mrs Staines explained. She did not look up as she asked, 'Find anything?'

'Nothing useful, I'm afraid.' said Eccles.

'Oh well ...' said Mrs Staines before shouting, 'You bastard!' Then she turned briefly to Eccles. 'Oh, not you love.' Pointing at the screen, she exclaimed. 'That wanker on there!'

The detectives quietly closed the door and left the house.

TEN

When the detectives had left, Jane sat on the edge of her bed and felt tears filling her eyes again. She had been very disturbed by their visit. She'd never really understood her father but now he had become an unpleasant mystery. Dundee and Eccles had implied that he was being framed for the death of that girl. Jane was not so sure. There was that unpleasant note and the parcel of clothes to be explained, and her father's comment on the last page of the unfinished novel. Even if he had not caused the death of that girl it seemed that he may have been involved in some nasty goings on.

She waited for her mind to settle before she made plans for the day. First she must go to an estate agent and get them to value that damned house, so that she could sell it as soon as probate was completed. Then she must find some cheap lodgings nearby until the house was sold. And while that process was going through she had to try to find her school friend Moira Evans and ask her what had happened all those years ago. But how would she find someone she had not seen for more than 20 years, who would probably be married and have a different name, or who might even have moved to the other side of the earth?

She needed someone to talk to. Until a couple of months ago that would have been Patrick. Whenever she was worried about anything he would listen patiently. It did not matter that he rarely came up with a solution to whatever the problem was, it was simply that he was a good listener. Quite often these little sessions ended with them in bed together. Patrick was good at that. It was Saturday morning so he was probably in bed with that girl right now.

Suddenly, her mood changed. She had things to do. What was the point of all this self-pity? She must make a new future for herself and sod bloody Patrick. She grabbed her coat and left the hotel.

The market was in full swing and Jane had to push her way along the crowded pavement to reach the estate agent. She remembered that there used to be one on the corner of the High Street and Church Lane, so she took her life in her hands and crossed the road. Surely, she thought, squeezing her way between eager shoppers, it would be sensible to turn the High Street into a pedestrian only area when the market took place. But the autumn sun was still shining and most people had smiles on their faces, so her spirits were lifted and, yes, when she reached the corner the estate agent was still there. The window was bright with glossy photographs, including a slide show of a very expensive country mansion. The business had a busy, successful feel.

Inside, there was only one agent not dealing with a client. The young girl behind the desk gave her a practiced smile. She was briefly reminded of Patrick's new girlfriend. The same bottle blonde hair, the same slim mini-skirted figure and rather overdone makeup.

'Can I help, Madam?'

'I'm *Ms* Downes. And I have a house to sell, eventually.'

'Please sit down. Let's get your details on the system.'

The girl tapped her keyboard and the screen cleared for a new entry. She smiled at Jane.

'I know what you mean about this Madam business. But it's what they tell us to say.'

'Well, let's go for first names then. I'm Jane and you are ...' She read the badge on the girl's smart blouse, 'Madeline.'

'Yes.'

Jane gave all her details, using the Old Vicarage as her address, though in fact she would simply use that as a poste restante.

A Perfect Alibi

'For the next few days you can get in touch with me at The Crown.'

At last, the entry was completed and Jane handed over a key to the property so that the agent could value it. She was about to leave when something else occurred to her.

'Do you also deal with lettings, Madeline?'

'For yourself? You'd better speak to Rita about that, unless ...'

'What?'

'Look, I shouldn't do this and I'll probably get into trouble, but you seem just the right person.'

'For what?'

'Well, my mum's looking for a new tenant for the little cottage next door to her house. It's small but very well appointed and it has a lovely view.'

'Expensive?'

'You'd have to discuss that with my mother. Shall I give you the address?'

'Where is this cottage?'

'Over the bridge. In the Lower Town. Julian's Hill.'

'I know it well. Those are large houses.'

'Yes, but the cottage is just in one corner of the garden. Probably built for servants, gardeners perhaps.'

'Well, my need is quite urgent. Will your mother be at home this morning?'

'She should be, you see, she's in a wheelchair these days.'

Jane imagined an elderly lady wheeling sadly about a large dark house.

'I'm sorry to hear that.'

'I'll give her a ring, just in case.'

'Please.'

The girl rang and her mother was delighted to hear about the prospective tenant. The girl passed a card with the name Mrs M Drew and the address of the house to Jane.

'Well, thank you, Madeline. You've been very helpful.'

Jane did not bother to go back to the hotel for her car. Instead she fought her way to the other end of the High Street, took a long set of steps down to the river and crossed the bridge. The river was still high but a couple of days without heavy rain had allowed it to drop to a safer level. The part of the town beyond the bridge was less grand and much less busy so she was able to move more quickly past the few shops until her route began to climb again on the other side of the valley. At the top was Julian's Hill, a quiet road with several splendid Regency style houses in large gardens. She had attended a party in one of these houses at the end of her schooldays and was embarrassed to remember the way she and her fellow pupils had behaved in that beautiful house.

The parents were away and their son, Derek, had foolishly announced that he was having party. There were dozens of gatecrashers and the house was almost trashed. She remembered the look of horror on Derek's face as he saw what was happening. Jane did not puke on the Axminsters, drop ash in the porcelain vases or have sex on the silken bedspreads, instead she had asked her boyfriend to take her home before the police arrived. Soon afterwards Derek and his parents moved away.

The house she wanted was at the end of the road with a large garden and a lovely little cottage in the corner, looking down into the valley. She didn't want to get her hopes up until she'd met Mrs Drew and discussed the rent, so she just glanced at the cottage and made for the front door of the larger house. She rang the bell and the door opened almost immediately, as if Mrs Drew had been waiting for her in the hall.

Jane was shocked to discover that the woman was not old, probably about the same age as herself. She was plump and pale probably from being confined to the house. Her fair hair, slightly greying, was cut short but her deep blue eyes gleamed brightly in the sunlit hallway.

'Mrs Drew?'

'Yes, do come in. You've come about the cottage? My daughter didn't tell me your name.'

She looked quizzically at Jane for a moment.

'Have we met before?'

'I don't think so. I'm Ms Downes, Jane Downes.'

'Well, I'll be damned ... you don't recognise me, do you? Well, of course you wouldn't. It's Moira. Moira Evans.'

Jane was unable to take it in.

'Moira!'

She bent down and gave her old friend a hug.

'This is amazing. You won't believe this, but you are exactly the person I was about to try and find.'

'Why? Oh look, come into the kitchen; we'll make some coffee and have a lovely chat.'

Moira turned her expensive looking and very manoeuvrable wheelchair around and led the way to the kitchen, which was a huge, high ceilinged room, with a large pine table and chairs in the centre. All around the sides were low work surfaces, designed to be accessible from a wheelchair and with every available gadget easily at hand.

As Moira got the coffee things together she asked,

'What did you mean when you said you were about to look for me?'

Jane knew that she couldn't just ask Moira about her father. Well, not yet anyway.

'I'll tell you in a minute. But what about yourself. I mean, it's wonderful to see you again but ...'

'Do you know, Jane, your face has hardly changed. It was just that sophisticated look and your smart clothes that confused me at first. You used to be such a gawky thing at school.'

'It's a long time since I wielded a hockey stick.'

They giggled briefly, like schoolgirls.

Moira served the coffee.

'Right, first this bloody wheelchair is the result of rheumatoid arthritis. It started about five years ago. No, to be honest I first knew something was wrong soon after John was born, but it's much worse now. I'm very lucky though. I have this lovely house and George makes sure I have everything I need.

'George?'

'Yes, George Drew. You probably remember his father – owned almost half the town – he's dead now. I married George almost straight out of school. You were meant to be invited to the wedding but we couldn't find you at the time. So, here I am with a well-off husband who can't do enough for me, and two super kids. What about you?'

'No husband, well-off or not, and no kids. Boring eh?'

They sipped their coffee in silence for a while. Then Moira asked,

'So, why did you want to see me?'

'My father died.'

'Oh, Jane! How stupid of me! I saw the report in the paper. You've been back for the funeral. How did it go?'

'It was quite upsetting. They found a body in his grave.'

'Oh shit. I read about that body but I never connected it with your father's funeral.'

'I've been thinking a lot about him lately. I don't think I ever really knew him.'

'Secrets and lies, eh?'

'Yes. That's what I wanted to ask you about actually, that time you came to stay for the weekend.'

Moira's face coloured slightly.

'That was a long time ago. What about it?'

'Well, after you left my parents had a terrible row. And I was never allowed to have friends to stay again. What happened?'

A Perfect Alibi

'Nothing much.'

Moira's face was now quite flushed.

'OK. This is how it was. I liked your dad. He was kind to me. Far more interested in me than my parents ever were. I suppose I had a sort of crush on him. It happens with adolescent girls. There was that one recently who ran off to France with her teacher. It's a phase some girls go through.'

'And?'

'It was the Saturday afternoon. You and your mother had to go out somewhere. Piano lesson I think. Your Dad asked if I would I like to see the study, where he wrote his books. I said yes, so he showed me some of his published books on the shelves and the one he was writing. He asked if I'd like to write something on his typewriter, sat me on his knee and while I was typing some rubbish his arms closed around me. Anyway, his arms came up until they were almost covering my breasts and he held them there. I didn't really mind. It just felt good to be held close like that. He may not even have noticed what he was doing. But then your mother came in and told me to leave the room. She said you were back and I should go and find you. She followed me out of the room and slammed the door.'

There was another long silence. Then Jane spoke.

'I suppose I guessed it was something like that. I mean when other girls had come to stay Dad was always more interested in them than in me. And you were very pretty with your long blonde hair and your lovely figure, almost a woman already.'

'Well, look at me now. Stuck in a wheelchair, growing fatter by the minute and my hair going grey. You're the good looking one now, Jane. You must have had loads of boyfriends. I guess that's why you haven't married, too busy playing the field?'

They both smiled. Jane decided not to tell her friend about Patrick.

'Another coffee?' asked Moira.

'No thanks. Can we talk about the cottage?'

'You'd like to view it?'

'Depends on the rent. And I should explain that I may not be staying very long. When I sell Dad's house I may want to move on.'

'Well, you could have six months' lease. You'll probably have sold your dad's house by then. Here's the key. Go and have a look.'

Jane walked across to the cottage. It was perfect. A lovely sitting room with a view over the river, a kitchen/diner and two small bedrooms, one with another splendid view. It was well decorated and more than adequately furnished. By the time she had locked up and returned the key Jane already felt completely at home.

While Dundee drove back to the station Eccles used her laptop to write a report of their visit to the Staines household. The new technology was such a boon. No more dashing back to the station to do the paperwork, or to check the files. It was all here with Wi-Fi available at the press of a button. These devices were now in all the squad cars. You could park up somewhere, use the machines and still show a police presence, which is what the public kept demanding. So, it wasn't all cuts and mergers. This was genuine progress.

She returned the laptop to its place and spoke to Dundee.

'So, what the hell has mummy's blue eyed boy been up to?'

'Dunno. And if it was him who stole that car, where the hell is he now?'

'I've been thinking,' said Eccles. 'He's a good looking lad. Keeps himself fit. Perhaps he's offering his services in some way. Toy boy? Escort? It would explain the money.'

'Or he might be a rent boy. That gravedigger seemed to fancy him something rotten.'

'Still doesn't explain his disappearance.'

A Perfect Alibi

'No, or that car being dumped in the pool.'

'It's been a long day, Jack. I say we drop the money off with forensics then call it a day. Leanne will be glad to have you home earlier for a change.'

'She's not there. Gone away for a couple of days.'

'Oh?' said Eccles in a worried tone.

Dundee didn't want to make his colleague feel guilty, but the day after he'd left for the Old Vicarage in the middle of the night Leanne had packed some clothes and driven herself and the kids to the home of an old girlfriend from her hairdressing days who'd gone up in the world and lived in a huge farmhouse a few miles away.

When he'd got home late and found the house empty he'd been distraught. But Leanne had phoned to tell him where they were.

'Just think it's for the best, Jack. A short break from one another and you can get on with your work without worrying about me and the kids.'

'Don't be daft. I'll be worrying about you all the more. And what about Charles? How does he feel about you and the kids landing on him?'

'He's not bothered at all. The place is enormous. Six bedrooms. And he still can't take his eyes of his beloved Tracey.'

She'd left him a microwaveable meal, which he washed down with a couple of cans of lager while he watched a load of TV trash till he fell asleep on the sofa. Just before he'd dozed off he had caught the second half of a documentary about people trafficking from Eastern Europe. Most of those trafficked were young girls for the sex trade, drawn to this country by promises of proper jobs in hotels and restaurants but who soon found themselves trapped into prostitution by unscrupulous villains, such as the Russian Mafia.

The girls who were interviewed had their faces hidden by a clever distortion technique and their words were spoken by interpreters. Jack felt enormous sympathy for these kids – that's all most of them were – and thought he would like to get hold of the men who had tricked them and deal with them as they deserved.

He was thinking about this when he heard Eccles saying something.

'What? Sorry, I was miles away.'

'I was asking what you were going to do with your evening now Leanne's not at home.'

'Hmm. One of those ready meals. Couple of cans. Catch a DVD.'

'Sounds really exciting.'

'You can join me if you like.'

'No thanks, but tell you what. I'm on my own as well, since Trish left. Why don't we have a meal somewhere? There's a place out in the sticks I've been meaning to check out, The Old Mill. Saw it recommended in the free paper. Leanne's hardly going to worry about you being with me, is she? Well?'

'Why not? But no shop talk.'

'Of course. That goes without saying.'

ELEVEN

The Old Mill was under new management and had been completely refurbished. Once it had been a working mill and the pond was still there, though they couldn't see it in the dark. The water wheel continued to turn behind a glass wall but merely as a spectacle, unconnected to any mechanism. The place was full of character and there were plenty of customers. Eccles had booked ahead and they were given a table for two in a quiet corner.

Dundee wore his usual evening out gear; sports jacket, open necked shirt and chinos. He was surprised to see that Eccles had made herself more feminine for once with a blouse and skirt and a touch of makeup, which softened her strong features.

The meal was good. Dundee made his usual conservative choices; soup followed by steak and ale pie. Eccles was more adventurous starting with pan fried chorizo and chilli squid. For her main course she chose a Cajun chicken burger with red pepper coleslaw and fries. She loved hot, spicy food. Everything was well cooked and served promptly by several pretty waitresses, studied appraisingly by both of them.

Drink was more of a problem. Jack didn't want to take advantage of the fact that Dawn was driving and in the end they settled on one glass of wine each and the house wine was quite satisfactory. Conversation was another problem. They wanted to avoid talking about the dead girl. Dundee was reluctant to discuss his marriage and Eccles was still fragile from the break up with Trish. So, they settled for sport which they both enjoyed. Eccles was a rugby fan and Dundee had played regularly until he had dislocated his shoulder. He still played cricket from time to time, for a local team, when police duties allowed and Eccles followed England's progress in the tests, especially as this was an Ashes tour in Australia.

After this they moved on to gossip about their colleagues, mainly friendly, except when they got to DCI Wentworth.

'The man's a disaster. His management skills are non-existent.'

'Not sure about his detective skills either. I mean it's obvious that someone is trying hard to frame Richard Downes, but Wentworth is convinced he did it.'

'Hey, we said we wouldn't talk shop.'

'You're right. Sorry.'

'How are the twins getting on at school?'

'Really well. Karen is hard working, already beginning to read and Sean's so sociable, he gets on with everybody.'

'Won't this break from school upset them?'

'Oh, they're still going to school. Leanne takes them and collects them apparently. It's a bit of a trek and it must be using up a lot of fuel. But it's only for a few ...'

Jack broke off. Dawn's attention had been drawn to the entrance of the restaurant where two customers had just entered.

'Well, well,' said Dawn. 'Look who's just arrived.'

Dundee turned to where Eccles was looking. Two young women were removing their coats. One of them was struggling out of a quilted jacket. She was short and rather overweight. The other one slipped off her simple black overcoat to reveal a shiny red mini dress. PC Grabowski looked absolutely stunning.

The two young women went to the bar. While her friend was ordering their drinks Grabowski glanced around the room. When she noticed Dundee and Eccles her face broke into one of those delicious smiles. Each wondered if the smile was meant for them.

Grabowski picked up her drink, whispered to her friend and they came over to the table.

'Hi there,' she said. 'This is Melanie, my flatmate.' To Melanie, 'This is DI Dundee and DS Eccles. Our two best detectives. May we join you?'

'Of course,' replied Eccles, 'But no shop talk. I'm Dawn and this is Jack.'

She signalled to one of the waitresses and two extra chairs were brought over. While the remains of their meal were removed, Jack got up to settle them into their chairs. He felt his hand briefly touch Grabowski's shoulder.

'Are you eating?' asked Eccles. 'We've just finished.'

'Oh no,' said Grabowski, 'It's far too expensive for us here. I've only just joined the force and Melanie's still a student. We thought we'd just come out for a drink and see what the place is like. You never know. We might meet some knight in shining armour and get invited out one evening. Then we can say to our knights that we know The Old Mill is very nice.'

She laughed lightly and the others joined in. Jack longed to look into those splendid blue eyes, but instead directed his attention to Melanie.

'What are you studying?'

'Forensic science, would you believe. Only my second year. A long way to go yet.'

'Definitely no shop talk then,' said Dawn.

'If you don't mind me asking,' said Grabowski, 'Do you often meet like this?'

'Not really,' said Jack, rather harshly.

'No,' added Dawn, 'but we'd both had a long day. Jack's family is away and I had nothing to go home for, so we thought ...'

Grabowski looked at Jack, rather disappointedly he thought. 'Your family?'

'Yes, my wife Leanne and our twins, Karen and Sean. They're visiting an old friend of my wife's.'

Suddenly, a bright light flashed nearby. At first Jack thought there'd been a flicker of lightning, but then he looked up and saw Dan Matthews with a camera aimed at their table.

'Excuse me!' he said, lurching out of his chair and making for the reporter, but Matthews had scuttled away. Jack rushed out of the restaurant, almost knocking a woman over. By the time he'd helped her up and apologised the reporter's car was already pulling out of the car park.

'Shit!'

He looked around the poorly lit car park, wishing he had driven himself. He punched the roof of the nearest car. Dawn came out to join him.

'Hey, calm down. What's going on?'

'It's that bloody reporter from the Star. If I'd caught him I'd have smashed his camera. Anyway, let's settle up and go home. I'm in no mood for socialising now.'

'That's OK. I've paid the bill, but perhaps we ought to say goodnight to the others.'

'Could you do that for me? Tell them I'm not feeling too well.'

'OK. Here're the keys. Get in the car.'

TWELVE

When Jack Dundee got to the station next morning he was met by an irate Wentworth.

'In my office. Now!'

A puzzled Dundee followed the Detective Chief Inspector into his office where a newspaper lay spread out on the desk.

'What the fuck's all this?'

He pointed to the headline.

'Detectives party while killer runs free'

Below the headline there was a photograph of Dundee and three women sitting at a table in a restaurant smiling happily with drinks in their hands.

Dundee didn't bother to read the report. He knew exactly what the tone of it would be. He tried to stay cool.

'It's that bastard Matthews, Sir. At the Star. We've crossed swords several times. Now, he's got it in for me. Eccles and I were having a meal at The Old Mill and discussing the case. My wife's away for a couple of days.'

'Of course, I recognised Eccles. Hard looking bitch. But who are the others?'

'Well, one of them's a new recruit downstairs. She was with Harris when that body was discovered in the grave. So, she recognised Eccles and me and came over to say hello. The other one's her flatmate. They just brought their drinks to our table. They weren't eating.'

Wentworth had calmed down. He sat at his desk.

'So, before they arrived you were discussing the case.'

'That's right, Sir.'

'And what conclusions did your two big brains come to? Before the others joined you.'

Before Jack could answer Wentworth took another look at the photograph and pointed at Grabowski.

'That one's really something. I hope you're not getting mixed up in anything, Jack.'

'I don't even know the girl really, Sir.'

He was glad that Wentworth was still studying the photograph as a slight flush came to his cheeks. Jack tried to distract the DCI.

'Any news on an ID for the body, Sir?'

'We're getting nowhere with that, the only two missing students have turned up. One had moved in with her boyfriend and the other was homesick and went back to Slovenia. We've a missing au pair but she's dark haired and 12 stone. Cheesy and Vice are still working on the sex trafficking angle, but nothing concrete so far. However, we've got something about that money from forensics.'

'Oh?'

'That money and the folder had prints all over them.'

'Presumably from Staines?'

'Yes, but here's the interesting part. The same prints were found in several places at the Old Vicarage. On the mains lead for that missing laptop for a start.'

Dundee whistled, 'Well, well. Anything on the car in the pool?'

'Yes, it belonged to Downes. DVLA confirmed it.'

'So, Staines is definitely in the frame, Sir.'

'Yeah, and I reckon when they look at the car they'll find his prints all over it.'

'Sounds very likely, Sir.'

'So, he dumps the car and scarpers. But where does he go without transport? Well?'

There was a moment's silence before Dundee went on, 'Well, Sir. I've just remembered something a very observant old bird who lives on the hill told me.'

'Go on.'

Dundee and Eccles were on their way to speak to Peggy Dickson again when Dundee's mobile rang. It was Leanne.

'Hi love. How are things?'

'Don't "Hi love" me. I've just seen the Star.'

'So?'

'When the cat's away the mice will play.'

'It's not like that at all.'

'Who is she Jack? That girl ogling you?'

'Leanne for God's sake ...'

'I knew something was going on but ...'

He wanted to hand the phone to Eccles to explain but she was driving.

'Look love. I'm working at the moment. Can I call you back later?'

'No you can't. I'll be at the solicitors.'

'Leanne, this is ridiculous. Please come home then we can sort things out.'

But Leanne had rung off.

THIRTEEN

The whole team was gathered in the CID room. Wentworth opened the proceedings.

'So, this geriatric Miss Marple on top of the Brown Hill says she heard a car go past her cottage in the early hours. Then she heard a van or something do the same.'

'Actually, Miss Dickson is an intelligent, observant woman. She was Ward Sister in a Birmingham hospital in her younger days.'

Dundee was in a foul mood and he'd had Wentworth up to here.

'Old people get muddled,' insisted Wentworth.

'She is only in her late sixties,' put in Eccles.

'Well, whatever. I think we're in the realms of fantasy.'

'So, how do you explain the disappearance of Staines, and all that money he left behind?'

'And his prints all over The Old Vicarage?' added Eccles.

'I've got something that might help,' said Cheshire. 'I've had a report from West Mids. Apparently, they raided a brothel in Hansworth recently. One of the girls spoke good English. She'd been brought over from one of the Baltic States, Poland, I think. Thought she was going to work in a hotel. But the thing is she said she was worried about her friend, who'd been brought over by the same gang. This friend had suddenly disappeared. She gave a good description of the girl and she sounded very much like our victim.'

'No photo I suppose.'

'No such luck. But if she came over here she might be able to identify the dead girl if it's her.'

'Thanks Cheesy,' said Wentworth. 'It's good to have something more than ludicrous speculation. So, we need this kid over here as soon as possible. DS Eccles, can you arrange that?'

A Perfect Alibi

The girl, Sabine, sat beside Eccles as she drove back from Hansworth. She was very disturbed. At first she did not trust Eccles. She said that the police in her own country were not to be trusted. And when the police in Birmingham had raided the brothel they had treated the girls like scum.

'We did not want to do those things. Those men brought us here by force. They took our passports. They keep us prisoners. We came here to have proper jobs.'

Gradually, as the journey continued, Eccles convinced Sabine that she was now safe. She would not be blamed for her life in the sex trade. They just wanted her to help them identify the other girl.

Sabine burst into tears.

'My poor Maria!'

Eccles said nothing for a moment. She glanced at the girl and saw her tears.

'How long have you been in England?'

'About half year, I think.'

'Your English is very good.'

'I work hard at school. My teachers say I should go university. Here, I practise, even though I hate.'

'What about Maria?'

'No, only little bit. She had not much, what you say, intelligence. Said she did not need. Because she pretty.'

'You had known her long?'

'All my life. Born in same street. Same school. She younger than me. I look after her like sister. Always I try to protect.'

Tears came again.

No, thought Eccles, this girl is not pretty, just another young girl, with the gift of youth, a reasonable figure, blonde hair probably made blonder, good skin, strong features and large blue eyes, red rimmed now and full of tears.

The girl went on.

'Always, I try to keep her safe. Maria do silly things. Not care. Drink too much. Smoke dope. Go with men. Get us in this mess. But even, in that place, I try to protect. But suddenly she gone. Disappear. I ask. I worry. No-one know where she is.'

At last they arrived at the mortuary, where Dundee was waiting. He started to approach but Eccles shook her head. She took the girl into the mortuary where the attendant pulled out the relevant drawer and uncovered the victim's face.

Sabine gazed down for a moment at her lifelong friend, whispered something in her own language, before turning, burying her head in Eccles's shoulder and howling.

'Maria. My dearest friend.'

Dawn put her arm around the girl, looked up and nodded at Dundee, who was waiting in the corridor, looking through the glass partition. The girl had almost collapsed so Eccles helped her out of the room. Dundee had disappeared.

Eccles took the girl across to a nearby café and found a quiet corner table.

'Sabine. Can you tell me how you and Maria came to England?'

'It was Maria's fault. She saw advertisement. Girls to work in English hotels. Very good pay. Maria said she going, so I go too. We packed and went to place. Man took our passports. I knew it was bad place. Bad men. I tried to get away but they not let me.'

Sabine kept looking around, speaking in a low voice, as if someone might overhear and she would be in trouble. Sipping her coffee, she continued.

'We were blindfolded. Taken to place where airplanes flew. Put on small plane. I did not see but heard. First went to some place hot. Locked in cellar for one night. Then on another plane. To another place. Cold. Wet. Again, our eyes were covered. Put in big van. Taken to big house like hotel. Maria in one room, me in next. Then Maria sent away. Special place they say, because

A Perfect Alibi

she pretty. They would not tell me. Then they take me to other place. It was brothel.'

'How did you know you were in England?'

'I look out of window. Big bars to stop me climbing out. The names of the shops and things like "garage" and "supermarket". I learn these in English lessons.'

Dawn saw Sabine glancing across to the counter.

'Would you like something to eat?'

'I have no money.'

'I can get you something.'

'Soup and some bread?'

'Of course. The soup of the day is tomato soup. Is that all right?'

'Please.'

'By the way, my name is Dawn.'

She went to the counter and ordered the soup and a roll and a cappuccino for herself. When she turned around she saw Sabine trying to sneak out of the café. She caught her at the door and persuaded her to sit down again.

The waitress brought the soup and Dawn's coffee. Sabine sipped the hot soup, then asked,

'What will happen to me, Dawn?'

'You are a victim, not a criminal. I have to return you to the station, but I will do everything to help you. You have been very helpful to us. If the authorities decide that you can go back home ...'

Sabine's face showed terror.

'Cannot. They kill me if find me.'

'Then I will do everything I can to prevent that happening. And if you have nowhere to stay you can have a room in my flat. I will take responsibility for you. For your safety.'

'I would like that. You have been very kind, Dawn.'

'And you have been very brave, Sabine. Now, finish your soup.'

Eccles and Dundee sat in the Saloon Bar of The Pheasant in the High Street sharing well-earned drinks. She had just returned from Hansworth, having tried to make it clear to the officials at the Detention Centre that Sabine was not guilty of any crime and that she had been very helpful to the police. Dawn said that she would vouch for the young Pole when required and that there was a safe place for her to stay when needed.

'From what this girl told you,' said Dundee, 'it's obvious that those bastards bringing in the girls have got a real business going. And that lad Staines may well be involved. We need him and we need him now.'

'I suppose you're right, Jack. But I just can't see our Peter as a criminal mastermind, can you?'

'Perhaps it was Richard Downes, alias Dirk Barker, pulling the strings.'

'Do you really think a mid-list crime writer would get involved in something like that?'

'Hmm,' muttered Dundee.

They both sipped their drinks in silence for a while, until Dundee said regretfully, 'Well, Wentworth's taken it out of our hands, now. It's over to the Serious Crime Unit. And I suppose they'll have to inform Interpol. Remember what that girl said about stopping first in a hot country?'

Another pause and another sip each, then Dawn asked.

'So, how are things with Leanne?'

'She won't speak to me. But now we're off the case I'm going to go over there to sort things out.'

At that moment, someone appeared beside them and Grabowski asked.

'Is it OK if I join you?'

A Perfect Alibi

FOURTEEN

Jane had now been living in the little cottage for almost two weeks. She just adored it. The heating system was not entirely reliable and there was no off street parking for her car, but these were minor quibbles when she was able to wake in the morning and admire the view across the river to the ancient town on the other side. Sometimes, on these early winter mornings the valley was filled with mist so that the town across the valley seemed to be resting on a cloud. But the best thing about Jane's new life in the little cottage was that she had only thought about Patrick once or twice the whole time she had been there.

She visited Moira most days, and when the weather was suitable she accompanied her on outings, in her adapted car. They discussed all manner of things, sometimes reminiscing about their schooldays, but more often planning Jane's future. The Old Vicarage, according to the agent, was not going to make as much as she'd thought, so before long she would need to earn a living again. Moira offered to employ her as a carer but Jane thought that might spoil their friendship.

She had met Moira's husband several times and really liked him. He had no airs or graces. He was a strong, active man, who still liked to get involved in the manual side of building work but he was also a shrewd business man who had managed to keep going during the last few difficult years in the construction industry and was now benefitting from the recovery. It was obvious that he was very fond of Moira and did everything possible to make her life as easy as possible.

Part of the problem with her father's house was that for a while it remained a crime scene. The police examined it very carefully, even digging up some of the garden in case there was more than one body. Peter Staines's fingerprints were everywhere, as well as her father's, but most disturbingly the fingerprints of the young woman who had been found in the grave prepared for her father were also discovered in her father's bedroom, the banisters, and the hallway downstairs.

Once the police had left the house was valued. The agent explained that for some purposes the house was too large and for others too small, but he was optimistic that the house would eventually sell for a reasonable sum.

Jane was increasingly worried about what kind of man her father had been. He had had a liking for young girls, but he had not harmed Moira or, to the best of her knowledge, any other girl. Apparently, he had become a lonely recluse in his later years. Perhaps his wife's death, even though they had not been close, had affected him. In order to try and understand him better she had brought one copy of each of his books from the study to the cottage – the rest had been given to charity shops in the town – and she spent her evenings reading each one carefully, as if they might give her some clue to the man he had become.

There were 11 novels in total and she began to spot similarities in the themes and characters. There was a murder in each story, sometimes more than one. The victims were usually young women, sometimes as young as their mid-teens, and before they were murdered they had usually been held captive. She found the sadism hard to deal with but she began to have some slight sympathy with the perpetrators because they had all suffered from rejection, which she felt she understood.

She took Moira to see the Old Vicarage. Moira had a good eye for property and might be able to suggest how to make it more saleable. This was not the house where the incident between Moira and her father had occurred. It was not the house where Jane had lived as a child, or had ever lived. As they wandered from room to room, Moira thought the house gloomy and suggested that it was strange choice for someone to live in on their own. Perhaps it was a good place for a writer to live because he could so easily withdraw from all distractions.

Moira asked, 'Did your father always live in this area?'

A Perfect Alibi

'Oh no, I think he came from the south. Sussex or Kent. I don't really know.'

'Didn't you ever want to know?'

'Not really. He was just my dad, who spent his days in his study, writing books. I spent most of my time with Mum. I know plenty about her background. She came from another part of the country, up north, near Whitby. She still had a bit of an accent.'

'Yes, I remember. I liked the way she spoke. Did she have family?'

'Oh yes, her mother was still alive and she had a brother and sister. But they didn't approve of Dad. Thought he was very strange. Mum and I went to visit them occasionally, always without Dad. I loved those times. They were so open and friendly. But when Mum died that was it. I've hardly seen them since.'

'Wouldn't you like to know more about your father? You know, what he was like as a child? Where he grew up? What sort of parents he had?'

'Yes, I would, but I'm almost afraid. His books are so strange. They suggest a very disturbed man.'

They went to the church and Jane put some fresh flowers on her father's grave. There was no headstone as yet. There were a couple of floral tributes, decaying now and hardly visible because of the condensation inside the cellophane wrapping. She lifted each one in turn. The first was from her father's publisher with a short formal message of condolence. She threw the flowers and the message on the rubbish heap. The other bunch, quite a tasteful mix, also had a printed note probably dictated over the telephone.

'Sorry to hear you've gone, Dick. I hope you managed to forgive me for what happened all those years ago. Couldn't make the funeral because of my legs.

Your old friend, Tony.'

Jane was intrigued. What did happen all those years ago? She removed the card. The florist's name was printed on the back and she recognised it as one of the oldest established businesses on the High Street. They would probably have a record of the person who had ordered the flowers. She needed to know more about her father's past life, even though she may not like what she discovered, and if she could contact Tony, that seemed like a good place to start.

She put the card in her handbag, left the grave and joined Moira who was waiting patiently in the car park.

It was now mid-November and the weather had changed dramatically. Gale force winds and lashing rain had stripped the leaves from most of the trees. The river had almost overflowed its banks and the cellars of buildings nearest to the river were already flooded. Then there was the first frost and the roads became lethal.

Inside the CID room the atmosphere was almost as cool as outside. With the investigation taken out of their hands it was back to the usual burglaries, small-time drug dealing, criminal damage and car thefts. Wentworth prowled about the room, bored stiff and picking fault with everyone. Dundee and Eccles had given full reports to the Serious Crime Unit and then tried to move on from the body in the grave.

DS Eccles had managed to convince West Mids Police that Sabine had been forced into prostitution. She was released as an asylum seeker, so long as Eccles took responsibility for her. So, the girl had come to share her flat and they had got on very well so far.

Dundee had not had much success with Leanne. She would not come home. She said she needed more time to think things over. But she had not continued divorce proceedings and Dundee saw that as a hopeful sign. He missed her and the twins dreadfully. His loneliness had made him less careful about his looks – unironed shirts and scruffy collars – and the house was becoming a bit of a tip, with discarded ready meal containers and squashed beer cans left on the work surfaces and clothes strewn across the floor.

One evening, he had just finished yet another microwaved lasagne, downed a couple of cans of lager and was about to sink into the sofa to watch television for a few hours when the doorbell rang. He opened the door to find Grabowski standing there, smiling that delightful smile and flashing those huge blue eyes. He stood looking at her, with mixed delight and trepidation when she asked, 'May I come in Jack?'

'Of course.' he said, but he was already embarrassed at the state of the house and the sweaty state of his unwashed body.

Grabowski entered and looked around.

'Oh Jack,' she said. 'You can't live like this.' She put her nose in the air and sniffed. 'I'll tidy up while you take a shower.'

Suddenly, she seemed much older than her years and very much in charge.

'I can't let you do that.'

'Oh yes you can. Then I want to talk to you.'

She took off her coat. For once she was not in uniform or dressed up but wore a simple tight sweater and jeans which made her look more enticing than ever.

'Go on,' she ordered. 'What would your wife say if she came home and found the house in this state.'

He went upstairs thinking, 'I know what she'd think if she came home and found you here.'

He showered and shaved, then dressed quickly in his one remaining clean T-shirt and some old, but clean, jogging trousers. When he came back downstairs, the place was immaculate. All the plastic containers and aluminium cans had been thrown into the correct recycling bins and the crockery and cutlery lay gleaming on the draining board.

'That's brilliant. You're an angel.'

'Perhaps. But I expect a reward.'

'Well, come and sit down.' His body stiffened as he wondered what that reward might be.

He led her into the sitting room and sat beside her on the sofa. He looked at the lovely young woman close beside him and was filled with desire. He put his arm around her shoulder and pulled her to him. But she resisted and struggled out from under his arm.

'Oh God, Jack. You've got the wrong idea.'

Jack was puzzled. Surely she wanted him to make love to her.

'You have a wife and children, Jack. I'm not the sort of girl who wants to break up a family.'

'But surely ...'

'You're a good looking man, for your age, and several women at the station would love to be sitting on the sofa with you, but I'm an old-fashioned girl and I'm here for another reason entirely.'

'Oh?'

Jack's body relaxed with disappointment.

'Which, on reflection, is probably just as immoral.'

Jack stood up.

'Well, you're certainly intriguing me. Would you like a drink, while you explain?'

'Sure. Do you have any fruit juice?'

'I think so.'

He went into the kitchen and found one of those cartons of juice that the kids usually drank at breakfast time. Luckily, it was unopened and in date. He poured two glasses, and added some vodka to his own. In a state of bewilderment he returned to the sitting room, but this time he sat in the armchair opposite his guest.

'Well?'

A Perfect Alibi

'It's like this Jack. I'm very ambitious and I want to move into CID as soon as possible. You are the best detective around – well, with Eccles of course – and I thought, if I could get to know you I could pick up some tips and maybe you could use your influence – see I told you it was immoral – and I might be able to get a transfer.'

She paused. Jack knocked back his drink.

'I see.'

'I did think about asking Eccles, but I know her sexual preferences and I was worried that she might get the wrong idea. Anyway, she is only a Detective Sergeant. You're the one who can really help me.'

They sat in silence for a while. Jack was worryingly disappointed, first that they were not about to embark on an affair, and secondly that the girl had shown herself to be so devious. Then he had an idea.

'OK. I'll do what I can for you. Not that I can make any promises. After all, you've only just joined the force, but there is one condition ...'

'Go on.'

'You go to see my wife and tell her that there is nothing between us.'

Grabowski smiled the wickedest of smiles.

'Would that be entirely true, Jack?'

'Now, I'm going to turn you out.'

Slowly, she rose from the sofa and made her way to the door.

'You really will put in a good word for me, if you get the chance.'

'Very well.'

'Oh, you're a sweet man,' she said and gave him a quick kiss on the cheek before hurrying out of the house.

Jack closed the door behind her and went back into the kitchen for a refill, without the juice this time.

Jane took the card from the flowers on the grave and visited the shop in Bridgeport High Street which had supplied it. The woman bustling about the shop in a flustered fashion seemed vaguely familiar. She seemed reluctant to stop what she was doing in order to serve Jane.

'Yes?'

'Do you have an address for the sender of this card?'

The woman glanced at the card. 'Fraid not. They usually pays by credit card. Probably got the phone number somewhere.'

A man's voice shouted from another room.

'You there, Doreen?'

'Serving a customer.'

'Well, make it quick. I need your 'elp.'

No wonder the woman was flustered, thought Jane.

'The phone number will do.'

The woman's lips curled.

'Not sure we can do that.'

'Why on earth not? The flowers were for my father's grave. I want to thank the sender.'

The woman didn't bother to enquire who the deceased might be.

'I suppose that's all right then.'

The woman found the receipt and wrote the number on a page from a notebook and handed it over.

'Doreen!' the man called again.

Suddenly, Jane remembered who the woman was. An older version of a very disagreeable girl she was at school with. She obviously did not recognise Jane and Jane did not bother to enlighten her.

When she got back to the cottage she rang the number. A man with a cockney accent answered.

'Hello. Who's calling?'

'Is that Tony?'

'Tony Morris speaking. And you are?'

'Jane. Jane Downes. You knew my father.'

'Bloody hell! Dick Downes's daughter! I knew your dad real well when we was kids. But I ain't seen him since we were both – what – 16. So, I'd no idea he had a daughter. But he always was a close bugger.'

'Thank you for sending those flowers. If you don't mind me asking, how did you know he'd died?'

'Well, thank gawd you don't say, "passed on" or "fell asleep". I can't abide them euphemisms. I saw his obit in The Times. Very short it was. "Crime writer passes away". See, even they're at it. They gave his dates and where he was born so I knew it was him. They give his pen name and all. Mind you, I never read none of his books. Didn't even know he was a bloody writer. So, Jane, how old are you? Or are you one of those women who won't tell?'

'I'm 38.'

'So, apart from saying thanks for the flowers what else did you want?'

'I'd like to visit you.'

'That would be nice. Don't get many visitors these days.'

'I don't have your address.'

'Got a pen?'

'Yes, and paper.'

Actually, she had her smartphone ready, but it would be too difficult to explain to the old geezer.

'I use an iPad myself,' Tony said.

Jane blushed even though he could not see her.

'Right then, here goes. Tony Morris, Brook House, Oak Lane, Little Gretton, near Ashford, Kent. Where are you now?'

'I'm staying here, in Shropshire, till I can sell my father's house.'

'Oh Yeah, I remember now. He lived in some place with a religious connection, didn't he? Quite ironic that.'

'What d'you mean?'

'I'll explain when I see you. Anyway, from where you are, you'll be coming down the M40 I guess.'

'That's right.'

'Got a Satnav?'

'Fraid not!'

'Right. I'll take you through it slow. Come around the M25 south, then the M20 to Ashford. Take the A28 towards Canterbury. After about five miles you'll see the sign to Little Gretton on your left. Carry on through the village, past the church – you can't miss that – then go right into Oak Lane. Brook House is first on the left. Bloody big place it is. Far too big for an old cripple like me. Got that?'

'When can I visit?'

'Any time. While I'm still compos mentis would be best. So, don't leave it too long.'

'You sound fine to me. Would tomorrow be OK?'

'No problem. See you sometime tomorrow then. If you get lost you've got my number. And I'm always here.'

She smiled as he ended the call. Tony sounded like a great guy.

FIFTEEN

Dawn could not sleep. It had rained for most of the day. Now, the wind was wailing down the chimney and rain lashed the window panes. She was glad her flat was in the higher town. When she and Dundee had crossed the bridge that morning she had noticed that the water had reached right up to the top of the arches. Another wet day and the river would burst its banks.

The day had begun well. Jack had come to work with a smile on his face. Leanne and the twins had come home. Grabowski seemed to have backed off.

The Serious Crime Unit had taken over the case of the dead girl, but had not made much progress. She and Dundee were now working on a series of burglaries from farmhouses on the Wolverhampton Road. That didn't stop them thinking about the case of the body found in Downes's grave or the missing man, Peter Staines, whom they assumed was involved. There were three mysteries that could not be solved until Staines was found or some more clues were discovered: firstly, why was the girl, identified by Sabine as her friend Maria, at the Old Vicarage; secondly, how had she died and lastly, why had she been thrown into Richard Downes's grave? But Eccles felt that there was an even more puzzling dimension. Who was it who was so keen to make Downes the villain of the piece?

Sabine had only shared Dawn's flat for about a week, but it was good to have another woman about the place. They shared all the chores and had lovely evenings laughing at all the crap on television. Sabine's English was improving rapidly. Now, it was only the occasional idiom that stumped her and Dawn would quickly explain. The latest was the cats and dogs which people said were raining from the sky. Actually, Dawn had found that one difficult to explain.

Sabine was reluctant to talk about her experience in the brothel. She described some of the men who used and abused her and this confirmed Dawn's opinion that women were better as partners. But she spoke openly about her life in Poland before she was kidnapped.

Her father had often been unemployed and her mother was always too ill to work. They lived in a tiny flat near the harbour. Sabine shared a room with a younger brother and sister. Her father often said that life had been easier under the Communists, but her mother preferred that they were an independent nation again. Her parents often argued about this. Sabine had been clever at school and wanted to train as a teacher, but when she was 16 her parents told her that she must find a job as a waitress or work in a laundry, so that she could help to support the family. In fact, she did get a job in a department store, and quite enjoyed that, but the pay was very poor and she found it hard to be polite to the better off customers, some of whom she suspected were attached to the Mafia. Now, the shops were filling up with good things but only tourists or a nouveau riche minority could afford them.

Sabine was not envious of Eccles's well paid job or her comfortable life style. She had been given refugee status because she had been trafficked into the country. As soon as her English was good enough she said she would seek work and help out with the bills. Dawn asked her if she would like to go back to Poland but Sabine was quite definite about that.

'I have nothing to go back for. Especially since my dearest friend Maria is dead.'

Dawn could not get to sleep, so she went into the kitchen to make a hot drink. As she passed Sabine's room she heard sobbing. She stopped by the door for a moment and the sobbing grew louder. Dawn tapped on the door and opened it. Sabine was sitting up in bed, with tears falling across her pale cheeks. Dawn sat on the edge of the bed. Sabine whispered.

'I think about Maria. She had sad life. Never really well, but she wanted so much to enjoy ...'

Dawn put her arms around Sabine's shoulders and asked, 'What was wrong with her?'

Sabine snuggled into Dawn's chest, like a child seeking comfort from a mother.

'She had something wrong inside. It began when she was about 14 or 15. She would not tell about it. Sometimes she went white and rushed away to toilet. I thought it was drugs but she said no. Sometimes she went very thin. I thought she might have what is called eating disorder but she say no. She was very brave. Just wanting to enjoy ... everything.'

Early next morning Jane set off for Kent. At last the rain had stopped. It was Sunday so even the motorways were fairly quiet, without those convoys of juggernauts, and she made good time. She stopped for coffee near Oxford and was approaching London by mid-morning. At the point where she should have turned on to the M25 she suddenly changed her mind and drove on along the A40 towards London, and at Hanger Lane she turned south into Ealing.

It was a cold grey day, but without rain or frost. The roads became busy again as she entered the familiar suburb. The population of Ealing had finally got out of bed and some were making their way to supermarkets or restaurants, a few perhaps going to church, or for country walks or simply visiting friends. She felt nostalgia for all the years when she had spent her Sundays with Patrick, rising late, and meeting friends at their favourite pub. But then she wondered why she was doing this. After all, nothing of hers was left here now. When she had given Patrick the address of the cottage, but not her phone number, he had boxed up all her belongings and sent them in a van up to Shropshire. She simply wanted to take one more look at the place where a large chunk of her life had been spent.

She parked in the quiet street of large Victorian houses, now mostly divided into flats. The plane trees were bare and the pavements slushy with trodden leaves. When she looked up at the flat no lights showed, even on this gloomy day. She had left, hurriedly, with a couple of suitcases, to stay with a friend. Then she had received the message about her father from the hospital and had driven up to Shropshire.

She still had her key, so if Patrick was out she would simply let her herself in and look around. After all, there may be a few books or CDs he had forgotten to send. If he, and possibly the girl, were in, she would just hand over the key and leave.

She went up to the first floor and knocked softly, but no-one came to the door. Perhaps he'd sold the flat, but then she saw the little name tag on the door. Tears came as she saw that he had crossed out her name. Angrily, she inserted the key and the door opened. Well, at least he hadn't changed the lock, but when she went inside she was shocked. The place looked like a tomb. Not a thing was out of place. She walked into the living room and then the bedroom. Everything was immaculate. She recognised all Patrick's things, neatly arranged, but there was no sign whatsoever that the girl had ever been here. Surely they could not still be sharing that tiny bedsit of hers. She was puzzled but now certain that she never wanted to come here again. She had been erased from Patrick's life just as her name had been crossed out on the door. She thought about her lovely little cottage on the hill and its view from the windows and knew that was where she belonged, at least for a while. She left the key on the kitchen surface, pulled the door to, and hurried away.

SIXTEEN

Jane wound her way through the labyrinth of the South Circular and at last reached the M25. Her detour had made her late so she put her foot down. At last she reached the M20, headed for Ashford and followed Tony's directions. Yes, there was the turn to Little Gretton. In the middle of the village stood the church and beyond that was Oak Lane. Tony had said that Brook House was big and it certainly was; a Georgian mansion of flint and dressed stone, beyond high walls and a decorative iron gate, which stood open. She parked next to a van, adapted to carry a wheelchair, and made for the handsome door, which opened before she could press the large brass bell.

Her host was tall, stooping, with tanned features and abundant silver hair. He was using a stick but he passed this from his right hand to his left and took her hand.

'Well, Well! Reckon you must be Jane.'

He gave her a kiss on the cheek.

'You don't look much like your dad, thank gawd. Oh, sorry that's rude. Come in. Come in.' He stepped back and balanced on his crutch as she passed him, then pushed the door to.

Jane began to explain.

'Sorry I'm late. I made a detour that proved unnecessary in the end.'

'That's life ain't it.' Tony chuckled. 'Full of unnecessary detours.' He pointed down the hall. 'First door on the right.'

She stepped into a lovely light room, where a meal had been set out on a large polished table. The wide floor boards were also polished and there was a magnificent marble fireplace, with a blazing log fire in it.

'Sit down for a minute and let me look at you. Then I'll tell you where you can freshen up and we'll 'ave a bit of lunch.'

She looked at the splendid cold feast on the table and asked, 'Is this your handiwork?' She wondered how he could have prepared such a splendid cold feast balancing on a crutch.

'No way! That's Mrs Taylor. My 'ousekeeper. She's gorn to see her daughter. Usually does on a Sunday afternoon. But she always leaves me lunch first. I can't even boil a bloody egg.'

Jane was intrigued. Tony's strong cockney accent seemed at odds with this magnificent house and its fine antique furniture.

Tony leaned across to pick up a bottle of wine and poured two glasses. The wine caught the sunlight and sparkled as it swirled into the glass. Jane was about to protest, but she needed something after her long drive.

'There y'are. Get that down you. That's quite a way you've come. And you ain't going back today. I've asked Mrs T to make you up a bed. We've got a lot to talk about.'

'But I haven't brought any clothes.'

'No worries. There's wardrobes full of 'em. My wife was about your size.'

'Your wife?'

'Yeah. Trophy wife they call 'em. Half my age. All boobs and bum. No fool like an old fool. She scarpered with the gardener a couple of years back.'

Taken aback by Tony's forthrightness Jane took a big gulp and emptied her glass.

'Right, you go and have a wash up – loo's just across the hall. Then we'll get stuck in to Mrs T's lovely grub.'

The lunch was very good. Cold meat, pies, boiled eggs, several salads, hunks of fresh bread and several glasses of a splendid wine. They ate in silence for a while, then Tony began to talk.

'For a start, you'll be wonderin' how a geezer like me, who can't hardly speak English proper, comes to have a house like this in one of the nicest bits of Kent. Well, the answer's simple. I won the lottery. Nigh on twelve million about ten years ago. And

A Perfect Alibi

I didn't go chucking it away, or spending like there was no tomorrow. No, I'd had too many years rubbing pennies together, so I made some careful investments, including this lovely pad and everything in it. So, I am as they say comfortably off, and I'm a quick learner. I say the right things and do the right things so that I am more or less accepted by the locals, who know they can touch me up for a bit of charitable giving now and then.'

'What about your wife? Wasn't she a drain on your resources?'

'That's a nice way of putting it Jane. But no, I made it clear when we married. So long as she could put up with me she could have a generous allowance, but if she dumped me she'd get nothing. It was all written down at the time. And to be fair, I wasn't much cop as a husband. Got this bloody arthritis soon after we was married. She stuck it for a while, then along comes this healthy young chap, full of vigour and spunk and it was a no-brainer really.'

'Any regrets?'

'No. I don't do regrets, Jane. Never 'ave.'

There was another silence. Jane thought about Patrick for a moment but then decided that Tony had got it right. No regrets.

Tony showed his visitor around the house, letting her explore upstairs on her own. Tony was a man who seemed to have grown into his house. It suited his large personality.

They finished the tour in the kitchen where they had coffee.

'OK. What d'you want to know about your dad?'

'Well, obviously, I knew him as an adult. But I know absolutely nothing about his childhood. How did you come to meet?'

'He was born here, in this village. His dad was the vicar. See what I mean? Born in a vicarage. Died in a vicarage. And when I knew him he was bloody atheist. The vicarage down here is a nursing home now. Anyway, I come here in the mid-fifties, taken in by Dick's mother, your grandmother. Apparently, they'd seen an ad for foster parents and felt guilty about this great big place they lived in with just the one kid. Also, I think they wanted a brother for your dad but his mum couldn't have no more kids. So, I come here when I was five.'

'Your dad was the same age as me. We shouldn't really have got on – him being an only child till then – but we did. I mean, he was all posh and I was a Barnardo's boy from Barkingside. But I think that was part of the attraction for him. I knew things he didn't, like bad language and petty thieving and so on. And I learned from him too, like how to read and how to speak proper, well a bit more proper than when I first arrived. So, we became inseparable. We both started at the village school and stood up for one another, us against them see, because neither of us was your typical village boy.'

'Then a few years later my real mother found out where I was. She was from Plaistow down by the docks. She'd given me up me when I was born, only a kid herself and no man around to help. She come out to claim me back. But when she saw how happy I was and how well looked after, she left me here. I never heard no more of her.'

'Oh, I'm so sorry.'

'Oh come on Jane. That was a lifetime ago. And to be honest I would have hated going back to her, in some grotty place in Plaistow. I'd never known her anyway and I loved this village and my life here. No regrets, remember. And there certainly weren't none from me.'

'So, your dad's parents went on looking after me – they never officially adopted me – but Dick and I, we sort of became brothers.'

'What was he like, as a boy?'

'Clever, very clever. I wasn't short of a few brain cells myself but he was different. Read a lot, a hell of a lot. He was a bit dreamy, romantic like. I was always more hard headed myself.'

A Perfect Alibi

'He wasn't sent off to boarding school.'

'No, I think his mum and dad were struggling a bit, financially I mean. But we both passed the 11-plus and went to the grammar in Ashford.'

'And you stayed friends?'

'Oh Yeah, thick as thieves. Until Victoria arrived.'

'Victoria?'

'Yeah, Victoria. She was really something. We were 15 when she arrived in the village. Her father had just been posted to the local RAF base. They'd been in Egypt. Then Nasser chucked them out. After that it was Cyprus and Malta. There were no married quarters at the camp down here so they were given a bungalow in the village. Then Victoria started at the girl's grammar school in Ashford, in the year below us. We travelled on the bus together morning and evening. She was tall and slim with long fair hair and golden skin from her years in the Med. She was good at sports, especially swimming. Your dad fell absolutely head over heels. But ...'

'But?'

'Well, you see your dad wasn't exactly handsome in those days. He still looked very young, short and scrawny like and he was very short sighted, wore a pair of them 'orrible national health glasses.'

'Yes, he always wore glasses when I knew him.'

'Me, on the other hand, I had matured early. I looked older than my age and girls fancied me. It was obvious from the start that Victoria preferred me. She was friendly enough to Dick when all three of us were together, but she often arranged to meet me on my own.'

At that moment, the kitchen door opened and Mrs Taylor returned. Introductions were made and then Tony took Jane into the sitting room while the evening meal was prepared. He poured two glasses of sherry and they sat in the firelight as night drew in.

'Who looks after all your fires?' asked Jane.

'That's Jeff. Jeff Hawkins. Sounds like one of them comic heroes don't he? He's the gardener and in the winter he also keeps the fires going. To be honest the central heating's pretty effective, but there ain't nothing like a real log fire.'

Jane watched the logs tumbling into ash and agreed. She picked up the story again.

'So, Dad lost out with Victoria?'

'It was worse than that. He was so obsessed that he didn't really understand what was happening between me and Vicky. Then Dick and me both passed 16 and took our O-levels. Your dad did really well and I managed OK in the science subjects I was interested in. Dick was going to stay on in the sixth form, while I applied for an engineering apprenticeship back in London. I was going to lodge with someone back in Plaistow.'

'Back to your roots?'

'Yeah, I suppose. So, come the end of term there was a party in some guy's house. His parents had gone to Spain. That's when it happened.'

'What happened?'

'Well, towards the end of the party Vicky and I slipped up to one of the bedrooms and there we were 'aving it away, when your dad walked in.'

'Oh God!'

'He was stunned. He just stared at us open mouthed. Then he left the room and never spoke to me again. He went off on some archaeological dig in Devon that summer and by the time he came back I'd moved up to London. I never saw him again.'

'Didn't you try to keep in touch?'

'At first I made an effort, but got nowhere. Dick's parents had lost touch with him as well. They thought he may have gone abroad. Soon after, his dad retired and they moved to Eastbourne.'

'What about you?'

A Perfect Alibi

'Me? I was young. I was doing something I liked doing. I fitted back into London life like I'd never lived anywhere else. Finished my apprenticeship and got a good job. Rapid promotion. The money attracted one woman after another. Then I got made redundant and the women scarpered.'

'What about Victoria?'

'Ah well, that's the odd thing. About six months after I went back to London she disappeared. Went into Ashford to a dance one night and was never seen again.'

By now the room was in darkness. Jane's thoughts were in a whirl. Tony got up and switched on the light. There was a soft tap on the door and Mrs Taylor entered.

'Dinner's ready, Mr Morris.'

SEVENTEEN

DI Dundee and DS Eccles sat at a corner table in the Regal Café just off the high street.

The detectives had just returned from a morning of investigations into the farm burglaries, following up a report that a white van had been seen near the latest burglary, which matched a vehicle that had been spotted near the first farm to suffer. But beyond seeing similar vans at both places the witnesses had nothing useful to report. Eccles had used her laptop to look for any stolen vehicles that might match the sightings, but nothing had come up.

They were not keen to return to the station yet, where the Serious Crime Unit had set up an incident room and practically taken over the place with their numerous personnel and all their special equipment. So, Jack and Dawn were taking a short break with a chance to catch up on personal affairs. It was a bitterly cold day with occasional showers of sleet so they were glad to get inside the fug of the café. A spotty teenage waitress brought over their coffees, spilling some from each cup into its respective saucer. She was very apologetic and explained that it was her first day of work experience and she was very nervous, so the detectives decided to accept her apology and poured the spilled coffee back into their cups.

'How are things at home?' asked Eccles.

'Leanne and I are walking on eggshells at the moment, but it's great to have the kids back.'

'So, what persuaded her to return?'

'Not sure. I'm just glad something did.'

He wondered if Grabowski had done as she promised and would he ever get a chance to repay her with a word in the right ear.

'How are things with Sabine?'

'We get on fine. She's got some horrific tales to tell.'

'Has she spoken to the Unit?'

'Of course, but she has no idea where the gang is based. The girls were always blindfolded when they were moved.'

'Those bastards think of everything!'

'Exactly.'

Dundee unfolded his paper and glanced at the front page. His eyebrows shot up.

'Oh, fuck this!'

He turned the paper around so Eccles could see. She read the headlines and slammed her fist down on the table making the spoons jangle in the saucers. She looked around but the few customers didn't seem to have noticed.

'Dead Girl in Open Grave Mystery

Local police incompetence

We've been informed by DCI Wentworth that the case of the dead girl found in the grave of a man about to be buried has been passed on to the Serious Crime Unit. Local detectives have made little progress, DCI Wentworth explained. They've failed to discover how the girl died or to catch the chief suspect, Mr Peter Staines.

Reported by Daniel B Matthews'

Dundee swallowed his remaining coffee in one gulp, then exclaimed angrily.

'Well, thank you Wentworth, for your vote of confidence!'

'Who wrote the piece?'

'Can't you guess? Look!'

She read the name of the reporter.

'Daniel B Matthews.'

'Daniel B. How bloody pretentious. Wonder what the B stands for?'

'I could make a few suggestions,' said Dundee. 'That's one Daniel I'd be delighted to chuck in with the lions.'

'Perhaps I should get a new partner; I'm being tarred with the same brush. But why's he got it in for you?'

'He tried to tap Leanne for information about a case I was on. Before your time this was. I got home and found him chatting her up. Perhaps I was a bit too zealous when I suggested he should leave.'

Eccles smiled. She finished her coffee, saying, 'Ready to face Serious Crime? By the way, did they speak to you much?'

'Hardly at all. I mean they read my report, asked me to clarify a couple of points but not much more. You?'

'Same, more or less. Went on about having a new perspective.'

'Well, I can't say I've noticed any progress. Have you?'

'Sod all. Have you had any ideas since we were pushed off the case?'

'I've had a few thoughts. First, *did* he have anything to do with the girl's death? Downes, I mean.'

'Hmm,' went Dundee.

'If not, who wanted us to think he had and why?'

'Well, it can't be Staines. He's not been around to post notes or deliver laundry.'

'Unless he arranged it before he did a runner.'

'I suppose that's possible. Anyway, who else might know what was going on?'

'To my mind there's just one candidate. Bennett.'

'The cleaning woman?'

'Exactly. She was often around. She might well have seen something. Perhaps she found the girl's clothes. She could have posted that note and sent back the laundry.'

'But why? I mean if she knew something bad was going on why not give us a call?'

'Blackmail!'

'But who could she blackmail?'

'The daughter, Jane.'

'But she doesn't have any money.'

'She will have when she sells that house. And did I mention that Downes had a fair amount of cash in his account. He was doing pretty well, for a mid-list author. Some company bought the film rights on his last book, so his publishers gave him a hefty advance on his next. She will inherit quite a pile.'

'How d'you know all this?'

'I was next to Cheesy when he looked at Downes's accounts.'

'Naughty, naughty. And you think Jane would pay a blackmailer?'

'Perhaps.'

'I think she's already having doubts about her dad. She wouldn't want his reputation torn to shreds.'

'And you reckon Bennett knew what was going on?'

'Perhaps not everything. But it's amazing what you come across when you're doing a bit of cleaning.'

'I wouldn't know about that,' said Dundee with a smile. 'Anyway, I was thinking. I know we're off the case but we might make a call on dear Mrs B. See if she's OK. Just in a friendly capacity.'

In the end Jane stayed with Tony for the whole of the next day. In the morning, he took her for a guided tour of the village in his motorised wheelchair. Jane thought about Moira, also confined to a chair and realised how lucky she, herself, was to be able to walk without any aids. They visited the church, which was beautiful inside. Tony told her that for a brief while both he and Richard had been choir boys until a visiting preacher had tried to grope them in the vestry.

Next, they viewed the Old Vicarage, now a very expensive nursing home. It was much larger than the one where her father had died, and altogether more ornate – Victorian trying to be Medieval – and she found it hard to imagine her father living there as a boy. Mind you they only lived in a small part of the house, Tony explained. He told her about her father's love of classical music, which he had not shared, being more of a rock and roll fan. Jane did not remember her father listening to music at all.

In the afternoon Hawkins drove the two of them into Ashford so that Jane could see the school which Tony and her father had attended. He explained that it was much bigger now but was still a selective school, within the state system.

Jane enjoyed every minute of her time with Tony, he was such a lively character, but she could not relate the boy he told her about to the man she had known as her father, except perhaps as the disturbed teenager he had become after the Victoria episode. She tried to ask Tony more about the girl but he would only say that she had disappeared on her way home from Ashford and had never been seen again.

That night Jane dreamed about her father's funeral and saw the body of that girl, lying in his grave. Suddenly, the girl woke up, climbed out of the hole, with soil falling from her bare limbs, came towards Jane smiling and said, 'Hello, I'm Victoria.'

Jane woke sweating and just managed not to scream. Several times she repeated the words, 'What has he done?' At last, she managed to slip back into sleep and next morning she drove back to Shropshire.

A Perfect Alibi

Sophie practically demolished the door when Dundee rang the bell. Mrs Bennett opened the door as far as the chain would allow and through the gap the detectives could see the snarling dog with rows of sharp teeth growling menacingly. Dundee hoped that Sophie was being held back on a strong lead.

'Oh, it's you two again. What you want?' asked Mrs Bennett.

Eccles spoke in her friendliest tone.

'D'you think you might put Sophie in another room. Then we can have a friendly chat.'

'I suppose.'

The little dog was pushed into the sitting room and the door closed on her, still growling.

Mrs Bennett reluctantly removed the door chain and let them in. Her whole attitude seemed to have changed. Her face had hardened. Dundee decided there would be no tea and biscuits for them this time.

She led them into the conservatory.

'Not sure why you're here. I saw in the paper you'd been taken off the case.'

'That's true. We are no longer on the case. But you were so helpful when we called last time, we just came to see if you were alright. The whole thing must have been a terrible shock to you.'

Eccles had hit the right note. The woman began to thaw.

'You'd better sit down.'

They did so. Dundee could still hear Sophie's low growl and hoped that the door to the sitting room was firmly shut. Mrs Bennett went on.

'Well, it was a shock in a way. But on the other hand ...'

'Yes?' Eccles asked. Dundee let her do the interviewing while he studied the woman's face. There was a shrewdness in the tight lips and narrowed eyes which he hadn't noticed last time.

'Well, one shouldn't speak ill of the dead. But he was definitely a bit peculiar. Mr Downes, I mean.'

'Peculiar?'

'Yes, I mean. He never went anywhere nor had any visitors. Except that lad, Staines. And I don't know what he was there for. I mean he wasn't a gardener. Old Downes never bothered about the garden. And he didn't cook or clean for the old man. I did wonder ... Well, it's like I told the other lot. I wondered whether there was anything ... y'know ... sexual ... between them.'

Her cheeks went pink when she said this.

Eccles kept calmly on.

'Did you ever see anything which may have led you to think ...?'

'Well, I once saw that youngster walking about in his underpants. I could have died of shock. But he said he'd spilled something down himself.'

'That's very interesting. Oh, by the way, talking about dirty clothes, the forensic team found nothing in the laundry basket.'

The woman did not look directly at Eccles as she replied.

'Yes. The other coppers told me that. It's a real mystery. Perhaps I just sent the stuff to the laundry without thinking. I mean, I was in quite a state, you know.'

'Of course, I fully understand. Do you think you could just jot down the name of the laundry you used? They must still have the clothes.'

Dundee wondered why Eccles was asking Bennett to do this when they knew perfectly well which laundry she had used, but he said nothing. The woman wrote down the name in Eccles's notebook and handed it back to her.

'Well, thank you again, Mrs Bennett.' said Eccles as she stood up. 'You really have been very helpful.'

Dundee stood as well.

Mrs Bennett smiled for the first time.

'I'll see you out.'

A Perfect Alibi

Once they were back in the car Dundee asked Eccles.

'Did we learn anything new?'

'Oh, yes. I think when we visit the laundry we will find that the girl's clothes never got there. And when we compare this writing with the note that was sent to Jane I think we shall find that the writing is very similar indeed.'

EIGHTEEN

Jane had taken her time driving back from Kent and it was already dark when she reached Shropshire. The motorways had been difficult with heavy rain and constant spray from those enormous lorries. As she approached the town she began to notice signs at the side of the road.

'Bridge Closed.'

'Flooding.'

'Alternative Route.'

There was an arrow pointing towards the bypass with its much higher bridge. If she had been heading for the upper town she would have had to go that way but instead she drove towards the lower town and then up the hill towards her new home.

She couldn't park immediately outside and it was raining again as she dashed across to the cottage. She felt very sorry for those who lived near the river. Their houses would almost certainly be under water by now.

Luckily, the heating came on straight away and she was able to take off her damp coat, skim through the few letters on the floor, and pour herself a large gin. There were a couple of messages on her answerphone. One was from the house agent informing her that a prospective purchaser had viewed the Old Vicarage and would be making an offer when the probate process was completed. Tomorrow she must go and clear out her father's things. She had been putting it off for far too long.

The second message was from Patrick. She had changed her mobile and not informed him, but because he had her address he had been able to discover her landline.

'Hello Jane. Sorry I missed you. Thank you for the key. I would like to speak to you sometime.'

He sounded rather depressed. Good, so he should be. What did he want to speak to her about? She didn't want to speak to him ever again.

Tony had asked her to let him know that she had arrived home safely so she phoned him and again thanked him for her enjoyable stay.

'You're welcome anytime Jane,' he said. 'And look, stop worrying about your dad. Move on kid. Remember, no regrets!'

After a quick shower, she microwaved a ready meal, ate it with some rather limp salad, filled another glass with gin and went straight to bed. But she could not sleep. In spite of Tony's advice she could not stop thinking about her father. Had he been involved with Victoria's disappearance? What about that Moira business? Had he had anything to do with the girl in the grave? Why were his novels always about the murders of young women? Why had he left that note at the end of his unfinished manuscript? What was it he couldn't do anymore?

At last she fell asleep but then that dream came again. The girl with long fair hair rose out of the grave, came towards her smiling and said, 'Hello. I'm Victoria.'

Jane took two of the sleeping tablets that she had been prescribed when Patrick first left her. She swallowed them down with another gin. Her eyes closed almost before her head hit the pillow and she slept and slept.

Next morning, she woke late with a slight headache. She went to the window and was astonished to see that the whole valley was under water, like an inland sea or a fjord, sparkling under the late November sunlight, which hurt her eyes and made her headache worse. Thank God the rain had stopped. Perhaps now the water would drain away.

Her doorbell rang. She put on a dressing gown and went downstairs. When she opened the door she was met with the flash of several cameras. She quickly closed the door again. When she looked out of the window she saw that several cars were parked on the road near the cottage, and that a small crowd was standing outside her door.

The doorbell rang again. She ignored it and went upstairs to get dressed. It continued to ring at intervals and someone shouted through the letter box, 'Miss Downes, we need to talk to you.' When Jane came down again she opened the backdoor and ran across the garden to Moira's house. She kept looking back towards the cottage, but no one seemed to have noticed her.

When Moira let her in Jane was aware that her friend was looking very serious. They went into the kitchen. Moira asked, 'Coffee?'

'Yes please,' replied Jane. 'Moira, what the hell is going on?'

Moira passed her a large mug of coffee and a copy of the local paper.

'I think you'd better read this.'

Jane looked at the headlines and gasped.

'Local Writer involved in Girl's Death

Following an anonymous tip-off the Serious Crime Unit is investigating the possibility that local author Richard Downes, better known by his pen name Dirk Barker, the author of several lurid crime novels, was involved in some way with the death of the girl found naked in his grave.

Mr Downes died two months ago and was buried at St Michael's Church, Olverley, near Bridgeport. He lived formerly at the Old Vicarage, in the village. He was admitted to the local infirmary following a severe stroke and died a week later. He is survived by a daughter, who is at present living in the district.

Mr Downes may well have had an accomplice, Mr Peter Staines, who has not been seen since the night before the girl's body was found.

Another thorough examination of the premises known as the Old Vicarage will begin as soon as a search

warrant can be obtained. The Press has been advised to keep away from the premises and wait for further information from the police.
Daniel B. Matthews'

Jane remained silent and reread the article. At last the silence was broken when Moira asked, 'Do you think there is any truth in this, Jane?' She pointed at the newspaper.

When Jane looked up there were tears in her eyes, 'I don't know Moira. I just don't know.'

Moira covered Jane's hands with her own.

'You poor thing! You don't deserve any of this.'

Suddenly, Jane sat up decisively.

'Moira, I need your help.'

'Of course.'

'First, I need to avoid that lot out there. I must get away.'

'Where will you go?'

'I'll stay with Tony.'

'Tony?'

'He lives in Kent. I've just come back from there. He was a kind of a brother to my dad when they were boys. No one will find me there.'

'You're sure he'll help?'

'Absolutely sure!'

'And how can I help?'

'I want you to go across to the cottage, go in by the back door, I left it open, and fill a suitcase for me.'

'But I can't get up the stairs.'

'Oh shit, I hadn't thought.'

'You can borrow some of my clothes. I know I've put on weight but we're about the same height.'

'Moira, you're brilliant.'

She saw her friend smile for the first time that morning.

Jane felt in her pocket.

'Luckily, I brought my phone with me.'

'Oh no! You mustn't use that. I've got a spare one you can use. But how will you get away from here. Your car's out there on the road. As soon as you walk out they'll be all over you.'

They both considered the problem. Suddenly, Moira smiled again.

'I've got it. My car's in the garage. We can get into it from inside the house, without being seen. Then if you lie down on the back seat, I'll cover you with a blanket and I can drive straight out. This is quite exciting really, isn't it?'

'Well ...' Jane wasn't so sure.

'Then I can phone George and ask him to hire a car and bring it to wherever you want him to meet you.'

Now, Jane smiled as well. 'You've been watching too many spy films, Moira.'

'Well, I do rather like to live dangerously, if only in my head. You see if you're stuck in a wheelchair ...'

'Yes, of course ...'

'Where do you think we should meet?'

'Well, I'd like to have a quick look around the Old Vicarage before the police start going over it. I just might find something to explain ...'

'Right, so we need to get there as soon as possible. First let's get you some clothes. Then you can dress while I phone George.'

It worked a treat. Moira pressed the button to lift the automatic garage door and drove out, as if she was going to the shops. The reporters surged towards the car, then seeing that it wasn't Jane they moved aside and let the car through.

At the Old Vicarage, George handed Jane the keys to the hire car, then got into Moira's car and they drove away. Jane made for the door of her father's house and turned the key.

A Perfect Alibi

Peter heard cars draw up on the gravel outside and froze in panic. There was a brief exchange of voices and then both cars left. He relaxed a little, went into the converted coalhouse, dressed quickly and returned to the hallway, just as the door opened. For a few seconds they just stood looking at one another, until Pete burst out,

'Who the hell are you?'

The woman studied him for a moment, her heart thumping, then said, as calmly as she could, 'Well, I know who you are, Mr Staines. I've seen your picture everywhere. I recognised you at once in spite of the beard and the dyed hair.'

So much for the disguise! For a moment Pete thought of pushing past this woman and running out of the house, but instead he simply said, 'I didn't kill her. I was going to give myself up.'

'I'm Mr Downes's daughter. Did he kill her?'

'No. Well, I don't think so. It's hard to explain.'

For some reason Jane didn't feel at all afraid of this young man. She knew at once that he was not a killer.

'So, how long have you been hiding here?'

'I only got back last night. Like I say, I was going to go to the police.'

'Where have you been all this time?'

'It's a long story.'

'Well, I want to hear it, but not here. The police will be arriving any minute. I don't want to see them, or speak to the press, until I've heard your story. I'm on my way to a place they won't know about. I'd like you to come with me ...'

'But ...'

'Quickly! Grab whatever is yours. Don't leave anything behind. I'll bring the car around to the door. Be ready!'

Within minutes they were on their way and Jane didn't stop until they reached the first service station on the M40. She bought a coffee for herself and a large burger for Pete who had no money and had had very little to eat for ages. Then she went off to phone Tony. When she said she needed his help he said he wasn't surprised; the story had reached the national press. He agreed to let her come to Brook House with Peter.

On her way back to the cafeteria Jane saw the headlines on a newspaper stand and when she reached Pete she said they must leave at once. He crammed the last piece of his burger into his mouth, squeezing ketchup down his chin, and followed her out to the car.

Peter soon fell asleep, so she put on some soothing music and simply drove. She didn't stop again until they reached Brook House. Tony had told Hawkins and Mrs Taylor that he would be going away for a few days and so wouldn't need their services. He packed a bag and called for a taxi, but when it arrived he told the driver that he had changed his mind.

When they reached the house Jane put her car in the empty garage, as Tony had suggested, then she and Pete went into the house by the back door.

A Perfect Alibi

PART TWO

PETER'S STORY

NINETEEN

Peter Staines sat on the veranda, drying off in the warm sun after his morning swim in the villa's pool.

The view was fabulous. Mountains on three sides, the lower slopes softened with pine trees and nothing but bare rock above. On the fourth side the land fell away to the bluest sea he had ever seen.

He rang a little hand bell on the table and a young woman appeared.

'Buenos dias, Felicia. Would you bring my coffee, please?'

'Certainly Señor.'

'Peter.'

'Peter,' she repeated, with a smile.

He had been here at the villa for two days and he thought that Felicia might offer him more than just coffee if he asked. He found her very attractive with her slender bronzed limbs — mostly hidden by a modest black skirt and white blouse — her long black hair, neatly pinned up, her slightly teasing smile and dark, intelligent eyes. What on earth she was doing, living alone up here, as housekeeper, cook and cleaner for the monsters who had brought him to the villa, he could not imagine. He knew that she found him attractive, but that could wait. He was still stunned by recent events.

He had discovered from Felicia that he was somewhere in Spain. Life was comfortable enough, but rather boring, and there was always the nagging fear of what might happen next. He had nothing to do and could not contact anyone. The men who had brought him in the plane and then by car had taken the laptop and dropped it into the sea somewhere en route. They had also taken his precious phone, which he could never have afforded without the money from Downes, and there was no landline at the villa. They had told him not to try to leave but as he had no passport or money he had little choice. He had wandered as far as the fence yesterday, thinking he might take a walk to the nearest mountain, but he found a pair of fierce looking dogs running loose beyond.

When he thought back to what had happened that dreadful night at the Old Vicarage it was as if a cloud passed in front of the sun. Pete felt physically sick at the memory of what he had done. He knew that if the police interviewed him it would not be long before he confessed and he would end up spending most of his young life in jail. He had had to get away, as far away as possible. He had sat in Downes's car, in the garage, and emailed the organisation to ask for their help.

They gave him a map reference for a place just seven miles away and told him that he must be there at 1.30am. He was to bring the old man's laptop and was not to worry about packing a case or bringing his passport as everything would be provided.

Pete was about to collect the laptop from Downes's study and drive away when he heard another car come down the drive. He peeped through the garage doors, still slightly open, and saw a woman get out of the car and go into the house. She must be the daughter. Shit! Now, he would have to wait until she left again or went to sleep. Even if she locked the door from the garage into the house he knew where the spare key was kept. So, he got into the back of the car and stretched out on the seat for a couple of hours.

Just after midnight he got up and walked quietly around the house checking that all the lights were out, before opening the door which had not been locked. He moved slowly along the passage and pausing outside the sitting room door he heard loud snoring from inside. Pete knew that the stairs creaked in several places unless you walked on the side nearest the wall. The study door had been left open so he unplugged the laptop and carried it back downstairs. One of the stairs *did* creak as he made his way down. He stopped, but no one came to investigate.

In the garage, he placed the laptop on the passenger seat, opened the garage doors, put the gears into neutral and pushed the car out on to the drive. He carefully closed the garage doors and drove quietly away. He had just 40 minutes to reach the rendezvous.

Pete didn't have a licence but he knew how to drive. He drove carefully but at a good speed along the quiet lanes and used the Satnav on his phone to locate the map references he had been given. He soon recognised the hill he was making for, which he had often climbed on his mountain bike. When the Satnav told him he had reached his destination he got out of the car and waited. Soon, he heard the faint sound of another vehicle, becoming louder by the moment and then a large van with darkened side windows pulled up beside him.

Two men got out and moved quickly towards him and for a moment he felt very frightened, especially when he saw the size of them, with their wide shoulders and thick necks. This was a very lonely spot and he was here entirely on his own. He knew very little about the organisation, except that it was very powerful. He was the only one, still alive, who knew what had happened at the Old Vicarage. Unless they had a use for him, surely it was easier for them to dispose of him here and now?

At first, neither man spoke. Perhaps they could not speak English. One took the laptop from the car. The other opened the side door of the van and said, in heavily accented English, 'Get in, pretty boy.'

Inside, the van had several seats, like a minibus. Pete sat down and waited. In the light of the moon he watched as the men pushed Downes's car until it rolled away on its own. A few seconds later he heard a loud splash, then the men returned to the van and they drove off.

One of the men sat beside him, the other drove. They were both nasty looking specimens, with scarred faces and shaven scalps. They both wore expensive looking leather jackets. When

A Perfect Alibi

the one beside him leaned over and said, 'Phone!' his jacket opened to reveal a pistol in a shoulder holster. Pete took out his phone and handed it over. That was the last time the men spoke to him, although they shouted across to one another in some guttural language that Pete thought might be Russian.

They drove down the hill, through the village and then turned on to the Ludlow Road. Pete recognised some of the names of the villages, caught in the headlights, as they wound their way up and up before beginning the long descent towards the old town. He had done this journey on his bike. It was bloody hard work going upwards but then there was the exhilarating freewheel down again. The road was familiar as far as the historic town of Ludlow but he had never gone further south. From the odd glimpses he caught of landmarks in the moonlight Pete tried to remember the route they were taking.

Peter began to wish he had never got involved with Downes even though he had been well paid. What was the use of the money unless he could get home to collect it? Now, he had a choice of two evils. He could try to escape from these guys, but how could he do that when they were armed? And if he did escape how long would he have before he was picked up by the police and sent to prison for a long time? The alternative was to go along with them and see what they had in mind for him. He thought momentarily of his mum, and how worried she would be. But now that his phone had been taken from him he had no way of letting her know where he was.

The moon had disappeared behind clouds and there was total blackness outside, except where the lights of the van shone. Suddenly, the man next to him took a dark piece of rag from his pocket and blindfolded Pete. He felt sick travelling on without being able to see, but it was only a few miles before the van left the road and seemed to bump across a field before coming to a halt. He heard the van door slide open, then the man beside him gave him a shove and said, 'Out!' Pete stumbled through the open door.

'This is it,' thought Pete. He'd seen loads of films where the victim was blindfolded and told to kneel on the ground before being shot in the back of the head. But he wasn't told to kneel, instead he was pushed across the field. He could feel the turf beneath his feet. Suddenly, there was the sound of an engine starting up. Not a car or van this time. Far louder than that. More like the engine of a small plane.

Pete felt the draft from the propeller as they reached the plane. Someone pulled him, stumbling, up the steps, pushed him into a seat and fastened a belt across his stomach. He lifted his hands to snatch off the blindfold but felt something cold and hard smash into his knuckles. Someone slumped down into the seat beside him, then a door closed, the sound of the engine grew much louder and they began to move. Their speed increased rapidly until the bumping ceased and the plane left the ground.

When the blindfold was removed Pete saw that he was sitting in the cabin of a small plane. There were six passenger seats and beyond a partition he could see the pilot with another man sitting beside him. The two men who had collected him from the hilltop were sitting in the passenger seats, one of them close beside him, the other playing some game on a phone. Then he used the phone to make a call in a foreign language.

As the sun came up, Pete could see that they had reached a coastline and were beginning to cross the sea. He had absolutely no idea where they were going and the sound of engine soon lulled him to sleep.

TWENTY

Felicia lay on the bed, sweating from sex. Pete sat leaning against the cool wall of Felicia's room. Normally he would have smoked but he had no cigarettes. The room was in darkness.

Felicia's English was much better than she had originally let on. She had explained that this was only a temporary job for her. She would be going back to her village as soon as she had earned enough to pay her way to university in Seville. All she had to do was keep the villa clean and cook for the men during their brief stays.

'Do they own the villa?' asked Pete.

'Oh no, the owner lives somewhere else. He never visits.'

'So, what is it for?'

'You will find out, if you stay, but you must leave as soon as possible.'

'Why?'

'Because you are in danger while you are here.'

'I've been treated well enough so far. Life is good for me here, especially now you and I have become ... friends.'

She slipped on her underclothes and thin dress and came to sit with him.

'You don't understand.'

'Well, tell me.'

At that moment, they heard a car approaching up the single track road from the valley.

'Quickly. Go back to your room. Have a shower. Get dressed.'

She gathered up his clothes and handed them to him.

'Go. Now!'

He heard the urgency in her voice, fear perhaps, and hurried back to his room.

The car drew up outside. He recognised the gruff voices of the men who had brought him here and some strange half strangled cries. He turned on his shower and stepped inside. There was a knock on his door. It opened. But whoever it was must have heard the shower and left again. Then there was silence.

He got into bed, thinking about Felicia, and eventually fell asleep.

Next morning, he found the two men sitting on the veranda with Felicia serving breakfast. One of them stopped shovelling paella into his mouth.

'You must be ready to leave tonight.'

'Where are you taking me?'

'No questions. Be ready.'

The other man took a cigarette from his mouth.

'Make sure you are ready. Now, go. Leave us in peace.'

Pete and Felicia stood together on the veranda, watching the car wind its way down the hill away from the villa, and breathed a joint sigh of relief. He put his arm around her waist and smiled.

'Well, my friend, what shall we do today?'

She pulled away.

'You must leave as soon as you can!'

'I have no passport or money. I don't even know where I am.'

'You are about 30 kilometres from Malaga. That way!' She pointed to the west. 'There is a British Consulate there.'

'I can't do that. I'm wanted by the police in my own country.'

Felicia stepped back.

'What for?'

'Oh, don't worry, I haven't done anything really bad. I've been framed. Do you understand?'

'I think so. You mean that someone has tried to make it appear that you are guilty of something. Yes?'

A Perfect Alibi

'That's exactly it.'

'And what you did is connected with these men?'

'Indirectly, I suppose.'

While they were talking they walked into the villa.

'Well, I know that they are very bad men. They brought another man here, about two months ago. He was here for two days then they took him away again. But he did not go easily, they had to force him into the car. I heard his screams. They did not see me looking, but I saw what they did. One of them hit him on the head with a gun.'

'So, you think they'll do the same to me.'

'I'm not sure. They may have a use for you. But it will be something bad, I know.'

'What about you? Aren't you afraid of them?'

'They seem to trust me. I just do my work and keep out of their way. You see the money is so good. Things are very hard for young people in Spain. No work at all, except for the very lowest pay. If I can stay for one more month I will have enough to keep me at the university for a whole year.'

'Are you able to leave the villa? Visit your parents?'

'No, I have to stay here for whole time. Then the villa will be closed up and I can go home.'

Suddenly, they heard a knocking which seemed to come from the kitchen and a muffled voice speaking in a language neither of them recognised.

'Where's that noise coming from?' asked Pete.

They went into the kitchen but the sound was muffled. Then Felicia remembered something.

'There's a kind of basement for storage but it is always locked. The door is outside.'

'Where?'

'Around side of house.'

Pete followed her to some steps leading to a low door. He knocked on the heavy, padlocked door. His knock was echoed and the muffled voice came again from inside.

'Is there an axe anywhere?'

'In garden shed.'

Pete hurried across to the shed. It was locked, but there was a small window at the side. Pete picked up a stone and smashed the window. He put a towel from the kitchen over the broken glass and climbed in. He used the head of the axe to remove the glass still left in the frame, then hurled the axe outside and climbed back out through the window.

He was preparing to smash the lock on the cellar door, when Felicia called out, 'Peter. You're bleeding!' He looked down and saw blood dripping from his wrist. Felicia fetched scissors, quickly cut up the towel to make bandages and wrapped one around his wrist.

The banging grew louder again and a muffled panicked voice called out to them in terror.

Peter smashed the lock in one blow and the door swung inwards. A young woman rushed up the steps and collapsed on to the floor gasping for breath. Then she pointed into the cellar with her two hands still tied together. Felicia undid her gag. She muttered something and pointed to the cellar again.

Pete felt around for a light switch. Suddenly, the cellar was flooded with light and he saw two more girls, lying on the floor, gagged and bound. As he moved towards them the girls recoiled. Then he realised he still had the axe in his hand. He tried to show that he was not going to hurt them and used the blade of the axe to cut through the rope tied around the wrists and ankles of the nearest girl. She was trembling with fear but as the rope fell away she put her arms around him and sobbed. He removed the gag and the girl coughed. She pointed at her friend. Pete cut her free and the first girl removed her gag. They held on to one another as Pete ushered them up the steps and out of the cellar saying, 'You're safe now.'

'English! You speak English?' said the first girl he had freed.

Outside both girls hugged their friend. Felicia had removed the rope from her wrists but they were red-raw from struggling to escape. She was still trembling.

The girl who spoke English explained.

'Kristina has fear of small room. Also, darkness.'

'She has claustrophobia,' suggested Peter.

'Yes, that is it. So, she struggled and struggled. Almost out of her mind.'

'Felicia. Do we have any brandy?' asked Pete.

She nodded and went inside. The others went on to the veranda and sat around the table. Kristina gulped her brandy down. The others sipped.

'Do the other girls speak English?'

'Not like me. I have English boyfriend for a while.'

Felicia brought water and food. The girls had had nothing since last night. Anna, the English speaker went on to explain how they had all applied for jobs in English hotels. When they went to be interviewed their passports were taken away for processing they were told. That night they were taken to a small village outside Warsaw where they boarded a plane. It was all quite pleasant until they landed. Suddenly, the men tied them up, gagged them and brought them here.

'You must all leave here very soon. You too Peter.' said Felicia. 'Those men will be back this evening.'

'Few problems,' replied Peter. 'We haven't a passport between us. We have no money. And there's the dogs.'

'I can handle the dogs; I am studying to be a vet. Dogs are affected by drugs just as much as humans and there is some cannabis in the men's room. I can mix some with meat and throw it out to the dogs. They will soon become harmless.'

'That's brilliant, so long as it works.'

'Trust me,' said Felicia. 'Oh and you have to tie me up when you leave. And perhaps rub some of that blood from your arm on to my face.'

'I just hope to God they believe you.'

TWENTY ONE

Pete and the girls walked past the dogs, now sprawled lethargically on the dusty earth, and took the path Felicia had showed them on the little map she had made. She had also packed some food and plenty of water and given Pete enough money for them to take a bus from the village to Malaga. He had promised to return the money as soon as he could.

He had hated the business of tying Felicia up and leaving her in the cellar. He had torn her blouse, as instructed, then wet his arm and rubbed some of the blood on her face. He did not gag her, so that she could call out to the men when they returned.

'What if they don't believe you?'

Felicia shrugged. He put his arms around her and held her tightly. If he ever got out of this mess he would come back and find her.

It was very hot indeed. Pete was wearing a wide hat stolen from the men's room, and a cape which covered his arms. When they saw him the girls laughed and called him a peasant.

At last, the path entered a shady olive grove and they stopped for a while to drink. Now, it was his turn to laugh as he saw the sweat glistening on the girls' crimson faces. Luckily, their arms and legs were mostly covered.

The shade continued as the path entered a narrow valley between the mountains and on the other side they entered a plantation of coniferous trees. Pete looked at his watch and told them they must hurry. The last bus left the village at 4.30pm. Suddenly, they heard the sound of a plane approaching. They crouched under the thickest trees as the plane flew on and landed somewhere nearby. Pete had stopped going to church in his early teens, though he had once briefly been a choirboy, but now he prayed silently that Felicia would be safe.

A Perfect Alibi

Pete urged the girls to run and they just managed to get to the village and on to the crowded bus before it set off for Malaga.

As the bus rattled and shook its way down from the hills towards the city Pete thought about the way his life had been turned upside down because he had been greedy. He glanced across at the girls, who all smiled back at him. They were hot and tired but happy because they were free. He had helped them to escape from a terrible life as sex slaves somewhere in England. But what would happen to them now? Could they ever get back to their own country and, if so, would they be safe?

Unwittingly, he had become involved in a terrible criminal world. He had liked the idea of earning money so easily, but it had turned him into a fugitive and an accessory to the worst kind of crimes. Those men were ugly in body and mind. They thought only of the profit to be made from bringing those girls to England and using them as prostitutes. They were evil and some of that evil had rubbed off on him. Perhaps he should go to the police and tell them what had happened and how he could help them to find the real criminals. He had not killed that girl. But would they believe him? Perhaps if the girls with him now could tell the police how he had helped them, they would realise that he was not a wicked person.

At last they approached the city, the roads improved and the bus ran more smoothly. It was a beautiful evening as they got off the bus. Pete left the girls sitting at a pavement café, near the station, enjoying cool drinks, while he went to find the British Consulate. At last, he found it, in a splendid building, with the union flag fixed above a high bronze door, but a notice on the iron gates, which were firmly shut, told him that the office would not reopen until 10am on the following day.

'Well, at least I don't have to decide what to do about telling my story until tomorrow.' he thought. Instead, he must find somewhere for the girls to stay that night. He had only enough for the girls to stay in a really cheap room. He would have to sleep in a park or on the street, but at least the night was warm.

He made his way back towards the café, but as he turned the last corner he stopped and stepped back into the shadows. When he peered carefully around the corner he saw that a large black saloon had parked right by the café and that the girls were being pushed into it. He thought he could see a pistol in one of the men's hands. How had they discovered that the girls were here?

'Oh, my God, Felicia! What have they done to you?'

Pete heard the girls screaming but no one was brave enough to try to help them. He knew that if he tried he would be caught or shot. At least while he was free he might be able help the police put an end to this gang's operations.

The car moved away at speed; he knew what he had to do.

TWENTY TWO

Pete trudged the streets of Malaga feeling more and more depressed as the evening closed in. He had let those girls down. They would now be taken to England, as planned, and Felicia must be in danger, otherwise she would never have told those monsters where the girls had gone. That could not have been just a lucky guess. He seemed to be the only person not smiling as everyone else walked the streets enjoying the warmth, the music issuing from the clubs and cafés, and one another's company.

The sky became cloudy and the air oppressive. What on earth would he do if there was a thunderstorm? He had already decided not to pay for a place to stay for the night. And there was no point in going to the consulate and giving himself up now that the girls had been recaptured. Instead he would use the cash to buy a ticket for the first bus back to the village tomorrow and try to help Felicia, if it was not too late.

He was drawn towards the harbour where the air was a little fresher. Night fell quite suddenly and there was less street lighting in this district. He found a little park, not much bigger than a large garden. He slipped inside just before an official locked the gate and hid in some bushes. He crawled beneath a huge hibiscus and sat on the sandy soil.

He still had the cape he had worn during the day to protect his pale skin. Now, he wrapped it around as a blanket and lay down. He could hear nothing but the distant hum of traffic. Even the birds had gone to sleep. It had been such a strange, exhausting day that his eyes soon closed. When he opened them again the sky showed the first pale light of dawn.

Pete could not wait for the keeper to open the park gates, so he climbed a tree and reached for the top of the railings. There was one tricky moment as he balanced between the spikes but he managed to jump down to the pavement without catching his clothes or hurting himself. Just as he landed he heard someone call out something in Spanish. He didn't understand the words, but he knew from the way it was shouted that it meant 'Halt!' and looking up he saw a man in uniform a couple of hundred yards away, drawing a pistol from its holster, so Pete ran. Thank God I'm fit, he thought. A few moments later he heard a faint whistle, but by now he was among the crowds who were gathering around the harbour, with their fishing gear, ready for a day at sea.

He slowed down, mingling with the crowd, and entered a café. Someone had left a seaman's cap on the table while they went to the counter. Pete picked it up and walked out again. That policeman, or whatever he was, had not been close enough to recognise his face but he might remember his fair hair. Now, that was hidden under a sailor's cap.

He walked back towards the bus station. The night's clouds had lifted and the sun was already burning down from a clear sky. At least the hat would protect his head from the hot sun.

The first bus for the village was leaving in 40 minutes. He bought his ticket and counted the few remaining coins. There was probably just enough to pay for something to eat, and a bottle of water, which would be essential later in the day.

By the time the bus had climbed into the hills, around the narrow hairpin bends it was approaching noon and the interior of the bus was like an oven. The choice was between the stench of sweating humans with the windows closed or swirling dust if they were open and the latter won, so that when Pete got off the bus he was as dark as a native, and no one took any notice as he took the path back towards the villa. It was about four kilometres through the plantation and the narrow valley and he had to stop in the olive grove to catch his breath and drink the last of the water.

From now on he moved very carefully, keeping low and looking out for those dogs or any sign of the men. At last, he

A Perfect Alibi

reached the fence. His nose suddenly filled with a disgusting stench and then he saw the corpses of the dogs decomposing rapidly in the heat, each shot in the head. If they could do that to a couple of confused canines what might they have done to Felicia?

There were usually two cars at the villa but one of these had gone, to take those poor girls to the plane and their fate somewhere in England. Perhaps they had taken Felicia as well, in revenge for her part in freeing them. Pete was suddenly filled with anger. He was determined to find those bastards and bring them to justice.

As he walked around to the back of the villa he saw the other black car, shimmering in the heat. The danger was that one of the men had stayed behind and would be waiting for him. He moved to the side of the building where there were no windows, then crawled towards the door and listened for any movement from within, before stepping into the shaded interior. He had picked up a large stone from near the door as his only weapon.

He stiffened when he heard a sound coming from the room where the men slept, but quickly realised that it was the sound of a woman moaning. He hurried into the room and found Felicia tied to the bed, her clothes torn and with cuts and bruises on her arms and head.

He went into the kitchen for a knife and quickly cut through her bonds. She sobbed as she hugged him.

'Are you in pain?'

'No, these are tears of relief, because you are unharmed.'

'I don't understand.'

'They said that they had found you and that they would hurt you if I did not tell them ...'

Her tears came again.

He held her gently until she calmed down. Pete's anger returned.

'What did they do to you?'

'They knocked me about a little to make me talk.'

'Nothing else?'

'They did not rape me, if that's what you mean. Do you know why?'

He thought about those monsters. Surely they were capable of anything.

'Because they are gay. They both used to sleep in this room, but only one bed was ever used.'

How clever of the gang to use such men, so that the goods were not soiled before they reached their destination.

'Have you eaten?'

Felicia replied, 'I have no appetite but I need to drink.'

Pete fetched a large glass of mineral water, which she quickly emptied. Then she began to tremble. Shock thought Pete, but there was panic in her voice as she said, 'We must get away from here, as soon as possible. They left early this morning, but they will be back soon.'

'Shall I take you to your family in the village?'

'No, they would soon find me. And harm my parents. We must go far away.'

Pete remembered the car he had seen outside.

'Look, you have a shower and deal with those cuts and bruises. Then put on some fresh clothes. I'm going to check something.'

He went outside and crossed to the car. He couldn't believe his luck. The keys were in the ignition. I suppose they thought that no one but themselves would ever come up here. He turned on the ignition and waited until the gauge showed him that the fuel tank was almost full, then turned off the engine and ran back inside. He filled a cardboard box with food and drink.

When he returned Felicia was dressed, her hair wrapped in a towel.

'Do you have anyone you could stay with somewhere else in Spain?'

'Yes, I have an uncle and aunt in Northern Spain, near Santander, but how would we get there?'

'Pack a few clothes and join me on the veranda.'

A few minutes later she came out, with a small holdall, the towel now discarded and her lovely long black hair flowing free. He held up the car keys.

'Let's go!'

Soon they were speeding down the narrow roads towards the motorway that would take them northwards.

TWENTY THREE

It took Pete and Felicia two days to travel from southern Spain to the northern coast. The car was a powerful Mercedes saloon and it was the first time Pete had ever driven on the right hand side of the road. He drove carefully to avoid being stopped because he had no documents whatsoever. Felicia guided him towards Granada where they joined the E902 and he was confident enough to raise his speed.

Pete had only been to Spain once before with some lads from the village and then was only aware of sun, sand, sangria and rows of hotels designed to please the tourists. Now, he was travelling through the much less inhabited mountainous interior where the road wound its way through forested valleys, with glimpses of distant snow capped mountains above them and fast flowing rivers below.

There was just enough fuel in the car to get them to Madrid, where they parked the car in a backstreet and spent an uncomfortable night, curled up on the back seat. Early next morning they wiped the interior clean of their fingerprints and left the key in the ignition. Some opportunist would soon spot the apparent error, slip into the car and drive it away, so that Pete and Felicia could not be easily traced.

Felicia had enough money for two rail tickets to Santander, a sizeable city port on Spain's Atlantic coast. Practically all her savings had now gone so she would not be able to continue her studies. Pete vowed that when he returned to England he would immediately send her every penny of the money he had earned from Richard Downes. He wanted to forget all about that dreadful episode, and he had become very fond of Felicia.

The train passed through a very different landscape as it headed northwards. There were clouds in the sky, and everything was greener, more like England, with little farms and walled fields. When they left the train it was much cooler and they wished they had warmer clothing, but there was no money left, except to buy a cheap meal. Felicia began to worry that her relatives may not be at home but as her Uncle Ramon was a fisherman she could not imagine him leaving his boat for very long.

From Santander they hitch-hiked along the coast, passing long sandy beaches and several lighthouses on the headlands between. Because Felicia was a pretty young woman they had no problem getting lifts, and Pete's muscular body discouraged the, mainly male, drivers from trying anything on.

At last, they came to the small coastal village where Felicia's relatives lived. They were at home and very welcoming although they had not seen Felicia since she was 15, when she had stayed with them one summer for a wonderful holiday. She told Ramon and Aunt Marta what had happened at the villa and they were horrified. She did not tell them about Pete's earlier involvement with the villains, only that he had rescued her from a terrible fate. She telephoned her parents to explain where she was and that she would not be returning for some time but that she was safe and happy.

Her aunt and uncle took to Pete straight away, especially when they saw how fond of him Felicia was. Their house was small and Pete had to sleep on a sagging, lumpy settee in the main room, but as her aunt and uncle went to bed early, Felicia would join him for some quiet lovemaking after which he slept well enough.

Uncle Ramon invited Pete to spend a day at sea with him. When they left the little harbour the sun was shining and the sea quite calm but this late in the year the Atlantic was unpredictable and by the time they reached the fishing grounds the boat was pitching and rolling like a fairground ride and Peter's breakfast had become brunch for the fish.

However, Pete soon gained his sea legs and by the time the nets were ready to be drawn in he was able to help. The Spanish spoken up here was not the same as in the far south, but he quickly picked up the fishermen's language which consisted mainly of grunts and curses. The crew shared a snack of bread, cheese and wine before turning back to harbour. The sea had calmed again and this time Pete's food stayed down. By the time the catch had been unloaded and Pete and Ramon returned to the little cottage they were both very hungry.

After a superb meal of fish stew and freshly baked bread Ramon spoke to his niece but kept glancing at Pete. When she came to his makeshift bed that evening she told him what her uncle had said.

'He thinks you would be a great help to him. You have the makings of a fisherman. You are strong and already beginning to ride the waves. One of his crew has just left to take a job on the ferries in Santander. He could pay you very little but you could stay here for free.'

Pete felt one of the lumps of the settee digging into his back with Felicia's weight on top of him. He chuckled.

'They'd have to provide a new settee.'

Felicia laughed softly. Pete was very tempted. He had grown to like Spain. He had begun to love Felicia. And if he stayed he would not have to face a possible murder charge back in England. But those evil men and the bastards who ran that sex trafficking organisation would not be brought to justice. He was the only one who could really help the police with their enquiries. He owed that to the girls he had helped to escape, only for them to be recaptured, and for all the other girls who would be trafficked. But especially, he owed it to the dead girl from the Old Vicarage, the girl whose body he had pushed into Downes's grave.

Yes, he would be happy as a fisherman. He really liked Ramon and he would be doing something useful, something that suited his physical prowess, and he loved the fresh air and the sea.

A Perfect Alibi

Of course, as an illegal immigrant he would have no papers and if the authorities made enquiries he would not be able to help his new friends in Spain or those girls in England who needed him. It was one hell of a decision to have to make, but it was not a policeman or an immigration official who forced his hand. It was a young unemployed Spaniard, Juan, who had been hoping to be offered the job on Ramon's boat. He came to the house a few days later and asked Ramon where Pete had come from and how long he was staying. Ramon told him that Pete was from Holland and was on holiday with Felicia. When Pete went back home the young man could apply for the job.

Now, Ramon himself became suspicious. He asked Felicia to explain why her young man was in Spain. She decided to be half truthful. She told her uncle that Pete had been caught smuggling and had been forced to leave the country without papers, but now he was prepared to return and give himself up. When he had done his time in prison he would come back to Spain with the proper papers and they would be married. Ramon, like many men who made their living on the sea was sympathetic towards smugglers. He had been involved himself at one time, though only in a minor way and never with drugs. Marta was a romantic at heart and wanted her husband to help Pete. So, it was agreed that when the forecast was good he would sail to the coast of Cornwall and slip Pete ashore.

Pete was quite pleased that circumstances were forcing him to return to England, but he was not sure what he would do when he got there. He was going to miss Felicia very much and was hoping that if he helped the police to catch the gang his sentence for being involved in what happened to the girl at the Old Vicarage might be reduced. The main thing would be to convince them that he had not killed the girl, though he still did not really understand what had happened to her. He decided that when he got to England he would lie low for a while. The ports and airports and Eurostar would have been asked to look out for him but if he landed in a quiet Cornish cove in the middle of the night he could probably make his way undetected towards home.

The only remaining problem was money. He would have difficulty hitch-hiking across England in winter. In the summer he could say that he was on his way to a music festival, or to try surfing, but these were hardly convincing reasons in early December.

The day for the voyage to Cornwall arrived. The forecast was reasonable. Pete was decked out in some of Ramon's old clothes with a waterproof coat and trousers on top. They set out in the early morning as if they were embarking on a normal fishing trip. Felicia and Marta both shed tears. They did not come to the harbour to wave farewell as this would seem strange to any onlookers. Luckily, the young man who wanted the job with Ramon was nowhere to be seen. Ramon suspected that Juan was not an early riser and so would never make a fisherman.

Unless the weather got worse it would take about 48 hours to reach Cornwall, so dawn would not have risen when they dropped Pete on some Cornish beach. The rest of the crew had been told that they were going to fish near the Scillies so they had prepared for a longer voyage than usual.

The forecast was accurate and although it was choppy in the Bay of Biscay the boat coped well. When night came, Pete slept fitfully, not because the boat was rocking in the swell, but with all the doubts he had about his return to England and his worries about how Felicia would cope if he was given a long sentence.

As the boat continued on past the Scilly Isles the crew was told about the real reason for their voyage. They were just as happy to help a smuggler as their skipper and Ramon promised them a bonus when they got back to Spain.

It was a moonless night and the coast of Cornwall was just a dark blur above the starlit sea. Ramon gave Pete a hug before helping him into the dinghy and an outboard motor puttered into life as they moved slowly through the surf towards the sand. Pete expected a light to come on at any moment and illuminate a group of policemen or coastguards waiting for him. He removed his shoes and socks, turned up his trousers and dashed through the freezing waves and across the sand to the dunes.

Pete buried his waterproof trousers in the sand, and tied the top around his waist. It was a chilly morning but there was no rain. The clothes that Ramon had given him were bulky and warm. The sun was just appearing over the sea as he left the beach and began walking along a rutted lane leading inland. There was no sign of any habitation, but the lane must lead somewhere.

At last, he came to a road. There was no sign but he turned towards the sun, knowing that he needed to head east. Soon, a few houses began to appear, mainly the sort of bungalows that retired people built when they moved to the coast to spend their last few years living the dream. His mum would like one of those he thought, but he couldn't imagine her ever moving away from the village, unless she met some new chap and went off with him. Just about possible he thought, so long as the lung cancer didn't get her first. Then he suddenly remembered that he hadn't smoked since he'd been taken to the villa and he hadn't missed it at all.

For the first time in ages he thought about his mum. She would be worrying like hell about him. She probably thought, like everyone else, that he was somehow connected with that girl's death. It was too much of a coincidence. Dead girl found in open grave. Gravedigger's assistant disappears. He hoped that she hadn't found the money. That would convince her he'd been up to no good. But boy, could he do with that money now.

The little hamlet petered out. He passed what looked like a farmhouse and a bit further on he saw a barn. It was the perfect place to rest and eat the small meal wrapped in greaseproof paper and shoved in his jacket pocket by Ramon. In the other pocket he had stuck a small bottle of watered down wine. He thought of dear Marta pottering about the cottage. How kind she and Ramon had been. Then of course his thoughts moved on to Felicia. God, how he would miss her!

When he had finished his meal he stuck the paper and the bottle deep into the straw and set off again. After about half a mile he came to a junction with a busier road. This time there was a road sign pointing left to Truro and right to St Austell. The sun was coming from the right so that was the way he needed to go.

It was fully light now and there was already a fair amount of traffic on the new road. He tried to hitch a lift but without luck. He knew that people were suspicious of hitch-hikers these days, especially a young man walking along a country road at this early hour. He gave up for a while and just walked on. What he needed was some kind of lorry park or a roadside café where he could chat to the drivers and gain their confidence. He could say that his mother was ill and he was going home to see her, but that he hadn't had his benefits this week.

He walked on again, more slowly, for a couple of miles and was just beginning to feel tired when a lorry passed him, slowed down and drew up in a layby just ahead. Perhaps the driver needed a rest, but he hurried towards it just in case. He had just reached the cab when the driver jumped down.

'Wanna lift?' the driver asked in a high pitched Midlands accent.

'Yes, please,' he replied.

The driver removed her woollen hat and shook out some long blonde hair. Fuckin hell! It was a woman.

'Where yo headin?'

'The Midlands. Wolverhampton. Brum.'

He knew it was no good telling her exactly where he was heading for. She would never have heard of it.

A Perfect Alibi

'Well, you'm in luck mate. I'm tekkin a load of fish to Brum.'

The driver lit a fag and was sucking on it greedily. Pete wanted to join her, but had decided to give up for good.

'Well, gerrin, kidda.'

The woman chucked away the fag end and jumped back into the cab. The big engine throbbed and the cab shook. Then they were on their way.

They travelled in silence for a while. Pete surreptitiously glanced at the woman. She was older than he'd first thought. Probably In her forties. He guessed that her hair wasn't naturally blonde: it had that brassy look as if it had been bleached. Her face was handsome, with strong features. When she sat at the wheel she removed her jacket and showed her muscular arms, covered in tattoos. She handled the lorry very efficiently, with the minimum of effort. She noticed him glancing at her and smiled. Pete became nervous. Perhaps she'd picked him up on purpose. She'd want repaying in kind. Suddenly, she asked, 'Roight. So, what's yo story?'

Pete told her about his mother and his lack of cash.

She laughed, 'That's probably crap, but I don't care. An if you'm thinking you can mug me and pinch me cash I aye got none, and yo better know I'm a black belt in Karate.'

'I had no intention ...'

'And if you think I want yo body, you can think again. I can get that any time I like at 'ome.'

There was another pause while she eased the lorry on to the A38 and picked up speed, then she spoke again.

'See. I just like a bit of company. I done this journey so many times I could do it blindfold. So, tell me about yoself.'

This was going to be difficult but he'd stick to the basics and invent what he had to.

'I came down to Cornwall for the summer.'

'Thought you had a bit of a tan.'

'Got a job in a hotel. Did some surfin'. Then the season ended, the hotel's half empty, so they give me the push. I signed on. Did a bit of this and that. Then I get a call about my mum. But I'd just spent my last jobseeker's on a new board. So, I gotta thumb it. No luck at all till you come along.'

She smiled again. Her whole face softened.

'How old am yo?'

He added a year, 'Twenny two.'

'Got a girl?'

'Sort of. She was working at the hotel. Gone back to Spain now.'

She nodded. He was doing pretty well, he thought.

'Right, here's the plan. We stop for summat t'eat just before Exeter. Don't worry I'm buying. Expenses like. Then it's up the M5 and we'll hit Brum about one o'clock. Sound OK?'

'Brilliant.'

It wasn't all one way. He discovered she was called Dana. Joined the army as a youngster. Drove trucks in hot, dangerous places. Loved driving almost as much as she loved Keith, her husband, and the kids. He stayed home to look after them while she drove the lorry.

By the time they got to the outskirts of Birmingham they were pals. Dana pulled into the lorry park and squeezed in neatly between two equally enormous vehicles. She checked her watch.

'Gotta stop 'ere for a bit. Driver Regs. Bit later than I thought. This OK for you?'

'Perfect. Thanks Dana.'

'Get going kidda and good luck. Hope your mum's OK.'

She gave him a soppy kiss.

'Tarra.'

He walked towards the toilets, wondering about the rest of his journey. Reckoned he was about 30 miles from home. He was going to have to be careful now. No more hitching, just footslog, or perhaps he could pinch a bike. First he needed a map. Plenty of those in the shop, after he'd had a piss.

He walked along the service road out of the back of the place until he came to the main road. Then he walked westwards, but he hadn't gone far before it began to rain. He took the waterproof top from around his waist and put it on. It began to get dark. He'd forgotten how early night falls in England at this time of year. But in some ways, it was good thing. No one was going to take much notice of someone hurrying along the verge on a dark rainy evening, even if they saw him.

He was walking quickly now and soon found himself in real countryside. The road went up and down over little hills, through woodland and open country. He came across a church and stopped for a rest in the porch. He wasn't keen on churches, especially after that night near the open grave, but the porch had a seat on either side of the door and it was out of the cold wind that had risen, driving the rain into this face.

He hadn't eaten since Exeter and his stomach was beginning to rumble. Then he noticed a bike, propped up against the wall of the church, partly sheltered by a yew tree. It was an old-fashioned model with hub gears and dynamo lighting, but it was a bike and it wasn't locked.

Soon, he was on his way again on a bike with lights and wearing an orange waterproof jacket. Just a late night traveller getting home out of the rain.

Suddenly, there was the sound of a siren rapidly approaching.

'Bloody hell, that was quick,' thought Pete.

He jumped off the bike and flung it and himself into the hedge. The police car seemed to slow, then zoomed on by. Pete waited for a few minutes, realising now that in front of the hedge was a ditch, full of water. His trousers and shoes were soaked. He was tired, hungry and wet through. But he was almost there.

Eventually the rain stopped and the wind dropped. It took him three more hours to reach the village. He parked the bike outside a house and hurried on into a little wood. Now, he knew exactly where he was. At the other end of the wood he removed his waterproof top and walked along a footpath behind the houses lining the cul-de-sac. He opened a little wicket gate in a thick high hedge and crossed the lawn to a large house. When he reached the back of the house he found a low door into what had once been a coal shed. He upturned a flower pot, found a key, unlocked the door and went in. There was no coal in here now. It had been cleaned out and whitewashed. There was a camp bed against one wall with a wardrobe opposite and a toilet in an alcove. This was where the girl had been kept.

Pete thought about those girls in the cellar at the Spanish villa. For a moment he was filled with self-loathing, but he was also totally exhausted. He took off his wet clothes, lay down on the bed and was soon asleep.

TWENTY FOUR

There was no window in the little room, so when Pete woke he had no idea what time it was. He felt stiff after the long bike ride and he was very hungry. Coming back here had seemed the right thing to do, but now he began to have doubts. Obviously, he couldn't just stay in this room, but if he moved into the rest of the house someone would be bound to notice. He could go straight to the police, but would they give him a proper chance to explain? When he thought about all that had happened to him since the girl died he knew it would sound quite incredible. They probably wouldn't believe him and because he had disappeared they would assume he had caused the girl's death.

As he became fully awake he began to smell the scent of the girl. It was very faint now, but it was there. He began to sob for her and for himself. He had no idea why she had died, but he felt partly responsible. He thought about Felicia. Would he ever see her again? Before he had met her, girls were just part of the fun of being alive, to be enjoyed and then discarded, as he moved on to the next. But Felicia had begun to mean much more to him.

He tried the light switch but the power had been turned off. He used the small toilet that Downes had installed in the room. Had the police found this room or had they just assumed it was still a coalhouse? The door into the rest of the house was disguised as part of the oak panelling in the passageway.

He had not undressed properly last night, but simply removed the waterproof coat, his wet shoes and trousers. He began to shiver. There was no heat in the room. He opened the door into the hallway and listened carefully. Daylight was filtering through from the fanlight above the front door. Suddenly, he jumped as a clock chimed somewhere in the house. He counted the chimes. Nine o'clock!

He went into the kitchen. The fridge was empty and wedged open. The cupboards had been cleared. At least the water was still turned on. He found one glass left on the work surface, let the water run for a while, then filled the glass and drank. The cold water increased his shivers as he stood in his T-shirt and boxers. This house had always been cold, even in the summer. Now, it was December and he had just returned from a warm country. He dared not turn on the heating system. He ran upstairs and went into the main bedroom. The old man's clothes had not been cleared out yet. He found a dressing gown in the wardrobe. That would have to do for the moment.

Back in the kitchen he went carefully through each cupboard, then down into the cellar where he found that the freezer had been turned off. He remembered that the freezer would have been empty anyway. He had chucked out all the food before putting the girl's body into it. He felt tears starting again. 'For God's sake,' he thought, 'get over it. You did a stupid thing and you must suffer for it, one way or another.'

At last he found a tin of baked beans pushed right to the back of a cupboard. There was no power when he flicked the switches and no gas when he tried to light the cooker, so he spooned out the beans and ate them cold.

He could not go on living like this. He could just about manage to wait until it was dark and try to sneak back home. But the streetlights were always on around the estate and there would be young people around, chatting smoking, messing about. What would his Mum think when he turned up again after all this time? She'd probably have a heart attack. She had absolutely no idea of all the things that had happened to him since he disappeared.

The best thing would be to phone the police and ask them to collect him, but he didn't have a phone and the landline wasn't working. Christ, what was he going to do?

A Perfect Alibi

As he stood in the hallway, he heard cars draw up outside. He ought to hide but for some reason he seemed unable to move. Then the cars started up again and drove away. He sighed with relief, but suddenly a silhouette appeared in the glazed panels and the door opened ...

PART THREE
THE RECKONING

TWENTY FIVE

Living alone in an isolated cottage on the side of the Brown Hill had never worried Peggy Dickson until now. Of course, the weather often made things difficult with deep snow, high winds or torrential rain, but these were forces of nature and she knew what to expect and how to cope with them.

She was not ignorant of the world beyond her hillside. She listened to the news and occasionally watched her ancient television. She knew that dreadful things happened in the world all the time. She had been particularly horrified by the war in Afghanistan and the terrible suffering inflicted by the Taliban and she still remembered very clearly the dreadful business of the Black Panther and that local girl found dead in some sort of drain. She was not completely innocent sexually as most people thought. There had been a brief relationship with a man in Birmingham when she was a student nurse. She knew that all he wanted was the sex and he was prepared to overlook the fact that she was plain and plump because she was available. It didn't last long, but it taught her about men and she wanted no more of them.

She had never associated danger or evil with her beloved hillside. Her greatest pleasure was the view from her cottage when she opened the door in the morning and the evening stillness when she could hear the soft call of owls, the mysterious cries of the foxes and the sight of bats flickering in the dusk. Most nights just before she locked her door she would look up at the sky and identify the constellations as her father had taught her.

But since that car had been dumped in the quarry pool she had become nervous. She did not understand people who did things like that and they had brought an unwelcome dimension to her beloved hill. Peggy no longer slept quite so easily in her bed, always listening out for cars passing her cottage at unearthly hours.

She had even begun to consider moving down into the village, but she would only be able to afford a pokey place and her dogs would hate it. In the day time, her fears usually faded away. She knew every inch of the hill. She never failed to give her dogs their morning and evening walks. And as time went by and there were no more night time disturbances she began to relax a little and sleep rather more soundly again.

Then a few days ago that young man had come into the surgery and started asking questions. He pretended to be a patient and asked to make an appointment with one of the doctors. Then he began his questioning.

'I believe you're Mrs Peggy Dickson.'

'Miss.'

'Well, Miss Dickson, I've heard about your courage and your quick thinking.'

'Have you?'

'Yes, the way you faced those criminals and informed the police about that car in the quarry pool.'

'Well, I didn't actually ...'

'I know that DI Dundee and DS Eccles really appreciated your help.'

'I thought they were both very nice.'

'Yes, but unfortunately they haven't made much progress with the case.'

'It must be very difficult.'

'They've both been taken off the case now. But that doesn't make your contribution any less important. Most people think of you as a hero, very public spirited.'

'That's silly. I hardly did anything.'

'If you don't mind I'd like a photograph to remind me of what you did.'

And before she could object he'd taken a photograph and turned to leave, saying,

'Better cancel that appointment. It's not convenient after all.'

Next day there was an article in the Star with a photograph of Peggy. The byline said the article was by Daniel B. Matthews.

'Brave recluse of the Shropshire Hills, Miss Peggy Dickson, spotted criminal activity happening on the top of the Brown Hill. She immediately informed the police and her quick action may help to solve the mystery of the young girl placed in the grave prepared for local crime writer Richard Downes, alias Dirk Barker.

Her information was wasted on the officer leading the enquiry, DI Dundee, but the Special Crime Unit have now taken over the case and when they manage to catch those responsible it may be Miss Dickson's evidence which helps to convict them. We salute her courage and public spirited attitude.

Well done, Peggy.'

Matthew's article was syndicated and passed on to the nationals. He had a scoop and sensed a lucrative future for himself. Nothing like an elderly woman showing courage and quick thinking for a good story. Soon, the national press came to Peggy's door, but she had, very sensibly, gone to stay with an old friend in the next village and asked to be covered at the surgery for a while.

After a few days the fuss died down and Peggy moved back to her beloved cottage and her dogs.

But one night she woke to the sound of a large car crawling past the cottage in a low gear and parking nearby. She was not so much afraid as angry that these people should disturb her with their goings on, whatever they were. She was determined to find out, so she dressed quickly, put on her waxed coat and wellington boots, took the oldest, most obedient dog and walked stealthily up the lane.

It was a very dark night, with no moon or stars but she knew her path well. Soon, she saw the car, with its interior light on, and two men sitting inside, one of them using a phone. The man on the driver's side got out of the car. Peggy crouched low behind a gorse bush. She froze when she realised that the man was walking straight towards her.

She heard him unzip himself and then a stream of liquid splashed into the bush. Peggy did not move but her dog growled. Hearing this the man drew a powerful torch from his pocket and shone it on Peggy, who stood up defiantly to face him. The man called to his colleague, who came running across to join him. The second man took a pistol from his pocket, raised it and fired straight at Peggy. There was a muffled thud from the silenced weapon and Peggy was knocked back on to the ground. The dog licked at her mistress, then growled and leapt at the men. There was another soft thump from the gun and the dog was dead.

Eccles and Dundee were sitting in their office, which was much reduced in size along with their status since the Serious Crime lot had taken over the case of the girl in the grave. The rest of their team was scattered to the fringes of the CID room and even Wentworth had been pushed into a dark corner, behind two filing cabinets to give him a measure of privacy.

The detectives were discussing a tip-off they had just received about the farm burglaries. A dirty white van had driven down the lane to an isolated farm and parked in a layby. The farmer's daughter was off school that day, ostensibly doing revision for her GCSEs, but actually spending most of the day looking out of the window and shaking her head to the sounds on her iPod. She saw the van arrive and its occupants sit there as if waiting for something or someone. Her room was on the shady side of the house so they were unable to see her watching them. She had a feeling that these men were up to no good, so she picked up her phone and took several photographs of them and their van.

When the van left she went down to speak to her mother, who was baking bread for the bed and breakfast guests arriving that evening; part of the diversity of schemes necessary to keep the farm viable these days. Eventually, the sceptical parent began to take her daughter seriously, and that afternoon they went to the police station and asked to see DS Eccles, who they knew from her recent crime prevention visits to all the farms in the area. The photos were taken from a distance and the quality was poor, but Eccles asked if she could borrow the phone to pass on to the techies. Laura blushed with pride and immediately agreed. She didn't think there was anything particularly incriminating on her phone for once and DS Eccles promised to return it that evening.

She and Dundee were sitting in their overheated office – until recently a paper store – discussing strategy for that evening when Wentworth suddenly appeared, looking fatter and even more flushed than usual.

'Right, you two, DSI Page wants to see you. In his office! Now!'

They wondered why the DCI was prepared to act as messenger boy, but guessed he was just glad to get out from behind those filing cabinets. They walked across to the office, which had been Wentworth's, while the man himself went off to shout at somebody else. The officer who now sat behind Wentworth's desk could not have been more different if he'd tried. Detective Superintendent Page was tall and cadaverous, with pale skin and thin grey hair. Eccles thought he couldn't be as old as he looked, or he would have been long retired. Page didn't ask them to sit down, but instead lifted a copy of the local paper from his desk and showed them the front page. He stared at them both, then spoke in low growl.

'So, who the fuck's been talkin' to the press?'

'Not me, Sir,' stated Dundee. 'I hate the bastard who wrote that crap.'

'You, DS Eccles? Smartin' about being taken off the case?'

'No, Sir. Glad to be rid of it. It needed your greater expertise.'

'Yeah. It did indeed.'

Page smiled a smile that would have forced the most hardened felon to confess.

'So, who d'you reckon's spilling the beans?'

'No idea, Sir.'

'DI Dundee?'

'Beyond me, Sir.'

'Well, let me tell you something for nothing. I don't believe you. Either of you. I know you're still making enquires. In fact, I've had a complaint.'

'Complaint, Sir?'

'Oh yes, DI Dundee. A dear lady who used to clean for Mr Downes. Remember her?'

'Of course, Sir. Mrs Bennett.'

Eccles spoke up.

'We only went to see her to make sure she was all right, Sir. She had been upset by what happened to her employer.'

'So, it was just a social call?'

Dundee spoke up in support. 'That's right, Sir.'

'So, why then did you pass on a sample of her handwriting to be compared with the note sent to Miss Downes?'

'Just the usual routine, Sir. Purposes of elimination. You know.'

A Perfect Alibi

'No, Dundee, I don't know why two detectives should be interrogating an innocent woman – who has not long lost her husband – when they are no longer on the case.'

DI Dundee had begun to blush and even Eccles was looking shamefaced.

Detective Superintendent Page began to pound the desk with his fist and beads of sweat appeared on his head between the sparse hairs.

'I want you two completely out of my hair, and out of the way of our investigation. I have asked Wentworth to suspend you both for a week. And if I see either of you hanging about anywhere near the station, it'll be more than suspension. Got it?'

The last sentence was so loud that the detectives both jumped.

'Yes, Sir!'

'Now, bugger off!'

Wentworth was waiting outside the office.

'You bloody idiots. How the hell am I supposed to manage with two officers down and this burglary business as well? I'd sack you both if I could. Now, clear your desks and get out of my sight.'

TWENTY SIX

Eccles said she would drive Dundee home, so they dumped their few belongings into her car and made their way to the nearest café. Eccles felt stunned. This would go on her record. She was about to point this out to Dundee when he said,

'That bloody woman. She knows we're on to her, so she makes a complaint. To be honest, I'm glad to be shot of the case. But it won't help your career.'

Dundee ordered a cappuccino for Eccles and an Americano for himself and they sat away from the counter in the empty café. They waited in silence till their coffees arrived, then Eccles said, 'She decides blackmail won't work, so she takes cash from the press to tell her story.'

'The thing that really gets me is that Page's mob haven't got any further than us.'

'Right! And now these burglars will probably get away with it as well, for lack of manpower, or Wentworth mucking it up.'

'Damn,' said Eccles, 'I promised to return that kid's phone when we went around this evening.'

Dundee was about to suggest a way around this when Eccles's own phone rang.

'Yes, DS Eccles here. Who's speaking? Oh, hello Miss Downes.'

Jack frowned, his curiosity aroused, but knowing they'd have to pass her on to the Serious Crime Unit.

'Well, Jane. How can I help?'

Leanne was so happy she was singing quietly to herself. Her customer was under the drier so she couldn't hear her. She and Jack were together again. The kids were at school. She was back at the salon, in paid employment, and among friends.

It hadn't been easy getting back into the swing of hairdressing. Styles had changed since she left to have the twins.

A Perfect Alibi

Equipment had become more sophisticated. The customers' expectations were higher and the cost ... wow! But Stella, the proprietor, had given her an easy start, part-time for a week or two, then her first full week under supervision.

The customers had changed too. There was now a sprinkling of black and Asian customers among them, even in this old-fashioned market town, and even when the faces were white she sometimes heard languages which meant nothing to her at all.

That made her think about Grabowski — though of course she spoke perfect English — who had brought her and Jack together again. What a beautiful young woman she was. And so courageous to come out to see her and explain. At first, Leanne had been hostile and suspicious, but Agnieska — a lovely name that — had explained that she had only tried to get close to Jack because she knew he was generally considered to be the best detective at the station and she so wanted to become a detective herself. Gradually, Leanne was convinced and the clincher was when Agnieska described how Jack had treated her so coldly when she had called on him at home.

Leanne looked at this attractive young woman. If Jack could resist her then he was an even better man than she thought. She decided at that moment to go on a strict diet, perhaps join Weight Watchers or go to a gym. Next day, she went home and saw with amazement how clean and tidy the house was. Jack must have kept it that way for her sake. How could she ever have doubted him?

Last night they had had sex for the first time since her return. She had been more willing and responsive than for ages. Jack was the only man she had ever wanted, since the night they had met at that dance. He was a good looking young man then and so gentle when they made love. Many of her friends were envious. Some had even tried, unsuccessfully, to take him away from her. Of course, he was older now, but he had remained trim and kept his good looks. His hair was beginning to grey at the temples, but this only made him look more distinguished.

Her friend Tracey had been very kind to let her stay at the farmhouse and Leanne had certainly seen how the other half lived. The husband was considerably older and very well off. They wanted for nothing, but Leanne couldn't imagine how Tracey could share a bed with such an old and feeble man.

Leanne was miles away when she heard a beeping noise and her nose was assaulted by the smell of singeing hair.

'Oh, my God!'

She switched off the dryer and lifted it from her customer's head. The woman was asleep. Her face was quite flushed but there was no obvious sign of damage to her hair. Leanne sighed with relief. She began to shape the woman's copper tinted curls. 'Chestnut Dream' it said on the bottle. The salon phone rang. Another appointment? They were certainly busy these days. But then Stella gestured for her to come to the phone, and whispered, 'It's Jack. Urgent he said. It's all right. I'll keep an eye on Mrs Brown.'

Leanne was puzzled and slightly panicked as she lifted the phone to her ear. Jack usually phoned her mobile and only during her breaks. Her first thought was the twins.

'Leanne?'

'Yes, love.'

'Bad news, I'm afraid.'

Again, she thought about the twins. But surely if there was a problem at school they would have phoned her, not Jack. She steadied herself.

'Go on.'

'I've got to go away for a few days.'

'Go away?'

'Yes. Dawn and I have been sent on a course, bloody miles away.'

Well, he's safe enough with Dawn she thought.

A Perfect Alibi

'That's a bit sudden isn't it?'

'Wentworth thinks it's a good idea as we've been taken off the dead girl case. It's all about the latest advances in investigation. We should be flattered, I suppose. Bound to look good on our records.'

Leanne thought about the lovemaking last night.

'Yes, I suppose. But I'd just got used to having you around again and the kids will be disappointed.'

'I know. But with all the cuts and changes in the service I can't refuse, can I?'

'Of course not. We'll be OK. But you must keep in touch, Jack.'

'I will. I'm just going home now to grab a few things then we have to get going. It's a long way. Love you.'

She was about to ask where exactly when the call ended.

Leanne looked up and smiled across at Stella, saying, 'Nothing serious, thank God.'

Jane had spent the remainder of the afternoon dashing into Ashford for a pair of jeans, a couple of T-shirts and some boxers for Pete, while Tony showed him to his room. Pete was glad to put off telling his story for a while longer. On the journey down he felt that Jane could become a real friend. When they arrived at Brook House he had, at first, been intimidated by the huge mansion with its antique furniture, but he liked Tony immediately, with his cockney accent, his humour and his non-judgemental attitude. Both Jane and Tony had been incredibly kind and he knew that what he had to tell them would upset them, but after they had shared a simple meal they stayed in the kitchen and he knew that the time had come.

Jane started things off. 'How did you come to know my father?' She still found it hard to call him Dad.

'That old queer Angus was responsible.'

'Angus? Did my father know him then?'

'Oh no. You see, I was helping Angus with a grave when he began telling me about that drama group he belongs to. They were having difficulty casting one of the parts for their next production. I'd done a bit of acting at school and the way Angus described it they just needed a good looking young guy for a small part. Not many lines to learn but a chance to be seen on stage. Well, being stupid and vain I began to think about agents on the look out for talent and a future on stage and screen. Ridiculous really, 'cause I can't act for toffee.'

'But you went along for an audition?'

'Yeah, I read the part. Just a few lines. But what convinced me was the girls.'

'As they would,' said Tony with a touch of sarcasm.

'There was one girl, about my age. It was her first time too. So, we helped each other learn our words and ...'

'Go on,' said Jane.

'There was this older woman, probably about 40. The director's wife. Anyway, she made it obvious she fancied me.'

'Did you fancy her?'

'She was quite attractive, but it got embarrassing. The director guy was jealous and took it out on me, kept putting me down. But I stuck it out and did the part. I was probably awful but ...'

'So, what has this to with Mr Downes?' asked Tony.

'He came to the show one night, don't know why. He didn't usually go out at all, he said, when he came to see me after the show. To be honest he didn't look too well. I'd no idea who he was. I was dead surprised when he said he lived in the village. I don't read much, so I didn't know he was a writer. He told me he lived at the Old Vicarage. I knew where it was 'cause I had a paper round when I was a kid. He asked me to go around to see him next evening. Said he had a proposition to make.'

'So, you went around to visit him?' said Jane.

'Yeah, and he was really friendly. Showed me round, told me about his cleaning lady, Mrs Bennett. He made fun of her, said she wanted to marry him. He asked me if I'd like a drink, went down into the cellar and got a bottle of wine. A really good wine it was. Expensive I reckoned.'

'What was this proposition?'

'He offered me a part in a film he was making.'

'A film?'

'Yeah. He said he was filming one of his stories. There was this one scene he was going to film himself. Didn't need a studio or a crew. All I had to do was make love to this girl, a young actress from some agency. He said he thought I would enjoy the work and he'd pay well.'

Pete suddenly looked at Jane and blushed.

'So, you agreed?' she asked.

'Christ, now I feel so ashamed and embarrassed.' He looked at Tony. 'Can I have a drink?'

Tony poured him a small whisky and one for himself. Jane shook her head.

Pete went on, 'Look, I know what I did was wrong. I wouldn't blame you if you told the police, but if you do decide to shop me, would you do two things for me first?'

'Depends what they are,' said Tony. 'If they're illegal forget it. You're in enough trouble as it is.'

'Wait,' said Jane. 'Let's hear what he wants. Go on Pete.'

'Well, I met this girl in Spain.'

Tony sighed. 'Not another girl.'

'Her name's Felicia. She's wonderful. I ...'

Pete wanted to say that he loved her, but he knew that Tony would probably laugh.

'I borrowed money from her so I could get back here. It was meant to pay for her studies. I've got that money at home, from Mr Downes, but I can't go home to get it. Do you think you could send some money to her? I'll pay you back. Really I will.'

Tony asked, 'How much?'

'About two grand.'

Jane's eyebrows shot up, 'He gave you two thousand pounds!'

Pete just nodded. 'A bit more than that.'

He couldn't look at Jane.

There was silence around the table, then Tony said, 'OK, you give me Felicia's address and I'll send the money in euros.'

'What was the other thing?' asked Jane.

'My mum,' said Pete. 'She'll be worried sick. Could you let her know that I'm OK, but not where I am and not to let anyone else know.'

'Yes, of course. But what if we decide to contact the police when we've heard you out?'

'It doesn't matter anymore. I deserve it.'

'We'll be the judge of that,' said Tony. 'Go on.'

'The first time I went around to the Old Vicarage we just chatted. Your dad wanted to know whether I liked girls, or if I was like Angus. He arranged a time for me to meet this girl and gave me a few hundred quid. "Just a starter," he said, "to cement our partnership." A few days later he phoned and I went around that evening. He told me that the garage was unlocked and I'd find a key on one of the beams so I could get into the house without coming to the front door.'

Pete paused. He went white, as if he was about to be sick.

'He took me down to that room, where I'd spent the night when you found me, Jane. Said he wanted me to meet the actress. He thought I'd like her very much.'

He paused again. Jane thought there might be tears welling in his eyes.

'He told me he'd had a room specially made. For the girl to stay in and for the filming. There was a camera fixed on the wall. The room had a secret door. When Downes pressed the panelling in the hallway in a particular place the door opened and inside, there was this girl ...'

Jane was beginning to hate her father. 'The girl whose body was found in my father's grave.'

Pete lowered his head and muttered, 'Yes.'

Jane's fists tightened. She was suddenly angry. Very angry! She thought of her father's grave and wanted to dig up his body and hit him as hard as she could.

'The girl lay there, stretched out on the bed, asleep, or drugged, I wasn't sure. She was smiling. Her long blonde hair like a kind of halo around her head and her long legs stretched out from a tiny skirt. She was lovely and I guessed very young, younger than me ...'

Tears formed and fell across Pete's cheeks. Jane was convinced that he had not harmed the girl, but her father ... she had begun to think he was capable of anything.

'We went out of the room and he locked the door again. He told me that the girl was called Victoria ...'

Tony glanced at Jane and they both whispered, 'Victoria!'

'He said that Victoria and I were to get to know one another, then when we were ready we could do the love scene. He said she was an experienced porn actress. She would not mind whatever we did and we were to make our lovemaking as real as possible. He gave me some more money and told me I was to come around again the next night. And to make sure that no one saw me.'

'I couldn't see anything wrong with it. I wouldn't force the girl, and if she was happy to have sex with me, then that's what we would do. I went home and put the money in a safe place. Remember, I was on fucking jobseeker's ... oh, sorry Jane. And all I had to do was to become friendly with a beautiful young girl and make love to her if she agreed.'

Pete began to tremble. Tony poured him another drink.

'On the phone Downes told me that when I reached the Old Vicarage I was to go through the garage and straight to the girl's room, so I knocked on the door and went in. She was awake this time. She seemed happy and very friendly. We tried to talk but she had hardly any English. She began to undress me and I didn't stop her. Then she mimed that the room was very warm and took off her own clothes. She was lovely, so eager. I couldn't resist her and soon we lay on her bed and made love. Of course, we used a condom, I'm not completely stupid.'

'At last, she fell asleep. I covered her with a sheet, put on my clothes and left the room. I heard Mr Downes calling me and I went up to his room. He was lying on his bed watching a large screen fixed to the wall. At first, I thought he was watching a porn film but soon I realised that the couple on the screen was me and ... err ... Victoria.'

'I was shocked and was about to say I wanted to pack it in when he handed me a large wad of notes, saying, "I know it's pathetic, Peter, but I can't do it anymore. You're young and virile, so you're doing it for me." '

Jane was squirming with hatred.

'Christ, what a pervert, I thought, but there was something I didn't understand. I asked why he couldn't just watch porn films. They were probably much more professional. "You don't understand," he said. "it has to be Victoria." I looked at all that money in my hand. I remembered how beautiful the girl was and that she seemed quite happy to have sex with me. But I knew it wasn't right and I decided not to go back again.'

TWENTY SEVEN

They used DS Eccles's car and sped down the motorway. The engine throbbed excitingly as the little sports car hit the nineties. Dundee let her listen to her type of music. He hated it but she was doing the driving. They were past Oxford in no time and headed towards London.

'What did you tell Leanne?'

'We're on a course. Latest methods of investigation.'

'She believed you?'

'Yes, we're getting on well at the moment. And so long as she doesn't check with the station ... What about Sabine?'

'She's fine. She's grown in confidence and her English is as good as mine. Probably better,' she added with a smile. 'She doesn't really need my protection any more. But we've become good friends.'

'She's probably very grateful for being rescued from her previous life.'

'Oh, she is. Very grateful. And when I explained that we were going to catch those bastards she was delighted. She still gets sad when she thinks about her friend, Maria.'

The traffic began to build up as they approached London and Dawn was forced to slow to just over 80mph.

'Do you think Staines is on the level?'

'Jane certainly thinks so. And I reckon she's a pretty good judge of character.'

'What, with a father like hers?'

'She had no choice with him did she? And Staines has every reason to want to assist the police.'

'Do you reckon we can do it? Just the two of us?'

'Not sure. Wait till we hear what he can tell us. But if we can crack it, I'd love to see Page's face. I hate that warmed-up corpse.'

'Even worse than Wentworth?'

'Oh Yeah. Wentworth's a pussy cat compared to him.'

The music changed to something more acceptable. It even had a bit of a tune. Jack sat back and listened for a while. They turned on to the M25. It was horrendous as usual, but if they could keep up a decent speed and there were no roadworks they might be off it again before the rush hour began. Damn! Just as he thought this Jack saw the sign flashing above them.

A neon arrow pointed left and another flashing bar showed that the lane ahead was closed. Soon they were crawling along at 50mph, hemmed in between two huge lorries, but at last the cones ended and the road widened out again. Dawn put her foot down and before long they saw the sign for the M20.

'This Tony must have a big house, to fit us all in,' said Jack.

'He has. Jane says there're six bedrooms and some attic rooms.'

'Wonder if he'll have a meal ready?'

'Christ, I hope so. I'm starving.'

They moved into the sitting room which faced the garden and the little wood beyond, so was not overlooked. Nevertheless, Tony closed the thick curtains before turning on the light. He didn't light the fire because he didn't want smoke to be seen rising from the chimney and the central heating was effective enough to keep the house warm.

When they were settled, Pete continued his story.

'I had no intention of going on with Downes's film or whatever it was, but I became concerned about the girl. What would happen to her left alone with that man in his big house? Where had she come from? Why did she have to be locked in that room? So, I got up early one morning, before anybody was about and went back to the Old Vicarage. I knew that the garage was usually left open and Downes had showed me the key kept above one of the beams that would open the door into the house.'

'Everything was silent; Downes was probably still asleep. I crept in and carefully climbed the stairs. The first room I came to was the study. The door was open and a laptop was switched on but the screen was blank. As soon as I touched the mouse the screen lit up. The website was called 'Sex Delivered to Your Door' and it explained how you could choose a girl and have her delivered to your home. To move on to the next stage you had to have a password. I took a wild guess and typed in Victoria. Suddenly, the screen was full of pictures of girls for you to choose from. Most of the girls had foreign sounding names.'

Tony said, 'Well, that ain't so bad, Jane. I mean, loads of guys use dating agencies.'

'Yes,' said Pete, 'but I soon realised it wasn't as simple as that. The girls on the site were naked or very nearly and none of them looked particularly happy, like they were being forced to pose.'

'I began to understand that whoever ran this site was loaning out these girls for sex. For a small fortune, they would deliver a girl to your home. You had to make sure she was kept in a secure place, so any bloke who used the service had to have a pretty big house with some kind of secret hideaway. If you got tired of the girl you could swap her for another one or you could keep her if you wanted – you know like a Thai bride or whatever – but you had to pay a huge sum of money, enough to compensate the organisation for lost rent.'

'The twisted bastards!' snarled Tony.

Tears were running down Jane's cheeks, 'No more twisted than the men who used the site. But I don't understand where my ... no, I can't call him that any more. Where on earth did he get all that money? He was never that well off.'

Pete spoke directly to Tony, 'Yeah, they are bastards. Really evil! I'll tell you all about them later, when we get to that.'

'Another strange thing. The girl knew hardly any English but apparently, your dad ...'

'Don't call him that! I disown him.'

'Well, anyway, he seemed to understand her language, whatever it was. I thought it sounded Eastern European, possibly Polish. You know we hear quite a lot of that these days, even in our area. Anyway, your father ... Downes ... was able to make her understand that if anyone came to the house – like Mrs Bennett I suppose – she was to be very quiet. He would warn her when someone was coming and tell her when they'd gone. She nodded to show that she understood.'

'What happened next?' asked Jane.

'I don't think you should hear this Jane,' said Pete.

'Oh no. You can't send me away now. I want to know exactly what that sodding man did. Every damned detail.'

'Are you sure, Jane?' asked Tony.

'Look, I've learned that my father ... *my father* ... was a pervert. He was also getting a lot of money from somewhere, probably illegally, and he might even have been a murderer. So, what could be worse? Go on Pete.'

'Well, just then I heard this moaning. More like an animal than a person. It came from Downes's bedroom so I went in and there he was, lying on the floor, unable to move or speak. His eyes were open but they didn't seem able to focus. His face was all twisted and he was dribbling from his open mouth.'

'Sounds like a stroke,' said Tony.

'Yes, I'd seen my uncle have one, so I knew.'

'What did you do?'

Now, Pete's eyes filled with tears. Jane got up from her chair and moved across to him. She knelt before him and took his hands in hers.

'Nothing. That's what's so unforgivable. I did nothing to help him.'

Tony whispered, 'Go on, Pete. You have to finish now.'

'Then I noticed the girl ... Victoria ... or whoever she was, lying on his bed. She was completely naked and she was lying

A Perfect Alibi

perfectly still. At first I thought she was asleep, but when I got closer I knew that she was dead. I felt her pulse but there was nothing. Her flesh already felt cold. I couldn't see any sign that she was breathing.'

There was silence in the room. Jane returned to her seat and buried her face in her hands.

At last Tony broke the silence to ask, 'Do you think Downes had killed her?'

'No. I don't know. There was no sign of any injury.'

'Go on.'

'Real panic set in. I knew that Downes needed help. The sooner you deal with a stroke the better. But if I called an ambulance they'd find the girl. Even if I just phoned I reckoned they'd probably be able to trace the call, so I left him where he was. I did nothing to help him.'

'He deserved it,' shouted Jane, her voice harsh with anger, 'But that poor girl ...'

'What happened next?' asked Tony.

'For a while I just stood there stunned. Then I saw it was nearly half past six and Mrs Bennett would be in at seven. I thought, at least she could deal with Mr Downes. He didn't seem any worse ... just lying there, sort of snoring loudly. I put a pillow under his head and left him. But if Mrs Bennett saw the girl ... Suddenly, this idea came to me. I got dressed and carried the girl down to the cellar. I chucked the stuff out of the freezer into the bin. I put the girl in it instead. It's a big freezer and she was so tiny she fitted in easily. I knew that your dad had forbidden Mrs B to go into the cellar. He didn't trust her with all his wine. Then I put the girl's clothes in the laundry basket. Next, I went down to the little room, wiped the scene with the girl from the camera and made my way out of the house by the back door. I crossed the lawn and went out through the garden gate into the lane. No one saw me on the way home. Mum was used to me being out all night and she's always slept late so she didn't hear me come in.'

No one spoke for a while. Pete could see each of them staring at him. He knew that their opinion of him had sunk to its lowest. But it was going to get worse. He had to go on.

'For a while I just went on as usual from day to day. I hated myself but I had no one to turn to. Not even Mum. I discovered from gossip in the pub that Mr Downes was in hospital, but there'd been no improvement.'

'No,' said Jane, 'he just lay there for days. I came up to be with him, but he didn't even know I was there.'

'Then I saw the announcement of your dad's funeral in the local paper and I knew that I had to get rid of the body before people started coming to the house. It was while I was helping Angus dig the grave that I had my most stupid idea.'

Tony saw Pete's face turn crimson with shame and guessed what he was about to tell them.

'I didn't have a driving licence but I guessed that if I waited till it was dark I could use Mr Downes's car to carry the body to the churchyard without being seen. I went down to the cellar, wrapped the girl's naked body in a blanket and carried it out to the car. Her slim body was no weight at all for me to carry. She was stiff after being frozen for a few days so I laid her on the back seat and drove up to the church.'

Tony was about to interrupt but Pete knew what he was going to say.

'I hadn't sat my test, but I knew how to drive.'

Tony nodded and Pete went on.

'I parked in the little car park behind the church, made sure no one was about, then carried her to the grave we'd dug earlier that evening. Her body was beginning to thaw out and give off this sweetish smell. I just about managed not to be sick. Then I removed the tarpaulin and pushed the girl's body into the grave. I was shaking with horror at what I was doing. She'd been a beautiful young girl and we'd been as intimate as any man and woman can be. I had absolutely no idea how she had died. I thought to myself she deserved much better than this, much better. And if I could ever find a way of getting revenge for her I would do so. But now I had no choice but to go on with my plan. I suppose, even then I could have called the police and given myself up, but I hadn't actually killed her and I didn't want to spend years of my life in jail.'

Tony burst out angrily, 'That's exactly what you should have done.'

Jane shook her head. 'I'm not so sure, Tony. After all, it was my dad who ordered that girl on the internet. And it might have been him who caused her death. He was just as much to blame as Pete but he couldn't be held to account. And the real culprits are the ones who delivered that girl to him in the first place.'

Tony turned back to Pete. 'So, what happened next?'

'I picked up the blanket and went back to the car for the spade. I covered the girl's body with a thin layer of soil from the heap at the side of the grave. The girl was small and slim and I thought no one would notice that the grave wasn't quite as deep as it should be. Once your dad's coffin was put on top the body would never be discovered and she would have had a sort of burial service as well.'

Tears welled again in Pete's eyes. He could not look at Jane or Tony. He was so ashamed at what he had done.

Tony frowned. 'So, how come the body was still visible next day?'

Jane broke in, 'I know the answer to that. You see, there was this heavy shower just as we got to the grave and most of the soil got washed away.'

'Yeah, I'd only managed a few spadefuls when I heard this man's voice up near the church, so I put the tarpaulin back over the grave, and scuttled away, taking the spade with me. As I crouched there I suddenly felt something beside me and wanted to scream, but then I realised it was a dog, panting and nuzzling my hand with its wet nose. I patted the dog's head in the hope that it wouldn't bark and when the man called again the dog went away. Then I heard him whistling as he came down the path towards the grave so I picked up the spade and ran like hell.

'And this guy never saw you?'

'Apparently, not. I got in the car and drove back to the Old Vicarage. I put the car in the garage and was just about to close the door when I heard Jane – well I didn't know it was you at the time – come down the drive in her car and ... well, you know the rest ...'

TWENTY EIGHT

Winter had definitely arrived and Peggy Dickson's body, and that of her dog, lay undiscovered under a light covering of snow, for a whole day, but one of the villagers walking past her house next morning had heard the other dogs howling inside and nervously knocked on the door. There was no answer, so she tried the handle and found the door unlocked. Inside was chaos. The dogs had scratched at the door, messed on the carpets and begun to tear at the furniture in their frustration. Once the door was open the dogs rushed out and ran up the hill followed, much more slowly, by the worried villager. When she finally caught up with them they had licked the snow from their owner's face.

When Wentworth was informed of the murder he shouted, 'Dundee! Eccles! Here now!' Then he remembered.

'What the fucking hell is going on? This is supposed to be a low crime area. How am I supposed to deal with another murder when I'm two detectives down?'

He stormed into Page's office and demanded to have his detectives reinstated at once. At first Page told him that as the murder was obviously connected with the case his unit was already dealing with, they'd better take on this murder as well, but when he looked at his own stretched personnel he changed his mind.

'Sit down, Graham. You'll have a bloody heart attack.'

Indeed, Wentworth was red in the face and breathing heavily as if he might succumb at any moment. He sat and mopped his brow with his sleeve, already stained from previous moppings.

'Can't you appoint someone from uniform as a temporary DC?'

'Come on, Sir. This is a serious case. Nothing a novice could handle. A very nasty murder.'

'Very well. You'd better recall Dundee and Eccles. Much against my better judgement, mind you, and if they mess up this time it'll be more than a suspension.'

Relieved, Wentworth went back to his so-called office and picked up the phone. There was no reply from Jack's home number. So, he tried his mobile, but that was switched off. Next he tried Eccles's flat. Sabine answered. 'No, Dawn not here. Gone away.'

'Do you know where?'

'No. For couple of days she say.'

He tried Eccles's mobile. That was also switched off.

'That's bloody strange,' thought Wentworth. 'Both phones switched off. Sounds like ... but I thought Eccles was a dyke.'

His heart was beginning to pound again. He took one of his tablets.

Suddenly, he remembered Jack telling him that Leanne had gone back to work. He called Cheesy.

'Jack's missus ... What's the name of the salon where she works?'

'Crowning Glory. In the High Street. Mind, if you want a haircut there's Joe's near the br ...' Then he remembered that Wentworth had no hair to cut ... 'Oh, sorry, Sir.'

Wentworth was too anxious to notice the insult.

'Got the number for Crowning Glory?'

'Yes, Sir. On Jack's file. I'll get it.'

A minute later he gave Wentworth the number. The DCI wrote it down, then asked, 'By the way, who was that kid in uniform that Jack recommended as a potential for CID.'

'PC Grabowski, Sir. But she's on leave this week.'

'Shit, shit and triple shit!' thought Wentworth, while he rang the number for Crowning Glory. A woman answered and he asked to speak to Mrs Dundee. The woman sounded rather annoyed, as she called out,

'Leanne! For you ... again!'

A Perfect Alibi

When Jack's wife came to the phone Wentworth asked if she knew where Jack was.

She replied quite crossly, 'I've no idea. But surely you must know. You sent him on that course.'

Tony loved having a house full of people. He'd always been of a gregarious nature. A typical Eastender in that respect. When his young wife was with him there were house parties every other week, and as well as local bigwigs some of the guests were minor celebrities, but there was always a good mix of ordinary local people as well. He could easily afford the necessary staff for such a lifestyle, but they were not here now, so he had to ask his guests to muck in. Jane became the cook with plenty of help from Pete. She hadn't done much cooking when she was with Patrick as he had a sophisticated palate and always wanted to eat out, but she knew the basics from her mother. She had cooked for herself when she lived alone, and Mrs Taylor had left the larder well stocked. Jane was in the kitchen preparing breakfast when Dundee and Eccles came down.

Last night, when Jack and Dawn had arrived, Jane had brought them up to speed and Pete had continued his story. They had agreed that the detectives could make notes but they were not allowed to interrupt. Pete had gone on to tell them all about the gang, his time in Spain, the girls and then, with some pride, how he and Felicia had escaped from the villa and finally how he had made his way back to England.

As Pete described everything Dundee and Eccles were astonished at the careful planning and resources behind the criminal operation.

'This really is big time stuff,' said Dundee. 'There's someone very clever and powerful behind all this.'

Tony spoke, through a mouthful of English breakfast.

'So, how can we hope to trace them? I mean I'm not saying you're not good detectives, but there're only two of you and we're not exactly a strong supporting team.'

As the enormity of their task sank in they all ate in silence for a while.

Pete felt relieved to get everything off his chest. He had expected to be arrested but the detectives said that they would sleep on it and decide what to do in the morning. Pete did not sleep well. He kept wondering whether he should disappear again, but he had come to like and respect Tony and Jane and felt that he would be letting them down if he bolted. Retelling the horrible events of the last few weeks had made him even more angry with the criminals behind this dirty business. Perhaps if he could assist the police in bringing the ringleaders to justice he would not have to spend so much time in prison and could soon be reunited with Felicia.

As they all sat around the breakfast table Pete asked, 'So, do I get turned over to the police?'

Eccles laughed. 'We are the police, Pete.'

They were such sympathetic listeners and so relaxed in their casual clothes that Pete had almost forgotten.

There was a pause then Dundee spoke. 'It seems to me that our priority is to find out where these bastards are based and stop the trafficking at source. We need your help to do that, Pete. You are the only one who knows how to contact the organisation.'

Eccles took up the lead.

'If we hand you over to the Serious Crime Unit they'll believe you were in some way responsible for the girl's death and simply stick you in jail, so the opportunity for you to help us catch those bastards will be lost.'

'But even with Pete's help what are we going to do?' asked Tony.

'I'm beginning to get an idea,' said Dundee, but it needs thinking through. Is it safe to walk in the garden, Tony? I mean will anyone see me?'

'Not if you stay around the back.'

'Right. When you've finished your coffee, Dawn, I want to talk it through with you.'

When she put the phone down Leanne was puzzled and angry. What was going on? Surely if Jack was on some training course Wentworth would know where he was? And it was very unusual for inspectors and sergeants to be sent on the same course. She went over to Stella.

'That was the school. It's Sean. They want me to take him home. Sounds like the flu.'

Stella did not look pleased.

'That's going to leave me very short-handed. But I suppose ...'

'Thanks Stell. It won't happen again. I promise I'll make other arrangements from now on.'

Stella watched her friend put on her coat and leave. She too was puzzled. She had heard Leanne complaining about the lack of male teachers at the twin's school and that had definitely been a man's voice on the phone.

When Leanne got home she made a cup of tea and sat at the kitchen table trying to work things out. Perhaps this is something that horrible man Page had arranged over Wentworth's head. Jack had told her what a nasty piece of work he was and that he and Wentworth didn't get on. Yes, that must be it, she decided. That was why Wentworth sounded so cheesed off.

She took her tea into the lounge and turned on the TV to distract herself for a while. There was a newsflash on the local channel about a memorial service for Peggy Dickson. Apparently, the police weren't prepared to release the body yet, as the investigation into her murder was ongoing. Leanne remembered Jack telling her what a brave and sensible person Peggy was and she was horrified to think that murders were happening in this quiet part of the world. She wondered for a moment whether Jack's sudden disappearance had anything to do with it.

She had a sudden thought that cheered her up. While Jack was away she would invite Agnieska round for a meal. She would be good company and the twins would love her. It would be a way of saying thanks for the way she had straightened things out between her and Jack.

She didn't have Grabowski's phone number, but she could probably be reached at the Police Station. When she phoned, however, she was told that PC Grabowski was on leave that week. Immediately, Leanne thought the worst. Tears sprang to her eyes as she assumed that Jack had arranged some time off and gone away somewhere with that young woman. But why had Eccles disappeared as well?

TWENTY NINE

Agnieska took a taxi from the station to her parents' home among the narrow terraced streets just to the north of Northampton town centre. She was using part of her week's leave to see them for the first time since she'd moved to Shropshire. There had been a Polish community here since the Second World War. There was even a Polish church. The community had begun to dwindle away during the eighties and nineties but had been bolstered by a new influx since Poland joined the European Union in 2004.

Her father had become a real Englishman but Agnieska's mother kept the Polish culture alive and spoke Polish most of the time, so Agnieska became bilingual. Her parents were very proud of their beautiful daughter but she was never spoiled, and because she loved them so much she never tried to hurt them. She did very well at school and even her teenage rebellion was mild. In her late teens her beauty became a problem. Boys hovered around like bees around a blossom, but mostly she kept them at bay.

Of course, Agnieska was not entirely the angel that her parents imagined. She had tried marijuana at a party but wondered what all the fuss was about, and she was not a virgin. At another party with school friends she had slept with a boy she quite liked. She found it painful and unsatisfying, but when she was at university she had had a brief affair with one of her tutors and found that she enjoyed sex with this more experienced man. When she discovered that he was married, with children as old as herself, she broke off the affair.

Mr and Mrs Grabowski were even more proud of their daughter when she earned her degree, but they were shocked and upset when she informed them that she wanted to join the Police. They hated the idea and saw it as a waste of her brains and her looks. Her father tried very hard to change her mind, quoting examples of policewomen who had been injured or even killed on the beat. Agnieska countered this by saying that as soon as possible she would move on to CID.

Her parents hoped that at least she would join the local force, dreading that she might instead choose the Metropolitan Police, which they considered the most dangerous in the country and were relieved when she joined the force in Shropshire, where serious crime was rare, and where Agnieska reckoned there would be less competition for CID.

At first she loved being home again. Her dad had retired but he remained fit and active, with work on an allotment and frequent long walks. Agnieska was proud to walk with him through the town parks and beside the canals. He was very knowledgeable about the waterways and she fondly remembered their holidays cruising around the local network in a hired narrow boat.

Something about her mother worried Agnieska. She seemed to have lost her spark. Agnieska tried to talk to her but got nowhere. Her mother was very pale and rather stooped for someone of her age. She asked her father whether he'd noticed a change in his wife. He said that he'd tried to find out what was wrong but she always shrugged it off.

'I'm going to take your mum on a Caribbean cruise. I'm sure that will give her a new lease of life.'

Agnieska was not so sure.

She spent an evening with some old school friends, but didn't really enjoy it. They seemed wary of her and she found them very shallow. One of them was a wife and mother, but she seemed already to be eyeing up other men. They all seemed to be more interested in so-called celebrities than in real life and one of them never stopped playing with his phone.

After a couple of days she became bored and restless. She missed the activity of her police work and her colleagues at the station. She became irritated by her mother's taciturn manner.

A Perfect Alibi

She couldn't see that much of her father, unless she was prepared to join him on the allotment and that was taking parental affection too far even for her. She had come home with the intention of staying for at least four days but was delighted when her phone rang, and she set off for Kent on the next train.

The phone call to Grabowski had been the end result of Dundee's long discussion with Eccles. Jane had watched them from the sitting room, noticing that Eccles often shook her head as Dundee talked, but at last she nodded, as they set off around the garden once more.

Jane had been thinking about her father. If, as a young man, he had killed that Victoria in a jealous rage then he was a fiend, no doubt about that. But if he had merely lusted after young girls who reminded him of his first unrequited love, then was he so different to Patrick with his girl from the office or even Tony with his trophy wife? At least with Pete it had been just youthful testosterone and a lovely girl, although her death remained a mystery.

At last, the two detectives came back into the house and asked for everyone to join them in the sitting room so that they could outline their plan. Jack stood with his back to the fireplace, reminding Jane of Hercule Poirot about to sum up his investigations, which would lead to a confession by the guilty person or a mad rush by that person to escape.

'I've had an idea about how we can find the traffickers, but we need Pete's help to contact them, and Tony's permission to make use of his home.'

Eccles interrupted, 'Will that be OK? Pete? Tony?'

'Fine by me,' said Pete enthusiastically.

'I'd want to know more before I agree,' said Tony.

'Right.' said Jack. 'With Pete's help we make contact with this organisation and you, Tony, choose a girl from their website, but she must be Polish.'

'Christ.' muttered Tony.

'When she is delivered you must show these guys a suitable room where you intend to keep her. We make ourselves scarce until they've gone. Then we tell the girl our plan.'

'And if she doesn't understand English?' asked Tony. 'After all, none of us can speak Polish.'

'Ah, but we have a colleague who can and she's on leave this week.'

'OK. If this girl can be made to understand. And if she's not scared out of her mind. What do we do next?'

Eccles continued.

'Tony contacts the organisation and says that the girl is not suitable and he wants to return her. Then we fit her up with a tracking device ...'

'What sort of tracking device?' asked Jane.

'We haven't thought that through yet. Any ideas?'

They all shook their heads, except Jane.

'I don't have any ideas, but I know a man who does.'

Jack and Pete followed Tony to the office where he kept his computer. Dawn went to find her diary where she had written Grabowski's number, and Jane picked up the phone to make a very reluctant, but necessary, call of her own.

THIRTY

For someone who had lived almost as a recluse for so many years the turnout at Miss Dickson's memorial service was remarkable. Of course, the way she had died had brought out inquisitive voyeurs and there was a posse of reporters, but most of those filling the little church were people who had known Peggy and her family as friends and neighbours for many years. These villagers had been shocked by the manner of her death and some would no longer even walk on the hill where her body had been found.

The SOCOs had discovered several clues near Peggy's body. The gorse bush was not only spattered with her blood but was also drenched in urine. As the urine was relatively fresh it was possible to extract some DNA but as no match could be found that was no help at all. There were also several boot prints, large and probably male close to the bush, but none of this evidence tied up with anything on police records. It was as if an alien had descended from another planet, murdered poor Peggy and returned from whence it came.

The post-mortem raised more questions than answers. Peggy had been shot at close range, as was her dog, by a pistol of unknown make. The bullets removed from her chest, and from the dog's skull, were unidentifiable and the spent shells had been picked up and taken away. A professional killing seemed the most likely, but why the hell should an elderly woman and her dog be executed in this callous way. The murder smelt of organised crime but what possible connection could Peggy Dickson have with that world. Of course, it was Peggy who had found the car dumped in the pool and when her statements were checked they discovered that she had told DI Dundee about another vehicle which had passed her cottage in the early hours of the same day.

It was really important to speak to Dundee, but he could not be traced. Page blamed Wentworth for this and Wentworth blamed Page. The tension in the CID room was almost tangible. It was while Wentworth and Page stood in his office trading sarcasm like a couple of cowboys toting guns in the saloon that they were interrupted by a junior member of the serious crime unit. The young man was black, handsome and spoke with an Oxbridge accent.

'Sorry to interrupt, Sir, but we've had a report of a possible sighting.'

Page was about to explode at the interruption but asked instead, 'Sighting?'

'Yes, Sir. Peter Staines.'

Page held out his hand and the young man gave him the report.

'Thank you, Parker. You may go.'

When the young man had left the room Page told Wentworth, 'One of our graduates. Fast tracked. Destined for higher things.'

Wentworth thought bitterly, 'Sign of the times. Black. Good looking. Probably a first class degree.' Three credentials he would never have. He knew he ought to leave Page's office but his curiosity was too strong and he hovered while Page read the report.

'Now, we're getting somewhere. A possible sighting at a service station on the M42. If it was Staines he was with a woman; about 40, short dark hair, smartly dressed. They drove off in her car heading south.'

Wentworth smiled.

'Downes!'

'Who?'

'Jane Downes. I've had my eyes on her all along. Dundee and Eccles didn't rate her as a suspect. She obviously pulled the wool.'

'But how does this help?'

'Because we know her car. If we find it, we've got her. And probably him as well.'

Page lifted his phone.

'Parker. Look through the reports. We want the number of a car belonging to Ms Jane Downes. Then put out an APB.'

Jane was amazed at, and rather worried by, the alacrity with which Patrick answered her request. She had used Tony's mobile, having read enough crime fiction to know how easily you could be traced using your own phone. Patrick had agreed to come to Brook House immediately; bringing some equipment that might be suitable for what Jack had in mind.

When Jane had first met Patrick he had been one of the techies in an electronics workshop and now, even though he owned the business, he still liked to play around with the latest gadgets. He agreed to pick up Grabowski from Ashford station where she was due in mid-afternoon. Jane wondered where they could hide his car, but Tony explained that they could use the coach house. They would just have to move a few things and even Patrick's Porsche would fit in. Jack and Peter cleared the space while Dawn phoned Agnieska and explained that someone would be picking her up at Ashford station. She sounded really excited at being involved with something the detectives were investigating. Dawn didn't tell her that the investigation was not official.

With Pete's help Tony had chosen a girl from the website. She was due to be delivered that night. So, now a room had to be chosen for her to be kept in, like a prisoner, so far as the bastards who delivered her were concerned. Tony thought hard about this and suddenly remembered the servants' quarters at the top of the house. When Dundee returned from the coach house Tony explained about the room in the attic and Dundee, Eccles and Jane went to have a look. They were horrified by the state of the room and got to work on cleaning it up, then they moved a single bed, a small wardrobe and chest of drawers from an unused bedroom on the floor below. They also found a commode in what had been the nursery many years ago. They tried to see the room as the traffickers would see it. The single window was small and high in the roof; you'd have to be mad to try to escape that way, and the room had a lock on the outside with a key in it.

When Patrick arrived, mid-afternoon, he was not at all keen to put his gleaming car in the coach house with its crumbling plaster ceiling and cobwebs everywhere, but Grabowski gave him a look that immediately persuaded him how important it was to keep the car out of sight. Jane's feeling about men was not improved when she saw how none of them could keep their eyes off this pretty girl.

Jane took Patrick for a walk around the garden to explain the situation and what they needed from him. There was an awkward silence for a while, but at last Jane spoke.

'How's ...?'

'Gone!'

'Gone?'

'Yes. I came back from the office early one day. Tracey hadn't gone into work, not feeling well, she said. I found her with Gary, from the workshop. Chucked her out, of course. Women!'

'I could say the same about men,' Jane snapped, with colour coming to her cheeks. Patrick looked away.

'I saw the way all you men looked at Agnieska.'

'Well, you must admit ... But the truth is Jane, I've really missed you.'

Jane stopped and faced him. He wasn't going to wheedle his way back into her affections that easily.

'Well, I haven't missed you. I've been too busy.'

'I behaved like a prick. I know that. I can quite understand how you feel.'

Jane did not reply. They walked on in silence for a while.

'Can you help us?' she asked.

'Well, you must tell me what it's all about, first.'

'OK, but you must listen all the way through, without interruption, and without any of your upper class, right wing, judgmental attitude.'

Patrick looked shocked. Jane had never spoken to him like that before. She told him about the dead girl in her father's grave and how the girl came to be in his house.

Patrick longed to point out that he had never liked her father, but he managed to restrain himself. Jane went on to describe Pete's involvement with the gang and how, with Tony's help, they hoped to discover where the gang was based and to catch the ringleaders.

As Jane told him the story his eyes widened and his mouth stayed open. When she had finished, he said nothing for a while and his features gradually resumed their normal appearance. At last he spoke.

'So, this girl who's coming here tonight will be sent back with some kind of tracking device on her person. Then ...'

'Dundee and Eccles are planning that now. Come on. I'll introduce you to everybody.'

'Just one thing, Jane. When this is all over, can we at least talk?'

'We'll see.'

There were so many people in the house Jane was beginning to struggle with ingredients for the evening meal. Eventually she made a sort of kedgeree with fish from the freezer, loads of rice and plenty of curry powder which everyone seemed to enjoy. While she and Pete sweated over a hot stove she asked him what he thought of Grabowski, thinking he would be as enamoured as the other men.

'Not my type,' he said. 'I prefer the Latin look.' Jane thought his eyes glazed over for an instant, as he stirred the rice, and realised he was thinking about Felicia.

Patrick had brought a couple of bottles of rather good wine with him, which he fetched from the boot of his car.

The others were wary of Patrick at first, with his public school snort and his Saville Row suit, but his wit and bonhomie soon won them over. Jane began to realise how much she had missed him, but was determined not to let it show. In her bitterness about his infidelity she had forgotten what an attractive man he was; slightly older than herself; tall and slim with wavy brown hair, expertly cut. She reminded herself that he was here for a reason, and that afterwards he would go back to London and she would have to manage without him. Anyway, there were more important things on her mind.

Dundee and Eccles had brought Grabowski up to speed and explained that she was to be an interpreter.

'What time is the delivery due?' she asked.

'Soon after midnight. Jack's going to play the part of Tony, because of the stairs. They don't know anything about Tony, except that he's loaded and lives alone in a large house. The traffickers will not even have heard his voice. Everyone except Jack will have to make themselves scarce from 11pm on. And there must be no tell-tale signs of other inhabitants. I'd like you to check that.'

Grabowski smiled with pleasure at being involved.

Sleeping arrangements had already been organised. Tony was to stay in his own bedroom, on the ground floor, which had been adapted for his disability. Jane and Dawn were to share one of the larger bedrooms, Jack and Pete another. Pete wondered briefly whether perhaps he was not really trusted yet and Dundee was there to keep an eye on him. Patrick and Agnieska each had small bedrooms to themselves.

Tony and Jack were about the same height and build, so Jack borrowed some of Tony's best casual wear to look the part of the local squire.

There was a nervous tension in the house. Tony was the first to go to his room, where he sat in a comfortable chair, so that he would not fall asleep. Gradually, the others slipped away, leaving Grabowski to check for any signs of other inhabitants. Jack sat in the sitting room, slowly sipping an extremely expensive malt whisky and trying not to keep glancing at the clock.

Just after midnight he heard a car approaching on the gravel drive and a few moments later the doorbell rang. He tried to compose himself as he moved into the hall and switched on the light. When he opened the door two huge men entered, dragging a drugged girl between them. Dundee noticed the bulge of a gun in one man's jacket pocket. They dumped the blindfolded girl on one of the hall chairs.

Handing Jack a small suitcase one of the men said, 'OK. You show us room.'

Dundee nodded, took the suitcase and led them up the stairs. They carried the girl like a sack of potatoes up to the attic. She moaned a couple of times but showed no other signs of life. One man supported the girl while the other checked the room.

He grunted again, 'Good.' Then they took the girl into the room and dumped her on the bed.

'OK. We go now.' He held out his hand as if to shake Jack's but Dundee turned away. He would have liked to thump the man on his bulbous nose, but looking again at the man he thought that might be like punching a brick wall. Anyway, there were two of them, and one of them had a gun. The man shrugged, grunted again and they went back downstairs. Jack heard the door close and the car drive away.

He stood for a while watching the girl slumped on the bed. He slipped off her shoes and covered her with a blanket. When he untied the blindfold and removed it, he gasped. The girl was so like Grabowski they could be twins.

A Perfect Alibi

THIRTY ONE

Next morning, Dawn and Agnieska looked in on the girl in the attic room. Dundee had locked her in last night because he didn't want her rushing off terrified into the Kent countryside. The effects of the drug had almost worn off and the girl was very frightened. She was huddled on the bed in a corner of the room with a blanket wrapped around her, but was still visibly trembling. As Agnieska approached, the girl tensed up and closed her eyes as if she was expecting to be hit, but when the young policewoman spoke to her in Polish the girl embraced her like a child holding on to her mother.

Dawn heard the torrent of Polish like background music while she stared unbelieving at the two girls who were so alike. Jack had warned her of this but it was still a shock. Perhaps the girl was slightly thinner than Agnieska, who glowed with health, and she was certainly paler.

The girl was still clinging to Agnieska as she spoke.

'What is she saying?' asked Dawn.

'She is asking where she is and if she is safe. Have the men gone? Will they come back? She is very frightened.'

The girl looked confused as Agnieska spoke in English to Dawn, and she began to cry again.

'I'm not surprised from the way Jack described them. They even put the wind up him. Tell her they've gone and that she is perfectly safe now.'

Agnieska told her this and the girl became slightly calmer. Then she spoke again in Polish.

'She wants to know who we are?'

'Tell her, just friends, who are trying to catch the men who brought her here. But we need her help.'

Agnieska told her. The girl threw herself back into the corner and spoke English for the first time, 'No! No!'

At last they calmed her down again and asked if she was hungry. She nodded, but shook her head when they suggested she come downstairs. She spoke to Agnieska, who interpreted.

'She is hungry. But she wants to stay here, with me.'

Dawn shrugged and went downstairs. The others were all gathered in the kitchen. She closed the door and put her fingers to her lips, before whispering,

'We have a problem. I don't think she will be able to help us. She is absolutely terrified. She's accepted that Agnieska is a friend, but she is nervous even of me. She's hungry, but she won't leave the room. I'll take up some toast and fruit. It's going to be a slow job gaining her confidence.'

When Eccles entered the room with the food the girl smiled. Well, that's a good start, she thought.

The girl had been talking to Agnieska about the village in Poland where she had lived with her parents and two brothers.

'It's the usual story,' explained Agnieska. 'Her brothers worked the farm, but it was too small to give them much of an income. Her father had died in his fifties and her mother was suffering from some debilitating illness, possibly caused by a chemical they had used on the farm. The girl needed work, so she answered an advert for a job in the nearest city for hotel work, but when she turned up for the interview she was given some sort of drug in her coffee. Later that night she, and some other girls, were taken by car to somewhere in the countryside. She was blindfolded, but as a country girl she recognised the sounds of the countryside at night. They forced her on to a plane with the other girls and after a long flight they landed in a warmer country. It was still dark when they landed. They were taken in a car to a place on a mountainside and locked in a cellar for the day. When it was dark they were taken back to the plane and when they landed again it was much colder. After another drive, they arrived at a big house where they were locked in rooms. They were given food and a change of clothes, and were

A Perfect Alibi

allowed to use the bathroom, but they were watched all the time by cameras in the rooms and corridors. After a day or two they were examined by a doctor, then men began coming to their rooms.'

Agnieska paused, before continuing, 'I tried to get more details but she broke down again. She is very frightened.'

'Well, if she's going to help us we're going to have to gain her confidence somehow, and she's going to have to trust one of the men.'

'Who would you suggest?'

'Tony. He's got such a friendly face. And in a wheelchair he won't seem a threat.'

'Yes, I suppose. But how the hell do we get him up here?'

'True. So, who else?'

'Pete. You could pretend he was your younger brother.'

'Right, let's try it.'

Dawn fetched Pete while Agnieska explained about her brother who was staying in the house. But as soon as Pete walked into the room the girl screamed, 'No men! No men!' rushed across to Agnieska and hugged her tight. The young policewoman shook her head and Dawn told Pete to go downstairs again.

Now, Dawn shook her head, saying to Agnieska,

'It's not going to happen is it? I'd better go down and explain.'

Dawn left the room. Eventually Agnieska managed to calm the girl down and get her back on to the bed. The girl rubbed her eyes and lay down with her head on the pillow. Soon, her eyes closed and she slept like a child being comforted by her mother after a terrible nightmare; a deep, calm sleep.

At last Agnieska was able to leave her and join the others. Jane offered her a cup of coffee and they all sat around the large kitchen table. At last Dawn said, 'Well, that's it then. There's no way that girl would have the courage to go back where she came from, whether she's tracked or not. So, what are we going to do with her? She has no papers. We can't just hand her over to the police.'

There was another silence until Tony spoke up.

'Tell you what. Mrs Taylor might help. She's the kindest woman I've ever known, always on the side of the underdog. If I introduce the girl as a helper for her, after all it's a big house and Mrs T has her work cut out to cope, the girl could stay, as another domestic so far as anyone else is concerned. What d'you think?'

'I think it's a brilliant idea, Tony,' said Jane. 'I've met Mrs Taylor and she's exactly as he says. And I reckon there are plenty of young foreign girls employed like that.'

'So, when we've sorted out this other business, I'll see to it. OK?'

'But,' said Jack, 'it doesn't solve our other problem. It looks like we'll have to abandon our plans to find out where the traffickers are based. OK, we've saved one girl from that dreadful life, but ...'

'Damn,' said Patrick. 'I was really looking forward to trying out that new tracking device.'

'I suppose it would have been better if I'd never come up with the idea,' said Dundee.

'Perhaps,' said Pete, 'but we all thought it was a good idea. We want to stop that lot, don't we? And if I'd been part of that it might have helped ...'

He didn't finish his speech, but they all knew what he meant.

It was Agnieska who spoke next.

'Look. It's a good plan. And I reckon we can still make it work.'

'How? The girl's scared stiff.'

'Look at me. You've all said we could be twins. I'm roughly the same age, and very similar in looks. When the traffickers come to collect the girl they'll just think I'm her. I'll wear some of her clothes, fit Patrick's tracker and go in her place. I'm a trained copper, a judo black belt. I can look after myself.'

DSI Page was really pissed off. He strode about the incident room as if he was still in the army, wishing he could tell his men to get a haircut and the women to go home and make the beds. This was the Serious Crime Unit; an elite unit, but what had they achieved? Sod all.

The possible sighting of Peter Staines had led nowhere. If it was Staines he had left the service station with a woman, but not in Jane Downes's car which was still sitting outside her cottage on Julian's Hill. They had checked all the car hire firms in the district but none of them had issued a car to a Ms Downes; no one even recognised her photograph. Dundee and Eccles had disappeared. And who had killed that old biddy on the Brown Hill? The only consolation was that waddling Wentworth, as he called him, had made even less progress.

The incident board was covered with reports and photos with arrows connecting them like a page from a children's puzzle book. In the centre was a blown-up photograph of the young girl on the mortuary slab. What had happened to her? Why did she die? And why was she found in someone else's grave? She was only a few years younger than his own daughter, who had emigrated to Australia to 'get away from her bloody father' her mother had told him. Now, there was a grandchild over there, and when he retired ... Christ, that couldn't come soon enough.

He had interviewed the Bennett woman personally and was coming to the same view as the missing detectives; that she was a vindictive, old busybody. She had no real evidence that Downes had had any contact with the girl found in his grave. The only possible evidence of any 'funny business' had been finding Peter Staines in the writer's house one evening. Her opinion that her employer was 'a dirty old man' was not evidence.

Suddenly, he saw Wentworth crossing the room towards him, with a smug smile on his face. Page picked up a piece of paper from a nearby desk and scuttled back to his office, but it was too late.

'We've got the bastards, Sir.'

'Oh no,' thought Page, 'not while we're still muddling along.'

'Which bastards, Inspector?'

'Those bloody burglars.'

Page sighed with relief, 'Oh, right. Good.'

'Yeah, it all went just as Dundee and Eccles had planned. Not that same evening, but the next. We were waiting for them. I leaned on them hard and one of them coughed up, told us where all the stuff was stored. Bloody great barn full of loot. Ready for eBay, most likely. Result!'

'Congratulations,' whispered Page without enthusiasm.

'And how's your case progressing?' asked Wentworth, smugly.

'Talk to you later,' said Page, holding up the piece of paper still in his hand. 'Something's come up. Got to make some urgent calls.'

'I bet you have,' said Wentworth to himself.

'Where's Daddy?' asked Karen.

'At work,' answered Leanne, brusquely. 'And don't talk with your mouth full.'

The twins sat at the kitchen table eating pieces of cake. Leanne knew that she shouldn't have bought the cake and should not have cut them both such large pieces, but she had a splitting headache and didn't want to answer a load of questions.

'What does Daddy do at work?' asked Karen.

Leanne had just crammed an even larger piece of cake into her own mouth. She almost choked, so took a gulp of tea before answering.

'He catches bad people.'

'But,' she thought, 'what is he doing at this moment with that Polish girl, with her pretty face and perfect figure?'

Then she remembered her own determination to lose some weight. She threw the rest of the cake into the bin and poured away the remains of the sweet tea. Instead, she poured a glass of water and took two paracetamol capsules.

Sean continued the questioning.

'What do the bad people do?'

'Oh, steal things, hurt other people, stuff like that.'

Karen thought this over then asked, 'What does Daddy do with the bad people?'

'Takes them to prison and locks them up.'

If only it was that simple, Leanne thought.

She noticed that they had both finished their cake and saw her chance.

'Right, go and wash your hands, then you can watch television.'

When they had gone, Leanne sat down at the table and lowered her head on to her arms. The pills would take a while to work. Meanwhile, her head was throbbing.

Soon, she heard the twins chuckling in the lounge. She went in briefly to check that they were watching something suitable before returning to the kitchen, taking a half empty bottle of wine from the fridge and swigging some straight from it. Then she sat at the table again and the tears came.

Just when things were getting better it had all gone wrong again. She loved her work and liked being back among friends. The kids had really settled at school and her days were no longer entirely devoted to them. She had money in her pocket, not much but it would soon add up. Jack had been so loving and attentive since she came home. Now, this!

Leanne heard another chuckle from the next room. Her headache was fading. Suddenly, she got up and began to start cleaning manically. She put the dirty plates into the dishwasher and wiped all the kitchen surfaces. After that, she got the vacuum cleaner from under the stairs and set about the hall carpet. When she'd put away the cleaner, she returned to the kitchen and began to prepare a proper meal for the twins and herself. While she was busy she didn't have time to think, and she didn't want to think.

When she called the twins in for their meal it was obvious that the cake had taken away their appetite. She forced some of her food down as an example and they pushed theirs around on their plates. At last, it was bedtime, so she gave them an extra long bath and read stories to them until they settled to sleep.

Back in the kitchen she dumped the leftovers into the bin, before moving into the lounge and slumping into a chair in front of the television with the wine bottle in her hand. She had turned the sound right down and was gawping mindlessly at the screen. Suddenly, she recognised part of the local landscape – Brown Hill – before the camera focused on the village church, filled to capacity for the memorial service for Peggy Dickson. Leanne turned up the sound slightly and concentrated on the news item. The newsreader reminded the viewers what had happened to Peggy and explained that the police were working on several lines of enquiry.

Leanne remembered Jack telling her about Peggy hearing those vehicles. It didn't sound much like an ordinary murder. She began to wonder whether he and Eccles were involved in some secret investigation. Perhaps Grabowski's absence had no connection with Jack's.

It had been a long, confusing, tiring day and Leanne decided to go to bed early, but before she undressed she stood at the window and looked out over the water meadows. The moon was bright and the river, still high but no longer in flood, shone like a silver ribbon in the moonlight.

She thought back to their lovemaking the night before last. Jack had been so tender and caring. His body was still as lean and strong as it had been when they first married. For a while she caressed her own body as if he was with her.

Suddenly, all her doubts disappeared. She knew that Jack was doing something secret and possibly dangerous but he was not with another woman, except Eccles and she was his support in a crime investigation, not his mistress. Leanne had tried Jack's phone several times that evening but it was switched off. She got into bed and put her own phone under her pillow. If he was trying to catch Peggy Dickson's killer she must be patient and let him do what he had to do. She closed her eyes and said a short prayer. Please God let him be safe!

THIRTY TWO

The girl was much calmer now. She seemed to have realised that no one in this house was going to harm her. Grabowski learned that her name was Milena and that she was just 19 years old. The men kept away from her room. She had stayed up there but had eaten all of the food Eccles had taken to her. Eventually, Mrs Taylor had come back to the house and Tony had told her that the girl was an illegal immigrant, who had run away from a nearby detention centre, and that she was going to stay in the house and assist her with the cooking and housework.

Mrs Taylor was immediately sympathetic. With the help of Grabowski she persuaded the girl to come downstairs into the kitchen. All the other occupants of the house made themselves scarce. The housekeeper explained, with Grabowski's help, what Milena's duties would be and soon discovered that the girl was very capable, having been largely responsible for running the home in Poland.

By late afternoon the two women were forming a bond. Eccles and Grabowski watched as the they walked down the drive towards Mrs Taylor's house, where the girl was to sleep that night, before taking up her duties next day.

It was very important that Milena was not in the house that night because the traffickers would be returning to collect the girl and take her back to their headquarters. Tony had emailed them to say that the girl was not suitable but that he would pay an extra fee to compensate the organisation. Of course, it would not be Milena they took blindfolded from that room but Agnieska and she would have on her the tracking device. Dundee, Eccles and Pete were to follow in Tony's van, containing the receiver which Patrick had installed. It wasn't the fastest of vehicles but it was suitably anonymous and would have no connection with any police business.

Meanwhile Jane and Patrick sat in the kitchen while she sewed the tracking device into Grabowski's bra.

'I had no idea you were such a good needlewoman, Jane.'

'There's a good deal you never bothered to find out about me, Patrick.'

Patrick coloured up and muttered, 'I suppose ...'

'And there's a good deal I'd rather not know about you. But I have to admit that this is a very clever device, so tiny but effective.'

'I hope to God it works. Agnieska is a brave girl.'

'And so attractive,' said Jane, then adding bitterly, 'I bet you'd like to help fit her bra on wouldn't you?'

Patrick winced and his face flushed even more.

'Still so angry with me, Jane?'

'Yes. It'll be a long time before I trust a man again.'

She bit off the thread and put down her sewing. 'Right. Go and find Agnieska and we'll try this on her.'

Dundee was, apparently, all alone in the house when the men arrived just after midnight. As before, they were men of few words but considerable menace. He wondered how many of these monsters there were, doing the business, carrying out their orders, in their black leather gear, like Hitler's bloody SS. Perhaps there were dozens of these mindless thugs, interchangeable and equally evil. Jack thought he recognised one of them, not by the face but by the thick gold necklace glittering between the lapels of his leather jacket. One thing was certain, whoever ran this show was making a packet.

They followed Jack up to the attic room, where Grabowski put on a performance worthy of an Oscar, with tears and trembling and loud Polish abuse. The men took no notice as they pinioned her wrists with wide sticky tape, fixed a blindfold over her eyes and jammed a piece of cloth into her mouth as a gag. The men did not seem to doubt for a moment that this was the girl they had delivered. Dundee was astonished by Grabowski's courage and was filled with guilt at having allowed her to face such danger.

As Agnieska was half carried, half dragged down the stairs Jack hoped that Pete was right when he had told them that these men were chosen for their sexual preference.

As soon as the men had driven off Dundee joined Eccles and Pete in Tony's van. The receiver was already switched on and was bleeping loudly, as they followed the car towards Ashford, then on to the M20, heading north. The clever thing about this piece of kit was that it not only gave an audible signal but it located the tracking device on a small screen using GPS.

Jane joined Tony in the kitchen and made some strong coffee for them both. She did not think that either of them would sleep that night. Tony had been upset all day at not being able to go with the others, and Jane was worried stiff on Grabowski's behalf. Patrick had not been allowed to accompany the others because the converted van had only the one wide seat at the front; the space at the back was for a wheelchair so there was no room for another passenger. They felt that Patrick had already made his contribution by supplying the tracking device and that otherwise he was not really involved in the investigation.

Dundee had told them not to expect any calls until the operation was over and, hopefully, the ringleaders were in custody, so there was no point in Tony and Jane staying up. From sheer exhaustion, they went to their rooms and tried to sleep. Jane eventually fell into a fitful sleep and when she woke again it was light and the birds were chorusing.

Her first thought when she woke was for Agnieska and although she was not particularly religious she sent up a prayer for the girl's safety. She didn't really know what Dundee planned to do once they discovered the headquarters of the organisation, but she hoped fervently that nothing went wrong, particularly for Grabowski.

She thought about her father. It was fairly certain that he had not murdered the girl, and it seemed likely that the note left on his unfinished novel referred to his impotence. There was still the mystery of the young Victoria and her disappearance though. Was he involved? And his knowledge of Polish? How the hell had he acquired that? The only identifiable crime he had committed was to become involved with the trafficking organisation.

Jane thought that she had been rather mean to Patrick and decided to call a truce. She made a cup of tea and took it to his room. She knocked on his door, in spite of the fact that they had been intimate for many years, but when he did not answer she just walked in. The room was empty and his bed had not been slept in. She felt alarmed but also slightly excited by his absence and after quickly slipping on some clothes she went out to the coach house. Patrick's Porsche had gone.

THIRTY THREE

Patrick tailed the van as it followed the large black saloon towards London, around the M25 and on to the M40. The roads were clear at this time of the night and they were making good speed. The van had to stay in range of the tracking device but stay far enough behind the other car, to remain unnoticed. There was nothing unusual about several vehicles travelling along the motorway together, but when they left the M40 it would be a different matter.

They passed High Wycombe and Oxford and continued smoothly on their way until Patrick glanced down at the dashboard and swore; his fuel was running low. He might make another 30 miles or so but after that he would definitely need a service station, and that might mean losing the other vehicles. He had plenty of power under the bonnet and it would not take long to catch them up as long as they didn't turn off the motorway.

After another 20 miles or so the needle was flickering towards the lower end of the red zone. If he didn't turn off at the next service station he would probably run out of fuel before he reached the one beyond that. A few miles further on he saw the brightly lit sign for the services and began to mutter 'fuck, fuck, fuck!' Then he was incredibly relieved to see the van indicating left and assumed that the car in front of it had done the same.

When he reached the pumps, the dark saloon was already filling up. Patrick took a good look at the man at the pump. He would remember that face. The idiot was dragging on a cigarette. Christ! How bloody dangerous!

Patrick pulled up to another pump. There was no sign of the van. They must have parked some distance away as the tracker would tell them when the trafficker's car left again.

Patrick glanced surreptitiously at the other car but could see no sign of Grabowski. She was probably lying on the back seat, out of it on some sleeping draft.

At last, the man removed the nozzle and replaced the cap. He used his card to pay at the pump, got back into the car and drove off. Patrick did not immediately follow. The other car could only go one way up the motorway, and his own car had the power to catch them up very quickly.

As he inserted his card to pay he saw the van emerge from the far side of the car park and make its way to the exit. Patrick got back in his car and followed. The fateful procession began again. Soon they turned off on to the M42. They left the motorway at Bromsgrove and headed west. A winding road took them to Kidderminster, then on towards Herefordshire. Patrick began to have a feeling about where they were headed. Soon they crossed the A49 and continued towards the Welsh border. They had travelled over 200 miles, but because the roads were quiet and the surface dry they had made good time. When Patrick checked his watch, it was 4.30am.

Suddenly, the van in front of him slowed down and pulled into a layby. Patrick guessed they did not want to be noticed following the other car on this quiet country road. The tracker would let them know where it was going, even a few miles ahead, as long as it was still working properly. He would have liked to make contact with the van and check but he had to stay just in range of the big car, in case the device *had* failed. Luckily, he knew this road really well. He dipped his headlights and watched the red glow ahead as the car wound its way down the narrow road through several little villages.

A few miles further on the Mercedes slowed again as it approached a high stone wall, and went through an enormous, elaborate, wrought iron gate, which opened as it approached and closed as soon as the car was inside. Patrick drove past the gate and followed the wall until he was out of sight, then he pulled over. The car had reached its destination, a superb Jacobean mansion, which Patrick knew intimately. This was Brampton Manor, the home of Lord Oxendale. Patrick had supervised the installation of a state of the art security system here just two years ago.

When Agnieska woke her head felt fuzzy, as if she had a very bad cold, and her limbs were too heavy to move. She knew she had been tranquilised with something last night; she had felt the needle going in. Those guys were not exactly skilled nurses. She hoped that the needle was clean, but then realised it would be. She was valuable goods, to be carefully maintained, for maximum profit.

She had no idea what time it was. Milena had not worn a watch so she could not wear one either. Her head began to clear a little. She studied the room she was in. There was no window but one solid looking door, which she guessed would be locked, and a smaller less impressive door. The room was sparsely furnished but clean and the bed she was lying on smelt freshly sheeted. It was, she thought, essentially a prison cell.

There was a camera in one corner so there was no part of the room where she could go without being watched except under the bed or possibly beyond the little side door. She got up slowly from the bed, still feeling slightly dizzy and made her way to the smaller door which led to a small en suite, containing a toilet, wash basin and shower. Whoever ran this place didn't want the girls wandering about the corridors. At least in here she could be private, she thought, but then she noticed another camera just out of her reach. 'Bastards!' she thought. 'I can't even have a piss without being watched!'

She returned to the bedroom where the small suitcase containing her belongings, actually they were mostly Milena's things, lay open on top of a chest of drawers. It was obvious that someone had searched through it but at least she would be able to shower and change clothes, except for the bra containing the tracking device, which she would have to wear until her colleagues managed to find her. 'I hope to hell it's still working,' she thought.

Agnieska sat on the bed and looked around again. There were no sharp edges to anything, no hooks to hang anything from and her manicure set with a small pair of scissors and a pointed nail file had been removed from her bag. So, even when things became desperate for the women trapped here it would have been difficult, if not impossible, to end it all. No wonder Milena had been so terrified. She had suffered unspeakable things in this room. For a moment Grabowski shuddered with the thought that dreadful things might happen to her if the others didn't get to her in time. Then she took a deep breath and said to herself, 'But they will. They will.'

There was a soft knock on the big door. Agnieska tensed. She did not speak, but got back into bed and pulled the bedclothes up to her neck, partially obscuring her face. A key turned, the door swung opened and a young girl, dressed in a pinafore with a little white cap on her head, came in and put a tray on the heavy wooden bedside table, which Agnieska had noticed was firmly fixed to the floor. The girl was short, rather plump and her face was badly scarred. It was not likely that she would have been employed here in the way that Milena had been, and Grabowski wondered whether this unappealing youngster knew the real purpose of this place. The girl stood for a moment studying Agnieska as if perhaps she wondered whether this was the same woman she was used to serving, but then Grabowski said good morning in Polish, in a voice as close to Milena's as she could manage, and the girl smiled slightly as if reassured.

Agnieska spoke a few more sentences in Polish but it was obvious that the girl did not understand, instead she pointed to the tray and left the room. Grabowski knew that she could easily have overpowered the girl and escaped from the room, but as the door opened for the girl to go out she saw a large, ugly man waiting to accompany the maid to the next room. Even if the minder had not been there Agnieska's attack would have been noticed on camera. No, escape was impossible. She must rely on her friends.

Patrick had been parked for only a few minutes when the van went by. He drew out and followed as it slowly circled around the high walls of the large estate. When the van pulled in opposite another entrance with much less impressive gates he parked behind it and turned off his lights. Soon the van lights were turned off as well. He flashed those of his own car. There was no movement from the van for a while. Obviously, his friends inside were discussing what this meant and how they should react, but at last Dundee got out of the van and approached the car. Patrick wound down his window and Dundee gasped with surprise.

'Patrick! What the hell are you doing here?'

'Sorry. I couldn't just sit at Tony's place while you were having all the fun.'

'Not much fun driving around in the early hours wondering where the hell we are.'

'Well, I know exactly where we are. And I know it's not a good idea to be parked near that gate. We need to drive on to the next village, where we won't be observed. Then I'll tell you all about it. By the way, is the tracker still working?'

'Oh yes, loud and clear, but it's not moving anymore.'

'Go on then quickly. It's only a mile or so. Park near the church. I'll join you there and fill you in.'

Dundee looked puzzled but did as he was told and not a moment too soon, as a man emerged from the gateway and began walking towards Patrick's car. He pulled away before the man had crossed the road.

Thank goodness that at this time of the year it would still be dark for at least a couple more hours. Patrick had often parked in the village during his work on the Brampton Manor security system because the village had an excellent pub with a splendid lunchtime menu. But now the village was asleep and they were in the only vehicles parked outside the church.

Patrick squeezed into the van with the others while he told them what he knew, with the tracking device bleeping away in the background.

'That place is called Brampton Manor. It's owned by Lord Oxendale. I supervised the installation of their security system two years ago. That's how I know the place. The good thing is that I know where every camera is placed and where the control room is situated. On the other hand, I know just how difficult it's going to be to get in.'

'You mean,' said Eccles in an acid tone, 'that this is the place where the girls are kept, till they're sent out to some rich pervert. And it belongs to a bloody Lord.'

'Yes, but we can't assume that he runs the show. He might not even live here. I know for a fact he has a place in Spain.'

'He certainly does,' said Pete.

'And possibly another place in Poland.'

'If that's true, then he's definitely mixed up in this business,' said Eccles.

'OK,' said Dundee with sudden urgency, 'Grabowski has done exactly what we planned. She's led us to the headquarters of the organisation. Now, we need to get her out of there, double quick, and we need help to catch as many of the bastards in there as we can.'

He picked up the phone which he had borrowed from Tony and called the number for the local police. He didn't give his name or his location, in case someone else was listening in, but knew that the police would be able to trace the call, whereas other listeners would probably not have the necessary equipment.

Dundee asked to speak to the highest ranking officer in the building. When a Deputy Chief Superintendent answered, he explained about the organisation and how it worked. The man listened patiently, but there was an air of scepticism in his voice as he asked to whom he was speaking. Jack put on the voice of a high ranking officer.

'I can't tell you that.'

There was silence at the other end and Dundee began to worry that the call had been ended. Then the Chief Super spoke again.

'Is this some kind of hoax?'

'Definitely not. All I can tell you is that we are a special team and we have been investigating this organisation for some considerable time. We have only just discovered where they're based and one of our colleagues has managed to infiltrate the organisation. If we don't get her out soon, she could be in danger.'

Jack felt someone tugging at his sleeve. It was Eccles telling him that the bleeping had stopped. The tracker had ceased to work. His voice was filled with panic as he spoke again into the phone.

'I have to go. Please get here as soon as you can. And ...'

'Yes?'

'It's likely that some of them will be armed. For God's sake get here pronto. It'll be the biggest bust of your career.'

In his panic Jack dropped the phone into the back of the van. He wasn't sure he'd switched it off. But there was no time to check. The sky was beginning to brighten. They had to get inside that place. Now!

THIRTY FOUR

As soon as she heard the click of the lock on the big door Agnieska got out of bed and began exercising. She was already pretty fit from her daily exercise routine and frequent visits to the gym but now she needed to be ready for anything. Soon, she had pushed the lethargy out of her limbs, then she showered and dressed. She knew she was being watched all the time. 'Dirty bastards!' she thought.

She was careful to make sure when she put on the bra that the tracker could not be seen. By the time she was dressed she was hungry. She ate the croissants and drank the coffee from the vacuum flask. It was good coffee and still hot. 'Like having a good breakfast before going to the scaffold,' she thought. She left some of the coffee in the flask and screwed the lid back on. The outer shell of the flask was made of plastic so would not make much of a weapon but the hot coffee inside might cause some damage if flung accurately into someone's eyes.

There was no chair to sit on, possibly because it might be thrown at an intruder, or at the camera, so she sat on the bed and wondered what the others were doing. Had the tracker brought them near? How long would it be before help came? What on earth was she going to do in the meantime? Agnieska had always been an active rather than a meditative type. That was partly why she had joined the police.

There were a few magazines on the plastic table. She picked one up and began to read but quickly realised that she should not be doing so, because it was in English and Milena could not read that language so she flicked through the magazine, looking at the pictures, then returned it to the pile.

She heard the key turn in the lock, followed by a firm knock on the door. Grabowski did not answer. The door opened and a man came in. He was tall and slim, in his late fifties she guessed, but with a full head of hair, expertly coiffured and probably dyed, making it incongruous in comparison with his face which had a healthy tan but was deeply lined. The man might have been quite handsome in his younger days but now he gave the impression of an overripe fruit, and he smelt sickly sweet like one as well. His clothes were obviously expensive, made to measure she thought, and his shoes had an incredible shine. The man smiled as he approached and Grabowski shuddered.

'Ah, Milena,' he said, in perfect Polish. 'How are you today? I like to visit all my guests at some time.'

His voice was exaggeratedly upper class. It reminded her of those audio books her father used to listen to. Stories about an upper class twit who solved all these murders. Some stupid name. Wimsey was it? Lord something or other anyway. Her father had an obsessive admiration for all things English, even the monarchy and aristocracy.

This man sat beside her on the bed and touched her hand. Grabowski's flesh crept, as they say. But she guessed that if he tried anything she could easily overcome him.

'Well, Milena, I gather things did not go well with your host. I wonder why? After all, you are pretty enough. Almost good enough to eat.'

He smiled as he said this and his teeth showed, very white, obviously false, but as threatening as a shark's.

'Perhaps, my dear, you were not in the right frame of mind. Perhaps you are too inexperienced. Perhaps we need to have a little practice first.'

That smile again. And the hand moved from her wrist to her shoulder and gently stroked it.

Grabowski tried to pull away, but the man was far stronger than she had expected. He pushed her back on to the bed and placed his hands on her upper arms. Then he got on to the bed and sat astride her, skilfully avoiding her knee jerks, something he had obviously done many times before. The soft bed underneath gave her no support from which to attack. Instead, she struck out wildly and caught him with her nails across his face. Now, he was truly incensed. He breathed deeply and spat out.

'Oh, we have a little wild cat. I love that in a woman. My greatest pleasure is in taming wild creatures.'

He pulled up her T-shirt and pulled it over her head so that she could not free her arms. Then he grabbed her bra and pulled it away. The catch at the back cut painfully into her flesh as it came away and the tracking device slipped out. He gazed at it.

'Well, well. What have we here? I don't like the look of this.'

As he held up the little electronic device to examine it Grabowski summoned up all her strength and tipped him off the bed. As he fell there was a thump, a gasp, then silence. Agnieska quickly scrambled off the bed. If he came for her again, she was ready, with her feet slightly apart and her body well balanced, as she had learned in all those judo lessons.

But he didn't come for her; he didn't get up from the floor.

Grabowski was tempted to go and look at him, but realised that would be foolish. What had happened would have been observed by whoever monitored the cameras. But the door was open and she had to get out of this room before the alarm was raised. She pulled down her T-shirt and made her escape.

The fact that the tracker had stopped working caused panic in the van. They must get Grabowski out of that place as soon as possible and that meant getting in. They all remained squashed in the vehicle, with Eccles sitting on Patrick's knee, as Dundee drove back towards the manor. They parked up next to the wall about half way between the service gate and the main gate.

'There's no camera on this stretch,' said Patrick, 'and there's a small wood on the other side of the wall. I remember suggesting that it was a weak point in their security but they didn't listen. Thank God.'

There was already a slight thinning of the night sky. They were going to have to be quick. They had one advantage. It had started to rain, quite heavily, so it was less likely that the patrols would be out. Jack, Dawn and Pete climbed on to the roof of the van, which creaked ominously, and then hauled Patrick up to join them. There was a clang of bending metal as the roof bent under Patrick's weight but Pete was already on the wall and jumped down on the other side. They heard him land heavily and then groan.

'Shit, I think my ankle's gone. You're going to have to put your feet on my shoulders as you come down.'

Pete grabbed their ankles as they came over the wall and guided them down so that they were able to land more gently, then Dundee, switched on a torch and began to lead them through the wood. Pete was limping badly as he followed them, but there was no way he was going to be left behind.

As they emerged from the wood Dundee turned off his torch. He peered out across a wide open space and could just make out a large building on the other side.

Patrick joined him and explained.

'These are the formal gardens. The Manor is square. We are facing the western side. We have to get around to the south side. That's where the control room is. But there's a camera on this wall, with night vision. They'll spot us if we walk out of the wood.'

Jack stepped back into the trees instinctively. They all huddled together under the branches which were just beginning to drip where the rain had forced its way through.

'So, what do we do?' asked Eccles.

'I suggest we stay in the wood and move around as far as we can. The trees end just where the building turns a corner. Then one of us is going to have to sprint to the wall. Both cameras will be near the end of their ranges there; there may even be a blind spot. Please God!'

A Perfect Alibi

Patrick paused, then asked, 'Which of us is the fittest?'

'That should have been me,' said Pete. 'But with this bloody ankle. Shit!'

'Then it's probably me,' said Dawn. 'I jog most days. But I'm not exactly a sprinter.'

'It'll have to be you, Dawn,' said Jack. 'I'm not so fast these days.'

'Keep low,' said Patrick, 'run like hell, and cover your head, there's a possibility they'll think you're a deer. There's a herd on the other side of the park, but they have been known to jump the fence and come around here for the grass.'

'I'd better grow some fucking antlers pretty quick,' muttered Dawn.

'You can't do that, but you can hold up a branch. You'll need one anyway.'

'What for?' asked Dawn.

'I'll explain when we get there. Come on.'

Dundee switched on the torch again and pointed it at the ground and they quickly reached the spot where the trees ended.

'Anybody got a knife?' asked Patrick.

'I have,' said Pete, 'Here.'

He handed over a lethal looking knife. 'It's for gutting fish. Ramon gave it me.'

'You keep it. You'll know best how to use it. I want you to cut a long straight branch – hazel would be best – at least four feet long. And leave some of the twigs on it. OK?'

'Sure.' Pete went off to find the right branch. He knew exactly what he was looking for. He and his mates use to make bows out of them.

'Now, Dawn. That's going to be your antler. Well, more like a unicorn's horn I suppose, but they might not notice. When you get to the wall stay really close. You can't be seen there. Move along until you see the camera; it'll be about eight feet up.

Swing your branch and knock the bloody thing off its perch. Then use your whistle and we'll come across to join you. Police still have whistles these days, I hope?'

Dundee nodded.

'Got mine. Thought it might come in useful.'

He handed it to Dawn.

Pete returned with a straight, sturdy pole about the length of a longbow. He'd left some of the twigs on it.

'Right,' said Patrick. 'It's now or never. It's getting lighter all the time.'

Eccles smashed the camera and the others ran across to join her, Pete limping in the rear. They moved towards a modern door in the wall beyond which, Patrick explained, was the CCTV control room and switch room for the Manor's electrics. It wasn't long before someone came out to investigate why the camera had failed. He may have been a simple workman innocent of the purpose of this place, but the team had no time to discriminate, so Dundee struck his head with the hazel bough.

As they entered the Manor they heard someone in the control room call out, thinking his colleague had returned.

'So, what's the problem, mate? Why's it gone on the blink?'

Patrick pushed open the outer door and all four stepped into the control room. The man sitting in front of the screens was not one of the monsters who dealt with the girls. So, when three men, one of them armed with a heavy staff, and a fearsome looking woman, surrounded him, he made no attempt to escape, and when Jack put his finger to his lips the man remained silent.

Patrick quickly checked for any alarm button. Pete found some spare cable on a shelf and the man was quickly bound to his chair. Eccles removed her scarf and tied it around the man's head as a gag.

Eccles pointed to one of the screens and said, 'Look! There she is!'

A Perfect Alibi

Grabowski found herself in a long corridor, with several doors on the same side as her own. This end the corridor was a dead end, so she could only go one way. Soon she spotted a camera looking straight down the corridor. She could be seen and had to get out of this place as quickly as possible. Her only chance was to walk normally along the corridor. They would not be expecting to see an inmate doing that and it may take some time before they identified her.

She had almost reached the other end when she heard voices. The language was strange, but the meaning was obvious. Two men, speaking urgently, probably armed, were coming to find her. With the element of surprise she might have overcome one of them, but not two. She had no other choice but to run back down the corridor, away from them, in the hope that she would think of something before they reached her.

A moment later she saw them enter the corridor. She wondered for a moment if they were the two monsters who had brought her here. When they saw her they stopped, then approached more cautiously, and she saw that one of them had a pistol in his hand. She put her hands above her head, in the gesture of surrender. There was nothing she could do against an armed man.

Just then she glanced towards the room she had left and saw the key in the door. If she could get back inside and lock the door at least she would have time to think. She jumped across to the door and grabbed the key. The man raised his pistol and was about to fire when the corridor was plunged into darkness. She fumbled for the doorknob, quickly opened the door, went into the room, and turned the key in the lock.

She sighed with relief. Surely the lights going out meant that her friends had arrived. And if Dundee had managed to convince the local police force they would have surrounded the place. She would soon be safe.

Suddenly, she was pushed face down on to floor. She felt something heavy on her back, strong arms grabbed her wrists, pulled them behind her, quickly wrapped some cord around them and tied it tightly. Then she heard that disgusting voice coming out of the darkness.

'Round two to me darling. Did you think you'd killed me? Sorry, but I'm much tougher than I look. I don't know why the lights have gone out. Perhaps it's something to do with that thing you were wearing next to your splendid breasts. Oh yes, I noticed ...'

The lights came on again.

'Ah, that's better.'

Agnieska heard the men outside in the corridor and the man sitting on her back called out in another language, which might have been Latvian, she thought, as she grasped some of the words.

'In here boys. I can't open the door for you. I'm otherwise occupied. Shoot at the lock, hand me your gun, then get out of here and find Tomas. Tell him to get the chopper ready for immediate take off.'

Agnieska heard the shot and the door swung open. The man handed the pistol to his boss, then hurried away.

At last, the man got off her back. The relief was tremendous as she felt the weight lift from her chest. She drew a deep breath and rolled over. The man was sitting on the bed, levelling the pistol at her. He smiled that ghastly smile again.

'Well, my dear. It seems I am back in control. I like being in control. I'm used to it. That's why I always carry a piece of cord in my pocket. You see, not all the girls want to give me what I want, so they have to be persuaded. What a pity we don't have time for me to control you. I think I would enjoy that very much.'

He paused as they both heard the faint sound of sirens from outside.

A Perfect Alibi

'But at least you can be of use to me in another way. Get up! Now! We are going for a little walk. Together!'

The voice was harder now; Agnieska had no choice but to obey. She struggled to her feet left the room and began to walk down the corridor, with the pistol pressed into her back, urging her along.

They saw Agnieska standing in the corridor and two men approaching her, one with a pistol in his hand.

'Oh, Christ,' said Pete. 'What do we do now?'

'This ...' Patrick exclaimed as he moved over to a lever on the wall. 'Jack switch on your torch. Now!'

As Jack's torch came alight, Patrick pushed the lever up. The lights went out and the screens died.

'That'll give Grabowski a chance. But we must get there fast. Pete, stand by that lever. Have you got a watch?'

Pete nodded.

'Give us five minutes then switch the lights back on. OK?'

Pete nodded again. He knew that his ankle would be a handicap in the rush to save Agnieska but at least he had something useful to do.

'Right,' said Patrick, who was turning out to be a very efficient leader. 'Follow me.'

As they ran along the corridors they passed cleaning ladies with trolleys and women, mostly young girls, carrying trays. Dundee shouted.

'Police! Go to the kitchen and lock yourself in. Don't come out until we tell you to. Go! Now!'

Some left their trolleys and trays and ran down the corridors. Others, who probably didn't speak English, were pulled along by their friends. Jack and Dawn followed Patrick as he led the way. They saw two men hurrying away down another route, but Grabowski wasn't with them so they let them go.

When they turned into the next corridor they were brought to an abrupt halt. There stood Agnieska with a tall, thin man behind her, pressing something into her back.

'So, my dear Milena, or whoever you are, your friends have arrived. Just a little too late.'

'Try anything and the girl's dead. Understand?'

Jack took a step forward but Agnieska shook her head violently.

'Do exactly what I say and the girl lives. We want that don't we? Such youth and beauty. You see that door. There's a key in the lock. Open it and go inside. Leave the key in the lock.'

Seething with frustration Jack opened the door. There was nothing else he could do. He felt angry with himself for putting Grabowski in such peril. He should never have allowed her to take such a risk. It was obvious from the look on Agnieska's face that the man was ruthless. If anything happened to her now, Jack would never forgive himself. He ushered the others past him into the room. There was a loud scream from a woman inside. Keeping the gun pressed into Agnieska's back the man pulled her across to the door and turned the key in the lock.

'Now, let's get going before the rest of the cavalry arrive.'

The corridors were empty as the man forced his captive towards the side door and past the control room, where no one would see them leave. Actually, Pete had switched the power back on and seen the whole thing on screen from the control room, but he had no idea of the geography of the building so he didn't know how to get to them. He had just decided to leave the room and start looking for them when he heard a sound outside in the corridor. He hid behind the door and peering through a crack saw a very pale and frightened Agnieska being pushed along by the man with the gun. There was nothing he could do, without possibly harming her. The outer door creaked open.

'Hear that. That's our means of escape. We're going for a little trip abroad, my dear.'

A Perfect Alibi

Pete heard it too. The whump, whump, whump of a rotor beginning to turn. He picked up the hazel staff which had been left in the control room and followed them. The rotors were so loud that the man didn't hear Pete coming up behind him. Pete lifted the staff and brought it down heavily on the man's head. He crumpled to the ground and the pistol dropped to the grass. Agnieska turned, saw Pete and hugged him, with tears flowing down her cheeks. There was the crack of a powerful rifle from across the greensward and Pete slid to the ground. Another rifle was fired from a different direction and silence returned.

With her hands still tied behind her back Agnieska knelt awkwardly beside Pete who lay face down in the wet grass. She saw the hole in his back and blood was oozing out into his jacket. When she looked up there were several men in flak jackets hurrying towards her. She shouted.

'Hurry. He's been shot. We have to get him to hospital.'

Two of the men dropped their rifles and hurried forward. Agnieska pointed to the gang leader lying prone on the grass and felt anger.

'And make sure that bastard doesn't get away.'

One of the men slipped handcuffs on to the unconscious villain, then picked up the pistol by the tip of the barrel, put on the safety catch and dropped it into his pocket.

More men in dark combat gear hurried towards Pete. There was no time to fetch a stretcher. He screamed as they lifted him and groaned as they carried him towards the helicopter, which they would use to fly him to hospital. Agnieska cradled Pete's head in her hands as they hurried across the grass. His eyes opened, saw her face and said, 'Tell Felicia I ...' but passed out before he could finish his sentence.

When they reached the helicopter Grabowski shouted above the noise.

'I'll go with him. My friends are locked in a room somewhere inside.'

Pete was lowered carefully on to the floor of the chopper and Agnieska jumped in beside him. Tomas, the pilot, was ordered to take them to Hereford General Hospital.

THIRTY FIVE

The Kent morning was clear and cold, with a touch of frost. Jane and Tony had woken early and were sitting in the kitchen over mugs of coffee, but their thoughts were elsewhere; wondering, hoping, fearing, what was happening to the others.

Mrs Taylor and Milena had arrived at 8am to begin their duties, offering to make breakfast for Tony and Jane, but neither had an appetite, so the cleaner and her protégé went off to make beds and generally tidy up after there had been so many guests in the house. Jane smiled at Tony as they heard the two women swapping words in each other's languages and giggling like schoolgirls.

When they had finished their drinks Tony and Jane decided to take a walk in the garden. It was difficult just to sit and wait for news, so they wrapped up warm and went out. Because there was no wind and the sun was bright it felt warmer than it really was. Tony was determined to try, however slowly and painfully, to manage without his sticks, so he took Jane's arm and they ambled along the paths, beside the flower beds where the bare earth would soon give way to the first green shoots of spring.

Feeling Tony's weight resting on her arm Jane wished that he had been her father rather than Richard Downes, then realised what a stupid thought that was. If Tony had been her father she would not be Jane Downes, in either name or personality. But there was a closeness with Tony that she could never remember having shared with her father. And now that she knew the truth, or some of it, about her father it was hard to feel anything but contempt for him. OK, so he had had an early disappointment in life; the girl he was in love with had chosen someone else, but life is full of knock-backs – look at her and Patrick – but you have to get over things and move on. And if the note at the end of the unfinished novel was about losing his virility, well, surely that was quite common in old age. She knew from her work in the lab that one of the causes of impotence was diabetes. The pharmaceutical company she worked for had tried to develop a cheaper alternative to the standard diabetic treatments. As part of her training she had learned all about that illness. Now, something began to ring a bell somewhere in her head.

There were the two types of diabetes. Type 2 was also known as old age diabetes, but type 1 could occur at a much earlier age, even among children, and it made life very difficult for the sufferer. She wondered what had caused her to think about this. It had something to do with the dead girl, but she couldn't get her head around that at the moment. And, oh yes, her father. He might well have been an undiagnosed diabetic. He hardly ever went to a doctor, his diet was poor, he drank too much, and he never took any exercise.

What else had made him the man he had become. Loneliness? It was possible after the death of his wife, but they had lived separate lives for so many years, and surely he had chosen to be alone. He had always maintained that it was a necessary part of a writer's life.

It did not excuse his bringing the girl into his home, but if his involvement with her could lead to the destruction of the whole organisation trafficking young foreign girls for sex then perhaps something good would have come out of all this.

Suddenly, her ruminations were interrupted by Tony's voice.

'Your Patrick turned out to be bloody useful didn't he?'

'I suppose so, but he's not my Patrick. He was unfaithful to me and I can't forgive him.'

'Was unfaithful, yes, but that's all over now. Surely, you can let bygones be bygones. Most men are slaves to their cocks.'

'You included?'

'Oh Yeah! Well, at one time. I mean a man sees a girl like Agnieska and he can't help himself.'

'She's certainly a lovely girl. I just hope ...'

A Perfect Alibi

At that moment the phone in Tony's pocket bleeped for attention. They both froze, then Tony leaned heavily on Jane, while he fumbled for the phone and handed it to her. She checked the screen and read the text to Tony.

'Mission successful. Many arrests but Pete hurt. Speak later.'

'Thank bloody Christ,' he said and they hugged each other as tears sprang to their eyes. 'But I don't like that bit about Pete.'

Jane felt her heartbeat increase as she read the text again, before handing the phone back to Tony.

'No, but it can't be serious or they would have said.'

'Who sent the text?'

'Dawn.'

Tony nodded and they walked slowly back towards the house.

Jane had liked Pete from their first meeting. He was a good looking lad with a well developed physique, but she didn't think there was anything sexual in her feelings for him. After Patrick's behaviour she had briefly thought about toy boys in a revenge kind of way, but with Pete it was his openness, his honesty. It was more like a maternal feeling that she had for him. He should never have got involved in her father's wicked scheme, but he was a typical lad who wanted to look good and have fun. That was difficult on jobseeker's allowance. He was young, full of testosterone and that young girl had seemed willing enough. Jane was sure that Pete would not have forced himself on her, and she was absolutely certain that he had not deliberately caused her death. What he did with her dead body was absolutely stupid, inexcusable, but she thought he had grown up since then. He had learned from his experiences. He had been desperate to help bring an end to the trafficking. And his love for Felicia seemed absolutely sincere.

Jane and Tony called Mrs Taylor to tell her the good news. They would have liked to share it with Milena as well but none of them could speak Polish.

'So, it's all over? That dreadful business with the girls?'

'It seems so, but unfortunately Pete has been hurt.'

'That's a real shame. Such a nice lad. Good looking too.'

'Yes,' said Jane, 'But surely it can't be serious.'

The phone rang again. Tony answered, and his face turned pale. He ended the call and put his hands out to cover Jane's.

'That was Agnieska. Pete was shot. He died on the operating table just a few minutes ago.'

THIRTY SIX

How different the church looked from the day of her father's funeral. Partly because winter sunshine was streaming through the tall windows, but mainly because the church was full. Pete had been well known and liked by many people in the village, and of course recent events had made him even more widely known.

That lady vicar who had been so kind to Jane was not officiating today. The Staines family did not want a woman priest for their son's funeral. None of them had been to church more than a couple of times in their whole lifetimes but they knew what was what.

At first, Jane had not wanted to come. The memory of her father's funeral was still vivid. She could still see the body of the young girl lying naked and dead in the bottom of his grave. There would be no grave today because after the service Pete's coffin would be taken to the crematorium on the other side of town for a small private ceremony. In the end, Jane would have attended this funeral, whatever the circumstances, to show her respect and perhaps, even a little love, for Pete.

Because the cause of Maria's death had not been found, a Coroner's Investigation was held to determine it. Jane had never intended to suggest to anyone that she thought she knew how the girl had died, but the idea had come to her in Kent, when she remembered her work in the lab. She had thought at that time that her father may have been a type 2 diabetic, later it occurred to her that the girl may have been type 1. When she talked to Sabine about the friend she had known for most of her life, it became clear to Jane that Maria had been a sufferer from at least her mid-teens.

In those last days at the Old Vicarage the girl had tried to explain her need for insulin but her father had thought that she was a drug addict and that her addiction should not be fed. So, gradually her blood had filled her organs with glucose until they had ceased to work properly. She became listless and disorientated and eventually her heart stopped. It was only at the investigation that Jane realised that the parents had to know, or they would spend their lives wondering what had happened to their lovely, lively daughter, so she mentioned her theory to the detectives who passed it on. The relief of Maria's parents at being able to bury their daughter and to know why she had died convinced Jane that she had done the right thing.

Sabine sat beside Dawn as the service began. She had been taken on by the police as an interpreter, for the growing Polish community in the district. Sabine had never known Pete. She was there for the sake of Dawn, whose eyes were glittering with the start of tears. Sabine's tiny, childlike hand was gripped fiercely by Dawn's powerful one, perhaps even painfully, but Sabine did not complain.

On the other side of Dawn sat another girl with tears flowing down her cheeks just as her long dark hair flowed down over her shoulders. Tony, who sat next to her had paid Felicia's air fare from Spain and Jeff had driven them up from Kent in a new van. The old one had been torched when the traffickers broke into it, cut the fuel line and chucked in a match. It was seeing the van in flames which had convinced the police that something serious was going on at Brampton Manor. The Superintendent had sent in his armed squad and in spite of considerable resistance most of Lord Oxendale's retinue had been caught.

Only one of them was killed as he aimed his rifle at Agnieska but hit Pete instead. There would be some very long sentences handed out in the near future. Lord Oxendale himself had been stripped of his life peerage, and the press had deservedly made him public enemy number one.

Since her return to Shropshire Jane had researched as much as she could about her father's life and those connected

A Perfect Alibi

with him. She had made one reassuring discovery. It was about his first love, Victoria. Her father had suddenly been sent out to Aden, where the rebels, or freedom fighters, according to your point of view, were beginning to cause problems for the British establishment. His family had gone with him and Victoria had contracted some nasty disease and died at the age of 17. It was a tragic story but at least the girl was not lying dead in some Kentish wood having been murdered by Richard Downes.

Jane also discovered that before her father met her mother he had spent a year in Poland, teaching English at a language school in Warsaw. He had grown into a reasonably good looking young man by then, though still short and slight. Jane wondered how many blonde haired, blue eyed young students had attracted his attention.

As the congregation sang the first of several dreary hymns, Jane looked towards the expensive coffin, and wondered who had paid for it. Pete had not made a will so the money he had earned from her father would pass on to his family and Tony would make sure that Felicia received the money Pete had promised her.

Jane's gaze moved on to the front pew where the Staines family stood alone. Mrs Staines was stifling a cough and pretending that she was choked with grief. Perhaps she was, or was it the effect of cigarettes? Pete's brothers, and their wives and girlfriends stood solemnly, mumbling through the words of the hymn. Neither of the boys had Pete's looks and it was obvious that neither of them shared his obsession with keeping fit. In fact, Mr Staines, who had turned up from somewhere, was the one who had the same well-toned physique as Pete, but above it was the face of a thug.

The hymn ended and the congregation sat down. Jane glanced around at the pew behind her. She smiled at Dundee, who winked back at her. He and Eccles had been reprimanded by their superiors for taking things into their own hands but this was balanced with commendations for their part in solving the mystery. Their success had been somewhat of an embarrassment to Page and his serious crime squad, which had been disbanded. Wentworth had returned to his previous post and Dundee was standing in for the DCI until she returned from her maternity leave. Eccles had also been temporarily promoted, to Detective Inspector.

Leanne was leaning heavily against Jack's shoulder. Things seemed to be all right again with that marriage. Leanne was really glad to have her husband back in one piece. And the twins had been delighted to see their dad's face in all the newspapers and on the television. It had not been appropriate for them to come to the funeral, so they were at school as usual.

On the other side of Jack was Grabowski. She had been very shocked by her experiences and needed a few days leave. She had lost that first flush of youth but had a seriousness about her now, which did not make her any less beautiful and would make her an even better detective.

The press was represented at the funeral by a young female reporter. Daniel B. Matthews had been reprimanded for publishing the identity of Peggy Dickson and so causing her death. Now, he was back to reporting on flower shows and other local events.

As the congregation stood for the last hymn, Jane looked around again, but could not see Mrs Bennett anywhere. She was not really surprised. That woman had probably seen more of her father in the last few years than anyone else. Pete had told Jane all about Mrs Bennett's scheme. There was a time when she had hoped to become much more than his cleaner. She was a widow and she fancied the idea of living in the Old Vicarage. She also liked the idea of being able to say, 'Oh yes, I'm married to a writer.' Downes had told him that she had done everything she could to get into her father's good books, without any effect. Then she tried another tack. She turned up one night in a fur coat and when she took it off she had nothing on underneath. Her father had just laughed, loud and long. From then on she was a woman scorned.

When she had found her employer lying on his bedroom floor she had called an ambulance, but once he had been taken away she searched the house thoroughly, looking for evidence of any misdemeanours. She had found the girl's clothing in the laundry bag, had laundered it herself and asked a friend with a white van to deliver it to the Old Vicarage when she knew that Jane was staying there. It was the beginning of her plan to blackmail Jane, but when that failed because Jane had simply disappeared, she decided go to the press and ask for a substantial fee for her story. Jane had briefly thought of unmasking the nasty minded woman but decided that she wasn't worth the trouble. No one was really interested in the sex life of a dead mid-list crime writer so, just like her beloved Sophie, Mrs Bennett's bark turned out to be worse than her bite.

A special place in the aisle had been reserved for Moira's wheelchair. Her husband sat beside her at the end of the pew. Jane had spent a delightful Christmas with them, telling them about the raid on Brampton Manor, and sharing a wonderful meal and plenty of wine. They were disappointed that she would not be staying on in the cottage, but realised that she needed to move on.

When the service ended the congregation filed out behind the coffin but Jane waited in her pew until the church was almost empty. She saw Angus standing by the pulpit, looking at the place where the coffin had been during the service. He was talking to himself but his thespian tones echoed around the stone walls.

'What a pity. Such a handsome boy.'

Jane approached him. He turned to Jane and his face was full of grief.

'I loved that boy, you know.'

He looked more closely at Jane.

'You're that lassie whose father's funeral was so rudely interrupted. That was a terrible thing.'

The tut that followed had a theatrical intensity.

'Angus,' Jane asked. 'Is there another way out of the church? I don't think I can face my friends at the moment.'

'There's a door leading out from the vestry. I'll show you.'

He unlocked the door and she left, making her way across the graveyard towards her mother's grave. There was no one nearby so she began to talk to her mother.

'Oh Mum, how did you ever come to marry him? Did you ever love him? Did you know what he was really like? How did you put up with him for all those years?'

There was silence except for the ugly rasping of rooks among the sycamore trees. Jane wished she had brought some flowers, but it had not seemed right when she was attending someone else's funeral. She went up to the gravestone and placed her hand upon the smooth cold marble.

'Mum, I hope you had some good times in your life. You were a good mother to me. I think I've inherited more from you than from Dad. At least I hope so.'

Next, she went around to the new part of the graveyard and approached her father's grave. There was no gravestone here as yet and she hadn't decided whether to have one erected. Perhaps it was best to leave the grave unmarked.

She didn't speak out loud to her father but she thought about everything that had happened since the aborted funeral.

It was time to decide what to do with the rest of her life. Probate had been completed and she had accepted an offer for the Old Vicarage, and if that all went as planned, she should be able to move on in a couple of months. The cottage was pleasant enough, and it had been great to meet Moira again, but too many people knew about her father and there were too many unpleasant memories in this district to make it possible for her to stay.

She thought about that girl from Poland who had died in her father's house. Perhaps for her sake she would go back to the laboratory and help to research something that would make the lives of type 1 diabetics easier to bear. It would be some sort of recompense. Yes, she would give it a try, but it would mean going back to London and finding somewhere to live.

Patrick had been unable to attend the funeral. He'd neglected his company for far too long. He had asked not to be involved in all the publicity surrounding the events at Brampton Manor but Dundee had told Jane how clever and brave he had been during their raid on the traffickers' headquarters. Was he to be a part of Jane's future? Could she ever forgive him for what he had done?

Perhaps.